SAINTS & SINNERS
BOOK 1

LUST

DEVON McCORMACK

Lust (Saints & Sinners #1)

ALSO BY DEVON McCORMACK

TWISTED RIVALRY
THE GUY NEXT DOOR
BFF: BEST FRIEND'S FATHER
BETWEEN THESE SHEETS
TIGHT END
TROUBLE

1

LUKE

I HURRY DOWN the field, running toward our team's goal.

Being a noob who's only playing a pickup game to get out of my dorm room, I wasn't expecting any action, but after a quick exchange between two of the guys, the soccer ball rolls straight to me. I know I must step up to the challenge, or my team is gonna give me hell. So I go for it, speeding up, figuring whether or not I can attempt a somewhat respectable pass to my roomie, Alexei. Even if I fuck it up, it will be less humiliating than not trying at all.

Unfortunately, Alexei's got a decent player from the opposing team covering his ass. Even within this game, I've seen enough of his skills to know he's gonna steal the ball the moment I pass it, so I push on.

In my periphery, I notice Brad Henning coming at me. Another impressive player from what I've observed during this game. I'm surprised he doesn't play for the school team.

I've only been here a couple of weeks, so I don't know too much about the students at St. Lawrence, but I've seen Brad around campus. Once I saw him park his motorcycle behind General Classroom, taking off his helmet and running his fingers through his brown hair, almost carelessly, but somehow managing to style it perfectly. He's friends with Alexei, and apparently some kind of sex god, but at the moment, he's a pickup-game rival tailing my ass.

Fortunately, nothing's as incentivizing as being stalked by a six-foot-something guy, so I kick and sprint. Might not know soccer, but track was my thing, so I manage to clear him, but before I can appreciate my victory, there's a tug on my shirt, and I'm jerked back before there's a shove against my shoulder. It's a powerful force, the weight of Brad's body colliding with mine, knocking me aside.

"It'll be fun," Alexei said.

"Everyone's real chill. We'll have a good time."

"You'll meet some new people. Come on. You can't stay cooped up in here all semester."

Maybe my roomie was right to push me out of my comfort zone, but when I hit the ground and roll onto my stomach, receiving a face full of dirt, I'm forced to reconsider whether this was such a great idea after all.

As I recover from the tumble, the other team is already racing to the goal with the ball. I spot a few uneasy looks from my teammates. They all know what Brad did, but none of them know what to do about it.

Alexei approaches. He's barely said, "Hey, you okay, man?" before I'm up on my feet, heading down the field.

After Brad scores, he spins around, raising his hands over his head. His team doesn't make a big deal about it, the way they did their other goals. Everyone knows it wasn't a fairly earned point.

As I reach their side of the field, Brad turns back to me. He must know what's coming after the stunt he pulled, but he cocks a grin. "Oh, Pretty Boy, nice try."

Pretty boy? The fuck?

His smile expands like he can't tell I'm fucking fuming.

"What the hell was that?" I shout. His teammates step aside, surely because they know I have every right to pummel his ass.

"Come on. It's all in good fun." He winks. "It didn't kill you."

"You'd think someone as good at soccer as you would know that was a foul." By the time I finish saying that, I'm in his face. Like a fucking moron. Not because he doesn't deserve this, but as I mentioned, he's a giant, and I'm barely five-ten. If this escalates into a fight, I'll get my ass handed to me.

But right now, I'm fucking fine with that. I'm not that confrontational, nor violent, but I've been in a few fights when I was younger and had to defend myself.

His gaze narrows. "I am good at soccer."

"Is that why you had to take a cheap shot?"

"Maybe I just enjoyed doing that."

I'm surprised by how tempted I am to take a swing. Although, I do want to hear what the hell that was all about before he grinds me into the earth.

"Besides," he adds. "This isn't an actual game. It's for a laugh. And I got a good laugh out of that."

My nostrils flare, but before I can charge, Alexei slips between us. "Hey, hey." His hand on my chest holds me off as he turns to my new enemy. "He's right and you know it, Brad. So how about you apologize?"

"Apologize?" Brad's forehead creases up. "I think Pretty Boy likes it rough."

He looks me right in the eyes as he says that, still with that smug grin on his conceited face.

Why does he keep calling me Pretty Boy?

That's not exactly an insult, but the way he says it, damned if I can think of anything else he could've said that could piss me off more. Even though he's gay, I know it's not intended as a compliment. Just to get on my nerves.

"Brad, you just fucking acknowledged what you did," Alexei snaps, and I have to say, though I'm just getting to know the guy, I like his balls because he isn't intimidated by this asshole either. Maybe because we might stand a chance if both of us jump him.

Brad steps closer to me. "I think Pretty Boy already knows another game he'd like to play."

He sizes me up, surely registering how quickly he'd have me eating dirt again. I feel his hot breath slamming against my face.

I'm straight, but as we stand there, facing off, all this rage and fury intensifying within me, my dick twitches. Maybe the start of a rage boner, but Brad is one of the hottest guys I've seen around campus, so even not being attracted to guys, it's hard not to appreciate. Fucking asshole got some good genes. Congratu-fucking-lations.

"What're you waiting for? Trying to figure out if you wanna kiss me?" he asks, clearly trying to rile me up.

"Sorry. Not into assholes."

"Bet you are," he says, cocking a brow. "Come on. Hit me. I want to see what you got pent up in that little body."

The way he's talking to me, it's like I did something to him personally. Whatever the hell has him like this is beyond me, but I learned a long time ago I couldn't hide from bullies, so it's on. "Fine by me, prick."

I'm about to lurch at him when another voice comes from nearby. "Okay, okay." Seth Spears sidles up beside Alexei.

I've seen Brad hanging around with Seth and another guy. The three of them seem to have a fucking aura around them, as though they're as special as their rich parents have surely led them to believe. Not a huge surprise to have guys like this at Georgia's prestigious St. Lawrence University, known for its impressive alumni and infamous five-thousand-students cap.

"There's no issue," Seth says.

"Like hell there's not," I spit back. "You saw what happened. He fucking just said what he did."

"But you don't mind."

Seth isn't just telling that to me, but to everyone, like he's inside my fucking head and knows how I feel.

"You don't mind," he grits out, gaze deadlocked with mine.

My rage intensifies, but another sensation immediately overtakes it, rushing in a wave through me. The knot in my chest relaxes with my shoulders. I struggle to pull my gaze from Seth's, but my body feels like it's being rewired. When he finally looks away, there's a serenity to me.

Brad's eyes aren't on me anymore, but on Seth. He looks about to redirect his rage at his buddy. But why?

Figure now would be a good chance to attack, but I suddenly feel sorry for a guy who would need to act up like that. Maybe he's just jealous that I was able to outrun him. And I don't have anything to prove.

Even as those thoughts come to me, I struggle with them. This isn't like me. I don't cool off after someone gets me that worked up.

"Hey, man, you okay?" Alexei asks.

"Yeah. I just... I don't even know... Can we just get back to playing?"

"You're good," Seth says, patting my shoulder.

Yes, I am. Everything's fine.

Brad stares at me as if waiting to see what I'm gonna do.

"Whatever. It is what it is," I say.

Why do I feel this way? Why did I say that?

I look at Alexei, whose jaw is clenched as he eyes Seth. He's got the same attitude as Brad, like Seth did something wrong, but all he did was calm me down, right? Isn't that what happened? But it's hard to know when even the event that led to this moment is becoming difficult to recall.

This shit is so weird, I'd rather get back to the game. Forget this ever fucking happened.

"He'll get a penalty kick," Alexei says. "Then we'll call it even. You think that's fair, Luke?"

"Yeah, that works for me."

Fortunately, they let one of the more seasoned guys score the kick for us, and then we get back to the game, everyone acting like nothing happened.

But the interaction with Seth and Brad plays on a loop in my mind.

Brad and I were about to start fighting, weren't we? You'd think I wouldn't have a question about that, but it's like I can't access the memories and emotions that led up to us standing face-to-face.

After the game wraps up, we head back to the men's dormitory. Like the main campus it adjoins, it has a Gothic aesthetic.

High arches. Vaulted ceilings. Stained-glass windows.

Decorating the exterior are a few statues of saints, angels, and the Virgin Mary—and even a few serpents and cherubs creepy enough to make me think the architect either feared religious imagery or had a hell of a sense of humor.

When we get to the showers on our floor, we divide up into the different stalls. Being one of the best universities in the country, you'd think St. Lawrence could invest in private restrooms in the regular dorm rooms, but no, we share a communal space like this is the fucking 1970s.

Six of the guys who were playing with us are showering, chatting with one another. Most everyone has been at St. Lawrence since freshman year, so they've all had a whole year to get to know each other. I, on the other hand, haven't even been here three weeks, so it's gonna take time to make friends.

As I scrub off, my mind keeps drifting through that awkward moment in the game, as if trying to remind me of something, and then it hits me like a fucking brick: Brad catching my tee and shoving me to the ground.

His asshole comments when I confronted him about it.

Heat flares in my cheeks as it all comes rushing back.

That fucking prick.

That *asshole*!

The knot in my chest is back, even stronger than

when I was about to pummel his fucking ass. But despite getting riled up again, I'm relieved it's all returning to me. And as I hear Brad chuckle in a neighboring stall, I'm about to rush out and take him on.

"You don't mind."

Seth's words float through my mind, stopping me in my tracks.

I didn't relax until he said those words. But why?

There's a wild thought that maybe what he said had something to do with my change of heart. But that's impossible.

My confusion around whatever the hell happened keeps me from starting shit back up. I finish my shower, throw a towel around my waist, and head out of the stall.

Seth and Brad are at their lockers, Brad's bulky physique on full display. The size of those muscles reminds me how easy it would have been for him to overpower me in a fight. Those biceps of steel, the flesh as taut as his abs, as he lets his thick dick hang out, assuring me that the rumors Alexei told me about him being a sex god are likely true. A reminder that the world isn't fair because a guy who's a prick shouldn't also know what to do with one.

As Brad finishes the combo on his lock and opens the door, he says, "You just gonna keep staring at it, Pretty Boy? Or did you want to play with it some too?"

I hadn't realized how long I was staring at his junk until he said that.

He turns to me, putting it on full, proud display. His flesh glistens under the fluorescent lights as he stands there, nude except for a necklace with a cross that dangles between his pecs.

I force my gaze to his, moving close to him again. Despite this rage in me, my dick twitches again and my mouth is watering. Gonna pretend it's just how hungry I am to kick his ass.

"I don't know what your fucking problem is," I say, bringing with me all the intensity I had before whatever the fuck happened that got me to calm my ass down.

"Hey, hey," I hear from beside me, and Alexei inserts himself between us again. He's damp, like he heard us starting up again and tossed on his towel quickly to intervene.

Brad and Seth glance at each other.

"You don't mind."

It's like Seth is trained in hypnosis or something, and that command was supposed to calm me down. It's a wild theory, but why are they looking at each other like they're surprised I'm coming at them like this, unless they thought that should have been enough to subdue me?

As Brad's gaze meets mine again, he says, "Alexei, don't stand in his way. If he wants to lose his temper, let him." He approaches me, puffing his chest out. I notice that dong wagging between his legs before he pushes up close. "Lil' Scholarship Boy's got a temper on him. Come on." His lips are inches from mine. "One punch. Just so when I destroy your ass, everyone knows you started it. Or we could kiss and make up?" He winks.

I must not be as pissed as when I was outside, since I'm able to restrain myself, think about the consequences of getting into a fight with him. I am a scholarship boy, and if it gets out that I was in a fight with one of their richy-rich kids, I can't imagine that's gonna do me any favors. And unlike most of the kids in this school, I don't have the money to get me out of a jam.

When I don't make a move, Brad sneers. "Good boy," he tells me, like a lapdog doing his bidding. "Now, unless you want to grab my cock and start jerking, if you don't mind, I wanna get some fucking pants on."

The heat in my chest sears, and I press my hands against his pecs and give him a good shove. Unsurprisingly, it only makes him stumble backward slightly. But that's the fucking least I can do to let him know I'm not afraid of his ass.

He snickers. "Ooh, I like it feisty. Look how hard you're making me already."

As I look, he's already got a semi.

"Dude!" Alexei says. "Put that thing away."

"Any volunteers?" Brad asks, which earns a groan from Seth, and I roll my eyes and head to my locker.

That may have diffused the tension for now, but given how Brad was on the field and how he treated me since, I already know I've found a mortal enemy at St. Lawrence.

2

LUKE

"WHAT THE HELL is that guy's problem?" I ask Alexei as soon as we get back to our dorm room.

He turns to me, wide-eyed. "Honestly, Luke, I have no idea. That is not the Brad I know. That cheap shot he made on the field—did you see how the other guys were acting? Everyone was thrown. Brad is a stand-up guy…usually."

"Tell me you know that's not true anymore. Or are you gonna put this on me because you've known him longer?"

I'm more than a little defensive since he's described Brad as his friend. And as cool as Alexei's been to hang with the past couple of weeks, I can't help judging him, just like I'm judging Seth for his association with that fucker.

Alexei throws his hands up in surrender. "Brad was in the wrong. I said that. You saw I had your back. I'm also a scholarship boy, and he's never said anything like that to me. This all blows my mind."

Well, shit. I'm taking this out on the wrong guy. I'm normally much more in control, but something about Brad Henning hits at a sore spot in me, beyond simply being pissed at an asshole. Like something about him is a threat to my very soul.

After losing both my parents by the time I turned fourteen—Dad to a brain aneurysm, then Mom to a car accident four years later—I pulled away from the friends I had and didn't try to make new ones. And when I didn't have friends anymore, or maybe simply because bullies could sense my vulnerability from everything I'd been through, I became a target, something my uncle Dan, who'd taken me in, had to put a stop to through school admins. Still, by sophomore year, I'd learned how to stand up to assholes like Brad even if it meant throwing a punch or getting my ass handed to me. So if this guy thinks he's gonna use me as his doormat, he's got another thing coming.

"I'll chat with him," Alexei says. "See if we can bridge whatever the fuck misunderstanding this is."

I toss my bag on my bed. "This isn't a *misunderstanding*. He went after me unprovoked. He didn't apologize. Just kept digging. And then Seth…"

I stop myself. If I mention what happened when Seth told me I didn't mind, Alexei's gonna think I've lost it.

"I'm sorry, Luke. You've been cooped up in here reading and watching TV, and I thought it might be nice to get out."

He's right. I knew I needed to push myself to get out. As one therapist told me a few years after my parents' deaths, *"You keep people at a distance. Do you think it's out of fear of losing them like you did your parents?"* As if my uncle needed to pay a hundred and seventy bucks for someone to pick up on that one. Although, as annoying as the advice sounded at the time, it's part of what got me hanging with Alexei and forcing myself to be more social.

It also reminds me that Alexei is not the one I should be dumping all this on. Unlike Brad, he's trying to be friendly. And it wasn't a total waste. In fact, after my incident with Brad, several guys and girls from the teams came up to me and made an extra effort to make me feel welcome. Brad doesn't represent the whole damn school.

"That said," Alexei adds, "if you don't want to go to a pickup meet again, I'll totally understand."

"Oh, I'm definitely going now."

He tilts his head, surely confused by my position.

"I've been around enough guys like Brad to know that if I give in, I'll never hear the end of it. I'm gonna show that fucker I'm not the kind of guy he can intimidate."

He smirks. "I knew I liked you." Then his brow tenses. "Hey, maybe that's what's up with Brad. Maybe he likes you…?"

"I seriously hope you aren't suggesting he was pulling

my pigtails. That's problematic behavior, not a sign of—"

"We both saw what his dick was doing in the showers. Might not be a healthy way of reacting or an excuse, but he's gay, and…Pretty Boy?" He chuckles.

"I don't know what you're laughing about," I tease. "I'm a hot motherfucker."

That's not really true. Not that I'm unattractive, but I'm probably average in the looks department.

We both burst into a laugh, and it's nice that despite how fucked up that shit was, I'm able to laugh about it.

But there's one thing I can't laugh about. Three words Seth said that echo inside my goddamn head.

You. Don't. Mind.

THE REST OF the afternoon and into the night, I'm googling shit like hypnosis, neurolinguistic programming, and the power of persuasion, with mixed results.

Some people swear by crap like hypnosis and NLP, while skeptics tend to believe in some ability to influence, but nowhere near as dramatic as what some of this shit claims.

Hell, if I hadn't had that experience, I'd be just as skeptical.

But that wasn't influence. I can't think of anything that could have taken me down from that rage other than being shot with a tranquilizer, and even that would have taken time to kick in.

Right after it happened, the details were hazy, like something I would've remembered from childhood. It had been enough to make me second-guess myself, but now all the details are back, rich and vivid. So graphic that I don't doubt what happened. And only with hypnosis have people claimed they could be totally transformed with just a keyword or phrase, ridiculous as that might seem.

But surely if Seth was running around campus hypnotizing everyone, people would notice. Although, I haven't been here long enough to know what everyone talks about.

The following morning, I'm in the communal kitchen for our floor. A few guys are in the dining area, watching *Judge Judy* on the big-screen TV. I'm standing at the stove, fixing an omelet, when Brad walks in.

"Morning, Pretty Boy," he says, glancing me over, his gaze lingering on my body a little too long, making me wonder if maybe Alexei was right about Brad's behavior. What if it was just an inappropriate way of approaching his attraction?

But that doesn't seem right. From what I've heard, he's messed around with a ton of guys, and if that was his reputation, people wouldn't think he was a stand-up guy, as Alexei put it.

As he opens the fridge, I glance his way and notice the protrusion in the crotch of his sweatpants. "You're having a very good morning, aren't you?" I say, deliberately pushing. He needs to know I'm not gonna sit back and take his crap.

He glares at me.

"Is that all for me?" I jab.

"Why, you need a smoothie for breakfast?"

The way he raises his brow, smirking, it has me thinking that if he wasn't such a fucking tool, we might actually get along. But since he's determined to be my archnemesis, it's now a game I must win.

"If I need protein, I have bars for that."

I glance around the dining area. The other guys are chatting or engrossed in Judge Judy's deliberations, and for the first time, Seth isn't right at Brad's side.

I've been debating about the best tactic. Confront just Brad, just Seth, or both at the same time?

Seth is much cooler than Brad, though. Seems like Brad struggles with controlling himself, which might work to my advantage if I can get him to slip up, admit that Seth fucking hypnotized me yesterday.

Christ, what the hell am I even saying?

As I flip my omelet, Brad pulls out some OJ, then rifles through the freezer, retrieving frozen fruits.

"I'm planning to come to the pickup game next week again. In case you thought you were gonna discourage me from that."

"Be happy to kick your ass again."

"Maybe you could show some integrity this time. Be

less of an embarrassment to your team."

He snickers, but it somehow sounds like a low, rumbling growl. My dick gets a little twitchy, which is fucked up, and I've been up too long to blame it on morning wood. I also notice heat in my chest, intensifying rapidly. I'd say it's just my anger at him, but it's stronger than anything I've felt in the past. Reminds me of why I got so fucking heated from the jump yesterday.

Brad fills the blender with frozen fruit, protein powder, and peanut butter, then mashes it all together. Meanwhile, I plate my omelet and grab ketchup from the fridge.

When Brad pours his mix into a glass, I set my plate on the counter near him and say, "That was an interesting trick your friend Seth pulled yesterday."

"What can I say? He's great at stealing." As he says that, he shoots me a look like he knows damn well I'm not talking about one of the impressive moves Seth pulled during the game. And I don't have to read his mind to know it's a bluff. Has to be. I saw the way he looked at Seth after he fed me that suggestion.

"That's not the trick I was talking about. I was referring to his *induction*." I use it like a hypno pro, based on my limited Google investigation.

Brad's brows shift closer as he winces. "Induction?"

"Real interesting how fast he calmed me down, don't you think? Maybe a little *too* fast."

This strikes a nerve. His eyes widen, and he studies

my face before glancing into the dining area. Is he worried the guys might hear? That I know something I shouldn't?

But then a mask of indifference slips into place, and he shrugs. "Seth has a talent for deescalating tense situations."

"I know what he did to me, Brad," I spit out, and he doesn't break eye contact this time, but his expression is frozen in place, not revealing a damn thing.

Finally, he says, "Really? And what is that?"

"He fucking hypnotized me." I keep my voice low because I can only imagine what the others would think if they heard me.

Brad's lips curl upward and his eyes close as he chuckles. It quickly turns into a laugh. "Of course. That's totally what happened. You got him." He moves closer and whispers, "Maybe cut back on the weed you do before bed. Or really, whatever you're treating yourself to."

He's much more relaxed now, which makes me think I fumbled on the hypnosis theory, but even if it's something else, I can't be *that* far off.

"Whatever the hell he did to me, I'll figure it out, so just let him know that if he tries his mind games again, it's not gonna be so easy."

That sobers him up. That impressive jaw of his tightens, but I've said my piece, so I turn my attention to my omelet, squeezing ketchup along the side for dip. A bit squirts out, scattering across the plate and—

"Fuck," I say as I notice a few drops across my tank. Now I've just given Brad Henning ammo. Here it comes.

I brace myself for the inevitable smart-ass comment, sure *Pretty Boy* will come up. I grab the hem of my shirt, and as I'm pulling it off to rinse it under the sink, Brad grips my wrist.

"Don't," he whispers, clinging to me. It's not a tight grip, but it's firm, and where he touches, a low, steady jolt of electricity pulses through me, exciting all my nerves. What felt like anger in my chest is now a powerful heat that sweeps through my body.

Our gazes lock, and I see a flash of panic in his wide-eyed expression. I'm fucking frozen in place, this energy coursing through me. My heart races, and my nerves are doing fucking somersaults in my chest.

With his free hand, Brad reaches into his shirt collar and pulls out his necklace, gripping it. The moment he does, he breaks our eye contact, and the sensation coursing through me cuts off.

"Good chat," he spits out, releasing my wrist. He snatches his smoothie off the counter and dashes off, leaving my body buzzing with life.

By the time he's in the hall, I'm able to catch my breath, which is when I notice the tent in my pants.

What. The. Hell. Was. That?

3

BRAD

"IF YOU'RE NOT gonna get into why you called this meeting, will you at least stop pacing?" Cody says. "You're making my anxiety flare up, and it's been bad enough lately."

I halt, steadying my breathing. Deep, measured breaths. "Better?" I ask.

"No. You're making me even more anxious that way. Just keep pacing."

As I resume my back and forth, my mind's all over the place. I'm a fucking wreck since my interaction with Luke this morning at breakfast.

"What the hell is going on?" Seth asks, trying to get it out of me after I finished rubbing one out in a restroom stall and grabbed him when he got out of his next class.

"We need to have a meeting. Later. With Cody."

"You can't give me more than that?"

"It's about Luke Waters, and I just want to wait, okay? Back off, and we'll talk about it later."

That whole discussion in the kitchen fucked with my

head.

That Luke remembered what Seth did to him.

Then how he started to take off his fucking shirt...and I about lost my fucking mind...well, my load, really.

Yesterday in the showers, after our fight on the field, my physical reaction to him was intense but only showed with a semi. This time it was overwhelming.

And excruciating.

Something's wrong. Very wrong.

Which is why I called the meeting at the old church this evening.

I check my phone. We said eight, and it's 7:56 now. Seth is punctual. He'll be here soon.

Cody, sitting at an old desk—one of many around this cellar—folds his arms, nestling his face in them like a pillow. Despite what we've done to straighten the cellar out, it's still just a bunch of junk—old boards and furniture—that we've rearranged so we can have our meetings.

A familiar sound comes from upstairs, and a few moments later Seth comes through the door at the top of the stairs. "So what the hell is this about?" He heads down, slinging his backpack around to his front.

I spit it out. "Luke knows what you did yesterday."

"What?" Seth reaches the bottom of the steps and sets his backpack on the floor.

"Wait, what did Seth do yesterday?" Cody asks,

LUST

pushing to his feet.

"Don't make this a huge thing," Seth says. "Sometimes they feel like something was a bit off, or like
something happened in the conversation they can't
remember. That's not weird. It's happened before. You
both know this."

"He said he thought you might have hypnotized
him."

"The fuck?" Cody says. "Seth, you used your fucking
powers on him? You didn't tell me that." He sounds
hurt, and I'm not surprised since they tell each other
pretty much everything.

"I didn't want to worry you while you were still
recovering," Seth tells him, referring to the spell we
performed last weekend here in the church cellar, during
which Cody received a name: Luke Waters. The one the
Guides warned us about.

Seth goes on, "And Mr. Bright Idea over here was
about to get into a fistfight with the guy."

"I was getting the ball rolling," I say, "to make his
stay here hell enough for him to want to leave."

After discovering Luke was the one we needed to get
rid of, we agreed we would fuck with him enough to get
him to drop out. I would start being an ass to him, and
Seth and Cody would use their powers gradually to make
his stay as unpleasant as possible.

I'm quickly realizing it won't be that simple.

"It was a little over-the-top," Seth says, "and you

23

nearly provoked him into a fight that might've gotten you both expelled."

"Maybe that would have been for the best," I say.

"You don't mean that, Brad," Cody says. "We want to save him, not ruin his chances of getting an education. He needs to leave here on good terms so he can enroll somewhere else. And just because he's gone doesn't mean we're in the clear. We need your powers here at St. Lawrence."

"No, I didn't really want that," I say. "I just…"

I hesitate. It's difficult to get into this next part.

How fixated I was on him on the field. Studying him as he flicked his nearly black bangs off his forehead. The pink in his cheeks when he really got going.

Then…what it felt like being near him. What touching him did to me.

Luke brought out something in me, and in a moment, all I wanted to do was keep him safe from harm. In a way I've never experienced before.

"Yesterday was the limit with my power," Seth says. "If you had gotten into a fight, I wouldn't have been able to get you out of it. I had to push on him *twice*. It didn't take like it normally does. I wonder how I fucked it up."

Which brings me to the shit that's been on my mind. "I don't think you did anything wrong. There's something messed up about this guy."

Cody studies me. "Something else happened, didn't it?"

Heat surges to my cheeks. "Are you reading me right now?"

"When did I get this inexhaustible power all of a sudden? I'm still fucking zapped from last weekend."

"Stop changing the subject," Seth snaps at me. "What happened with Luke?"

"I—I—just know there's something wrong."

"Say it," Cody presses. "You were fucking him, and something weird happened. It's not like we need to guess what it could be with you."

Seth grimaces. "When the hell did you have time to fuck him?"

I roll my eyes. I get why this is their assumption, and it's related, but damn, I wish my power wasn't seduction—though really, only right now. I definitely enjoy it most of the time.

"We didn't fuck. I already felt something on the field with him. I think it's what made me lose control. And after, when we were in the showers, I was giving him shit, he pushed me, and I felt this jolt move through me. It was intense. I had to use my amulet to keep myself from having a raging hard-on, but even that didn't get me down all the way."

"I did see that," Seth says.

"And this morning, I bumped into him in the kitchen, and fuck, I was like a stone as soon as I saw him. I was playing it off fine, but it wasn't just that. I wanted to fuck him like a goddamn animal—like wild, obsessive thoughts, the kind you get when you're thirteen. And then he started to take his shirt off—"

"In the kitchen?" Cody asks.

"He got ketchup on it."

Cody and Seth exchange a confused glance.

"This isn't the part of the story that matters. Anyway, him taking his shirt off was too much for me, and out of desperation, I grabbed his wrist to stop him, and holy fucking hell—I haven't done any hard drugs, but if that's what it feels like, I don't understand how anybody's ever able to get clean. I thought I was about to cream right through my pants."

Cody's face twists up. "It was hot until you said *cream*."

"Cody, be serious," Seth says. "Go on, Brad. Then what happened?"

"I got the hell out of there and had to bust one out in the restroom. Then I ran into you and called the meeting."

Seth bites his bottom lip, his gaze wandering before he shakes his head. "Brad, you're attracted to this guy? That's what this is about?"

I sigh. "*This* is why I didn't tell you this morning. I knew you'd blow it off. This isn't like when I fuck around with other guys. Something else happened there. He did something to me. *Is* doing something to me."

"And he must've fucked with your powers too," Cody tells Seth.

"Seems like it," Seth says.

"What if he's not just a victim?" Cody muses. "What if he's part of the reason it enters our world?"

"Technically, *we're* the reason," I say, guilt rising within me.

"No," Cody says. "Something dark sensed us that night, and because of the vision, we assumed that what we did unleashes it, but what if that's not the case?"

He's referring to a spell we did one night—when we fucked with our powers in a way we shouldn't have and felt something evil drawn to us, as though using us to find its way into our world.

"It didn't come into our world that night," Cody says. "And you remember how Luke appeared in my vision. What if it meant his power is connected to the genesis of that evil being?"

"Based on what you described," Seth says, "that would make sense. Maybe that's why the Guides warned us about him."

"That's all speculation, though," I say. "We don't have much to go on, but I was thinking…" I hesitate, knowing how this would go over before I get the words out. "Cody could go under again."

Cody's cheeks flush, his eyes watering.

Seth steps up to me. "What the fuck is wrong with you?"

Cody's trembling and shaking his head as his gaze wanders. "No, no. I can't do that again."

"Of course you're not fucking doing that. Brad's out of his goddamn mind." Even though he's talking to Cody, Seth's eyes are on me like he's trying to make a point—or about to hit me.

"It's only a fucking suggestion," I tell him. "I'm not forcing his hand. But you both know we need more information."

Cody turns away from us, still shaking.

"Cody?" Seth hurries to him, but before he can reach him, Cody steps away. "It's okay, Cody. We're not gonna make you do that."

"I would," he whispers. "It was just so hard last time."

"I know it was," I say, trying to soothe him.

Channeling's always been painful for Cody. He describes it like nails drilling into him. Last time, after finishing writing down the name he received from the Guides, he thrashed about, screaming at the top of his lungs. And even once he calmed down, he was shaken up. Much worse than the other times.

"It's just, it's all been so vague," I say.

"Cody, tell him why that's not happening," Seth says.

The fuck does that mean?

Cody takes a few breaths, regaining his composure. "Brad, I've been having panic attacks since that night. And not the kind where I can use my amulet to shake it off. These have been too intense. Something happened

28

last time, and it scared me."

"So that's not an option," Seth adds, like he needs to make that clear to me.

"I wish you had told me, Cody."

He nods. "I didn't want to worry you. Seth only knows because he's been there when some have happened."

Of course; they're roommates, so that'd be a hard thing to hide.

If I'd known it was worse than usual, I wouldn't have even brought it up.

"You're right," I say. "That's too much to ask of you, Cody. I just feel like there's more to all this, especially now that it's clear this guy can fuck with our powers. The Guides didn't warn us about that."

"That doesn't change anything," Seth says. "The plan is still the same: we get this guy to leave, and everything goes back to normal."

Oh, how fucking easy for Seth to say that shit, but executing this plan is a whole other story. "Now that we know he can affect our powers, I don't think this is something to drag out. We need to throw everything we can at him. From all angles. We must make his staying at St. Lawrence unbearable. And as we all know from what we read in his background check, he's legacy. Dad went here, but Dad isn't around anymore. And the fact that he didn't get in freshman year and still came back means he's determined because he has some kind of dream about attending St. Lawrence."

"Guy should have stayed at Emory," Seth says. "But you're right. You think you can keep your raging hard-ons to a minimum around this guy?"

"I don't know about that. Maybe I'll find a way to use them to my advantage."

"How will you—"

"Not sure yet. Working on it."

"We're in this together," Cody adds. "We'll figure it out. You guys tee him up, and when I'm better, I'll lay into him. Luke Waters maybe has a few more good weeks at St. Lawrence."

A surge of guilt hits me. What the hell are we doing to this poor guy?

But unfortunately, it's our only recourse.

I will tear down this whole goddamn school to get Luke Waters as far away from it as possible, as soon as possible.

4

LUKE

"Hey, Unc," I answer the FaceTime call.

I prop the cell on the phone mount affixed to my desk, positioning it so Uncle Dan and I can see each other.

"Just had a minute on my break," he says, "so thought I'd give you a call."

After my mom died, Dad's brother became my legal guardian, and he's definitely stepped up to take on that responsibility. Despite how busy he is with work, he always finds time to check in. And considering I'm not having an easy time making friends here, and my issues with Brad and Seth, not to mention a whole series of fucked-up thoughts around Mom and Dad not being around for this chapter of my life, it's nice to be able to talk to a guy who I can let my guard down with.

After he tells me a little about his day, he says, "Everything all right? You look stressed."

"Stayed up late finishing some reading," I lie.

Because even though I can usually talk to Dan about

just about anything, I can't tell him what's been occupying my thoughts lately.

Since I confronted Brad in the kitchen at the end of last week, I've become a paranoid fucker. Talking to him was supposed to answer my question, but now I have more.

What the fuck happened when he touched me?

Why did I have to run back to my dorm room and jerk off while thinking about him?

And why does my dick twitch every time I see him around campus?

I'm convinced this is something he and Seth did to me. I don't know how, but I intend to find out.

"If you're going to lie to me," Dan says, "then you should make up a more plausible story. Unless you became a totally different person than the Luke who left here, I can't imagine you weren't all over that reading. You're probably a few chapters ahead of the rest of the class."

I snicker. The guy knows me. "I was just staying ahead."

Again, a lie, but he can't know what's really stressing me out. No one can. If anyone would believe me, it'd be Dan, but considering the theories running through my brain, I'm not saying shit until I'm absolutely certain.

"Been thinking about a part-time job," I say to change the subject. "I know we agreed—"

"Let's just get you through this first semester. I make

fine money. Not send-you-to-St. Lawrence money, but I can cover you for this. It's not worth risking your scholarship or falling behind."

"You're right, you're right." Because if I don't keep an A average, I'm fucked out of tuition, books, and lodging.

"Looks like you're more settled in," Dan says. Now he's the one changing the subject. "I'm already seeing the clothes piling up on your bed."

"If you're gonna give me hell, then maybe I should hang up and get back to what I was doing," I tease.

"It's nice. Means you're comfortable."

"Eh…"

"Uh-oh. Knew I'd hit on something."

Fuck. Of course he did.

"Just some growing pains."

"You like your roommate?"

"Yeah, Alexei's cool. My only friend here right now. Some guys aren't great. And others don't seem very friendly."

I noticed this ramped up after my chat with Brad that morning in the kitchen, so I'm wondering if he spread some rumor or if Seth is running around performing his wizardry on our peers.

"Are you being bullied? You think you need to talk to an administrator?"

I hear the concern in his voice, as he surely reflects on the issues I had in the past.

"This isn't like when I was younger," I insist, and at his suspicious gaze, I confess, "But yeah, I might need to. Better than using fists." That's the right thing to do, and if there wasn't this fucked-up element to it that I don't yet understand, maybe I would have already talked to someone about it. "Sorry, but can we talk about something else?"

Dan reminds me that if I'm threatened, I need to report the incident to administrators, if not the police, before embracing a subject change. We talk about this conference he's looking forward to attending in a couple of months because it's in Hawaii. And once we're all caught up, I say, "I do have a little work I need to finish up before class. Then I have a pickup game."

"Pickup game?"

"I'm playing soccer with some of the other students."

"Soccer? This hasn't come up."

"Just a way to meet new people. Alexei talked me into it last week."

Dan chuckles. "Sounds good. I'm glad you're getting out and socializing, even if some of the kids are being assholes. Fuck, I shouldn't say that. I mean—*dammit.*"

Dan's worked so hard to stop cursing since Mom's death, when he decided he needed to be more of a positive role model for me. It's sweet of him, and we get a good laugh out of his fumble, then say our goodbyes.

I pack up and head out to Brit Lit, where Prof. Strauss lectures on the reading from last night, and we have a quick class discussion. After class lets out, as I'm passing his desk, he says, "Mr. Waters, could I chat with you for a minute?"

I approach his desk, waiting as he types on his laptop. I'm wondering how long this will take, but a minute later he stops and addresses me. "These short responses I assign in the first month are designed to help me gauge where my students are at, and I must say, I was surprised when I read your recent one."

I've always gotten props for reports and essays, so I'm ready for him to give me the sort of compliments I'm used to, when he says, "Yours was…substandard."

"What?"

"Overly simplistic. Like you were rushing. Or not really thinking it through. I expect more from my students. I know you're a transfer, so I suspect that has something to do with this. And I don't just speak for my own class—I can't imagine this was sufficient at Emory."

He's so matter-of-fact that I'm running back through what I thought was a sophisticated philosophical argument about God's fucked-up design of his garden in *Paradise Lost*. But clearly, I was mistaken.

"I'm sorry. Could I have a chance to rework it?"

"That's not how my class works, Mr. Waters. The grade you get is the grade you earned. I just wanted to give you a heads-up because you have another essay response for next week, and I'm really hoping you'll put the time in that the assignment deserves."

I spent an hour on that. I thought it was good. But now I'm like...fuck me. It's like the whole fucking school's against me.

The interaction really puts me in a mood, and though I've been dreading this pickup game all week, it's nice to have an excuse to let off some steam. I'm not a soccer player, but I'm impressed with how quickly I pick it up, mostly to piss off Brad Henning.

I'm still a fast fucker like I was when I trained for track. Guess all those years of desperately trying to run from my pain paid off, even if they never made the pain go away.

I use my speed to my advantage throughout the game, noticing Brad somehow manages to change positions so he can play defense to my offense every chance he gets. I return the favor, and during a play, as one of his teammates kicks him the ball, he takes off with it, calling back to me, "Come on, Pretty Boy. Show me what you got."

Damn, it doesn't take much for him to get me on edge, and I'm right on his ass when Alexei comes from the side. Brad looks like he's about to dodge Alexei before he kicks the ball between Alexei's legs and goes the other way so that I wind up slamming into him at full speed.

He's like a brick wall, stopping my body, but my leg kicks under his and he trips up, grabbing me as we both tumble to the ground. As we land, his weight crushes down on top of me.

"Fuck," I groan, but even with the pain, as our bodies are mashed up against each other, there's a rush of sensation. Not as intense as when he grabbed my wrist the week before, but still fucking electric, exhilarating. It drives me so wild, I can't even bring myself to get the fucking guy off me. I'm gasping, and I know it's not because he knocked the wind out of me.

Something hard presses against my pelvis, wedged between us. As he raises himself up on his elbows, he grunts. "Fucker, look what you did to me."

"Which thing are you talking about? I can't control your boners, dude."

"I meant running into me. And you don't have any room to talk about the other thing."

As he shoots me a glare, I notice I'm as stiff as he is, and it's not helping that our bodies are still tight against each other, neither of us making a move to pull away.

This is definitely gonna show in gym shorts.

God, he has a fucking pretty mouth. I could just kiss him right now.

Stop it. He's doing this to you!

Brad reaches in his collar, grabbing hold of his necklace again.

As he pushes off me, there's still a buzz from him being up on me, but now it's like my body wants him back on me, craving that sensation again. I'm fucking empty inside without it.

What the fuck are you doing to me, Brad Henning?

As I try to get up in a way that'll make my hard-on less obvious, I notice his isn't as bad, maybe because of whatever the hell he's doing with his necklace. Frustratingly, I'm the one who ends up getting looks and chuckles from the others on our team.

"Look who's getting hot and bothered from all the action," Alexei teases as we get into positions for our next play.

I roll my eyes, my gaze turning to the bleachers, where one lone student sits in the stands beside a backpack.

The guy looks familiar. Shorter than me, with blond hair. When I see him, he's typically with Brad and Seth, but I can't remember his name.

He's too far away for me to be sure, but I have this feeling he's looking at me.

He tilts his head, and Ross, our team captain, calls my name, pulling me back into the game.

I don't give the guy in the stands much thought until the game's over, but when I look for him, he's gone, which gives me an uneasy feeling. Of course, most things do when it comes to that crew.

After the game—which my team lost—I head back to the dorm to shower off. While I'm scrubbing myself down, I notice my dick's still a little aroused as my thoughts keep returning to the moment when Brad was lying on top of me. It felt good to have his weight on me.

Fuck, no, I hate that asshole. And I'm fucking straight!

But the more I fight it, the harder I seem to get.

I give my cock a stroke, closing my eyes and imagining Brad pulling back the curtain and coming in here, pushing against me, locking his lips against mine.

I hate myself for the fantasy, but I can't help what my dick wants right now.

I give my cock another stroke, when suddenly my fantasy shifts, and I'm a kid with Mom and Dad at Christmastime.

The hell?

Flashes of memories with my parents come flooding back. I'm very young. Making Dad's birthday cake with Mom. Going out to picnics at the lake.

My mind's out of control, taking me back through vivid scenes from my past.

I press my hand against the shower wall, taking deep breaths as I try to push them back, but the memories come even stronger than before.

I'm at the hospital with Mom. I can see in her teary eyes that the news isn't good. What's wrong with Dad? A familiar grief overtakes me. I'm back in that nightmarish moment.

As I struggle to pull myself from the scene, the image of the guy from the bleachers pops up.

Blond locks.

Eyes closed.

He's muttering something.

I focus on this scene, hoping that will keep me from going back to the memory.

He's in a dark room, kneeling on the cement floor in a chalked-out pentagram.

"I'm so sorry, Luke," Mom says, straining to go on.

"No," I say, returning to the image of the guy from the bleachers, seeing him muttering to himself, sweat beading down his forehead.

What the fuck are you doing?

In an instant I'm struck by searing pain that cuts through me, straight into my soul. I know this pain so well…the depths of despair. I collapse against the shower wall, steadily sinking to the floor as memories haunt me.

"Daddy's not gonna be okay, sweetie."

"Stop it!" I scream, thrashing about.

My words seem to summon the blond guy once again. His eyes pop open and he gasps, and then it's like I've been shot in the chest, my body propelled into the shower wall.

It takes me a moment to realize the hit knocked the wind out of me, and as I struggle to get some air back into my lungs, the shower curtain is drawn open.

Alexei stands outside, a towel around his waist, wide-eyed with worry. "Dude, you okay? What's wrong?"

I pat at my chest, straining, and he rushes in to help me to my feet. I finally catch my first bit of breath when he has me out of the shower.

A bunch of the guys are standing around us in a

semicircle, including Seth and Brad.

Despite the discomfort of having the wind knocked out of me, my mind has quieted from the memories, but I can't shake the image of their friend. Cody. Somehow I suddenly fucking know it like I know my own name.

But how is that fucking possible?

As my breathing steadies, everyone seems to ease up. Alexei helps me to my locker and into my clothes. "We should get you checked out at the clinic."

"It's okay. I'm feeling better."

"Dude, you were on the fucking floor."

"Can we not do this here, please?" I glance around the room…make eye contact with Brad, who's a few lockers over. I give him a pointed glare because I don't know how, but he had something to do with this.

Once I'm dressed, I talk Alexei out of taking me to the clinic, and we return to our dorm room.

I'm still rattled, but overall, I'm fine. At least those dark memories are at bay again. Now I just need to figure out what the hell all that weird-ass shit was with Brad on top of me and this Cody guy.

I settle into bed and pull out my phone, since I'm gonna have to google some of this crap, when I notice a notification from the St. Lawrence grade portal.

It's listed as Strauss's class.

He didn't tell me the shitty grade he gave me on that homework assignment, so I pull it up just to see. Already been a bad enough day, might as well get it over with.

Second Response: A+

My jaw drops as I reflect on that weird-ass conversation he had with me.

A series of scenes play through my mind:

Cody in that dark room, kneeling in the pentagram.

Brad grabbing my wrist, and that powerful sensation shooting through me.

Brad falling on me in soccer, and me feeling another exciting rush.

Seth's comment that's had my brain doing backflips ever since.

This shit isn't fucking hypnosis. It's something much darker.

And these guys are coming for me.

Hard.

5

LUKE

I TAKE A sip of my drink as I scan the crowd at Alpha Alpha Mu's party.

When Alexei first told me about it this afternoon, I struggled. Since I flipped out in the shower yesterday, I haven't bumped into Brad, Seth, or Cody. Not in the dorms, nor around campus. Not that I'm trying to avoid them, but I wonder if they're trying to avoid me after the stunts they pulled.

I must've mistaken your responses for someone else's, Prof. Strauss wrote back after I emailed to ask him about my mysterious A+. *Can't really say. Sorry about that.* I'm certain Seth, Brad, or Cody did something to him, just like Seth did to me last week on the field.

Since Cody did whatever the hell that was, my internet searches aren't about the psychology of persuasion or the subconscious anymore, but about—impossible as it seems—magic. Googling that made me feel like I was out of my goddamn mind, but I feel like I have to be open to any possibility. And it's all such a clusterfuck of mixed messages and varying perspectives that it's hard to know where to even begin as far as sorting out the bullshit from the truth.

There are spells for *everything*, from influencing someone's thoughts to making someone lust after you. Maybe all three of them have cast spells on me, but whereas Seth's and Cody's wore off quickly, Brad's lingers. It's been fucking with my head and dick since he seized my wrist.

But they've all got me freaked out. If it really is magic, given what I've witnessed already, who knows what they're capable of?

Despite having all this swirling in my brain, I try to enjoy some beer pong with Alexei and my St. Lawrence peers. But even as I chat up new acquaintances, I keep searching around, knowing damn well who I'm looking for.

Brad fucking Henning.

I'm probably an idiot for planning to confront a guy who's actively using magic against me.

I may not be able to fight off what Brad did to me, but I fought off Cody in the shower, and I could feel he was freaked out over it. So maybe if I let Brad know I'm figuring them out, they'll know I can google my own defenses against their powers, and they'll have to move on to a new, unsuspecting victim.

Is that the smartest move? Who knows? There's no rulebook for when your peers are trying to bully you with fucking magic.

Of course, even as I tell myself I'm here to warn Brad to get off my back, I fear I have some subconscious ulterior motive. That whatever he did to me makes me want to approach him. Just to be close to his body again. To feel the warmth emanating from his flesh. His hot breath against my face. Get a surge of that energy when he touches me.

Fuck, I need to stop thinking about that because it's making me hard again.

After beer pong, I head out to the back porch and struggle to focus as I chat up a girl who was on my team. Jess is so hot. Dark-brown hair, glasses, gorgeous smile. The sort of girl I'd be interested in if I wasn't so distracted. But as we're starting to get to know each other, my gaze shoots over her shoulder, drawn right to Brad, as if my body is now primed to find him.

"Oh, is that for me?" Jess asks, pulling her gaze away from my crotch and moving closer.

I chuckle awkwardly. "Yeah…" I lie because I know who it's for, and I hate myself for being this hard for that asshole.

I try to be discreet about looking at Brad. Hot as hell in his black biker jacket and jeans, he's talking with some guys I've seen around campus. Not his regular crew. He keeps glancing my way, but I can tell he's trying not to.

I want him to look at me again, but this desire is definitely whatever spell he has me under.

I'm craving his gaze.

I want him to get his ass over here. I want him to press his body against mine again. Treat me like shit, if that's what he wants. I don't care. He could bend me over right now and force himself into me—

Stop it!

"So what did you say your major is?" Jess asks.

"English."

"Really? What kind of work are you planning to go into?"

"English professor. That's the long-term plan."

I sense Brad's gaze burning into my cheek—or maybe that's just what I want to feel, but when I look over her shoulder again, he's staring at me, heading toward us.

"What are you majoring in?" I ask Jess as Brad steps up beside us, catching her by surprise.

"Sorry to interrupt," he tells Jess, "but do you mind if I steal this guy for a minute?"

She insists we swap numbers before I go, so while she takes my phone and inputs her digits, Brad and I stare each other down. He looks like, at any moment, he's gonna attack me. After she hands me my phone, Brad heads off into the yard, and I follow. He continues on through the back gate, leading me on a path into the woods.

Probably not a smart move to go with him into the woods, where he could kick my ass and leave me for dead. I wonder if I'm just feeling confident I'll be able to put up a good fight and escape, or if this is part of this sick lust I have for him, drawing me to him without regard for my safety.

We walk for a few yards before he spins toward me. He moves fast, and before I know it, he snags my shirt collar and shoves me against a tree. By the time my mind catches up with what just happened, I feel something sharp against my neck.

A blade?

Fuck.

I should've thought this through instead of blindly following; although, considering how it feels being close to him, I'm not sure I had a choice. Even with the threat of him slicing through an artery, I can't deny this chemistry and that it's hot as fuck being up against the tree like this. My body's as stiff as my cock.

"What the hell did you do to Codes?" he grits out, some of his spit landing on my bottom lip, and I try to play cool as I lick it off.

Is it just in my mind, or does he taste delicious?

"Codes?"

"Cody. You did something to his head."

"He was fucking with *my* head. I was just trying to make it stop."

"How did you know that, though? Who the fuck are you? What are you doing to us?" He presses the blade against my neck.

"What the fuck is the point of this knife when I'm

telling you what I know?"

"I don't believe a goddamn word that comes out of your mouth. And to think I was trying to help you."

Help me? If his goal is to confuse the hell out of me, mission accomplished.

His breath fogs before him as his gaze shifts to my lips. He wants me. I can feel it with every fiber of my being. And I want him. So fucking bad it's making my balls sore.

His gaze shifts down. "You're fucking hard right now?"

I check his crotch. "You are too."

We stand there in silence. His hot breath rushes against my face again. As it hits me, my body vibrates with desire.

He grunts. "I can't even think straight."

"I've been having that problem recently too, but I don't figure we mean the same thing. Now put the knife away, and let's have a fucking conversation."

His jaw tenses. I take his free hand and press it against my crotch, urging him to stroke me, and his eyes shut as his body trembles. He takes a breath, like he finally has some relief from the thick tension between us. Whatever he's done to me, it's clearly affecting him too.

"Fuck," he grunts. "I can't do this. I don't fucking like you."

"And I'm straight. But let's just rub one out, and then we can talk. Deal?" I can't believe I'm saying this.

I'm just that desperate.

He grits his teeth, his head shifting either way before he says, "Fuck it." He pulls his blade back and folds it up, sliding it into his jacket pocket.

After having a knife to my throat, the smart thing would be to run, but my rational mind isn't in control, just this potent, feral desire for this asshole. It's so powerful that I can't even blame myself for whatever's about to happen.

And I can blame him for all this once I get some relief.

I check to make sure no one at the party can see me behind this tree.

Brad unfastens his fly in no time, and as he starts to help with mine, I grab hold of his shaft.

"Damn, that's big," I say.

"The hardest you saw was in the showers, and that was nothing."

I pull my hand back and lick my palm, tasting him— *God*, he tastes good—before putting it back around his cock and giving him a few strokes.

He finally gets my fly undone and his hand under my boxers, rubbing my cock.

"Thank Christ," he says, as though we just needed to get to this moment so he could have some peace. Angry as I am that this is my life right now, at least I can enjoy the fact that Brad has to suffer too.

He shoves me against the tree, pushing close, until

his chest is against mine. He leans down, his face settling near my cheek before he slides his nose across it, inhaling. "You smell so good," he whispers before rocking his hips, his cock stiffening even more as he offers a bite against my throat.

I roll my head against the tree.

His teeth push into my flesh, shooting sparks from the spot right through me. It's the sort of experience that makes me forget all about our issues. Makes me forgive him every asshole thing he's done to me—even having a knife to my throat—as long as he doesn't fucking stop. Because if he does...*that* I'll never forgive him for.

"That's right, just like that, Pretty Boy," he says as I continue working his cock. "So fucking pretty."

My cock firms in his hold as he says the words, which sound like a confession rather than trying to drive home an insult.

"I shouldn't want this," I tell him. "I'm straight."

He snickers against my neck. "You mentioned. Mmmm. Not my Pretty Boy then, my Straight Boy. Even better."

He offers another nibble, then an open-mouthed kiss to the flesh.

His tongue and lips send waves of sensation through me. Can only imagine how good it'd feel wrapped around my cock, taking me to release.

I start to call out before his hand clamps down on my mouth, and I'm relieved one of us was thinking fast

LUST

enough to keep me from alerting the party to come out and watch the two guys jerking off behind the tree.

We work together in a wild frenzy—we're just strokes, breaths, pulsing cocks, and this steady rush of sensation that assures me this was the best way to end our agony. He presses his chest tighter against my body, and with my free hand, I grab on to the back of his head, drawing him closer as he continues making out with my neck.

"I'm about to come," he whispers into my skin before he bites at my jaw, and I feel his hips jerk and his cock throb before the warm sensation rushes against my abs.

I keep jerking for a few moments, reveling in the sensation of him marking me.

Like the only thing I ever needed in my life was to have a man dump his load on my body.

What is this?

What is happening to my goddamn brain?

I can hardly think straight before he pulls his cock away and releases me.

"That's fucking cruel," I say. "I got you off." He drops to his knees. "Brad, you fucking asshole—"

Before I can go any further, I feel a warm, wet surprise around my dick.

He doesn't hesitate. Doesn't question anything. Just goes to work.

All wet, wild tongue and lips.

This is a fucking pro, and he's so good, my eyes fucking water as my nerves celebrate his expertise.

He keeps going at it, then with his free hand, cups my balls. The pressure mounts quickly. Too fucking quickly.

"Brad, I'm gonna—"

He pulls off and says, "In my mouth. I don't care. I need it," before his lips slide back down the shaft, and he takes me to the hilt, deep throating me as my hips jerk about, and I feel the pressure finally release.

I place my hands on either side of his head, holding him in place, gasping from the intensity of the high. And even after swallowing me, he's still lapping my cum off my cock like a goddamn popsicle.

As I catch my breath, reeling in what lingers from the explosive release, all I can think is—

What the fuck did we just do?

6

BRAD

I FINALLY MANAGE to pry myself away from Luke's body.

That overwhelming desire, which felt like it was splitting my soul in two, has let up, and for the first time since I approached him, I can think clearly.

I take deep breaths as I recover from the frenzied workout we just shared.

I wish I'd been strong enough to resist him. But as I intuited his desires, felt his every sexual wish, I found myself totally submissive to them. In that moment, Luke was my master, and I his humble servant, dedicated to his pleasure. As I tasted his skin, felt his hard girth, all I could think was, *Do what you want to me. I'm all yours, Luke Waters.*

"This isn't good," I say now that I can appreciate just how out of my mind he made me.

"That wasn't good for you?" Luke asks, sounding skeptical as his brows tug closer together.

I shoot him a dirty look. "Not what I meant, and

you know it."

He only jerked me off and I blew him, but it was more exciting, more fulfilling, than any fuck I've ever had. I'm still reeling, my body surging with relief from caving to the urges he's stirred since that first pickup game.

I fasten my fly, and Luke does the same, but I notice he's not trying to wipe me off him. He's still stained with my cum, and I love that just as much as I love the taste that lingers on my tongue.

Fuck this guy for what he's doing to me.

I'm about to restart my interrogation when he spits out, "Why are you doing this to me?"

The hell?

"What kind of gaslighting bullshit is this? *You're* the one fucking with *us*."

"I have no idea what you're talking about."

"Liar!" His denial evokes an impassioned response that isn't just feral lust and desire. I start toward him with the same intensity as when I had the blade to his throat.

Not that I would have used it. I wanted to intimidate him into revealing his wicked plan. Being that close to his body, feeling the heat he gives off, taking in his scent, I don't know that I even have it in me to harm anything that brings my body so much pleasure.

"What did you do to Cody, asshole?" I press.

"What did he do to me?" He moves ever closer, his

hands clenched at his sides.

I'm worried all that desire is about to hit me again, but I'm relieved to discover our jerk-off and BJ session quieted those impulses, at least temporarily.

"He was in my fucking head, wasn't he?" Luke says. "I wasn't imagining that."

"Like you don't already know," I snarl. Don't even know where the hell that came from. Like with most things that involve Luke Waters, seems safe to blame him for the primal responses he activates in me.

"Why bring me out here if you're gonna continue being evasive?"

"Why did you come to St. Lawrence, Luke?"

He looks stunned. "St. Lawrence has one of the best English departments in the country, and I'm an English major."

"Bullshit."

His face scrunches up. "They're ranked third in the US, between Harvard and Yale."

"I meant that's a bullshit reason. There's another one."

His gaze wanders, and he bites his bottom lip. "My dad went here, okay?"

"I already know that. We did a background check before you came here. And I don't give a fuck what you tell most people about why you came here. Why did you *really* come here? What are you trying to do to us?"

His head jerks back, his eyes widening. "You guys are

the ones fucking with me. Seth that day on the field. Cody bringing up all that horrible shit from my childhood. And then you...you...look what you just made me do."

He might as well have slapped me. "*Made you do?*"

"I told you: I'm straight."

"You think you're the first guy who's ever told me that?" Although I must admit, when he said it, that made messing around even hotter.

"I've known I'm straight as well as I've known anything about myself, but suddenly I come here, and I..." He glances at the house, lowering his voice when he turns back to me. "You're doing something with my head like your friends did. Like when Seth made me back down from fighting you. Is that your game? You find straight guys and make them hard for you? I hope you know what that makes you: a fucking sexual predator."

It's a sobering accusation, and his scowl appears sincere. In case there is any truth to what he's saying, I quickly defend myself. "I don't have the ability to make anyone attracted to me. My power makes people's desire for me stronger, but it must already be present. So yeah, I've helped a few bi and gay guys figure their shit out, but I'm not coercing people to fuck them against their will, so don't put this on me."

He's still eyeing me suspiciously, like he doesn't buy it. If this is an act, he's damn convincing.

What am I saying? It has to be a fucking act!

"You just said your power. So you admit you guys are fucking around with… God, this is so fucking dumb, I don't even want to say it."

I chuckle because some days I find it hard to admit to myself.

"Magic." He says the word through his teeth, softly, like he's embarrassed. Reminds me of how Seth, Cody, and I felt after we stumbled across this stuff.

"Like you don't already know that."

"I didn't know it until you guys started bullying me. And you guys weren't exactly subtle."

"That was the point. And now that you know our secret, it's time to cop to yours. Where did you learn how to use your powers?"

"I don't have powers, Brad."

His continued denial makes my rage flare up again. "Shut your lying mouth. You know how long it's taken us to get to where we are? We found out about this shit last year, and we've been training ever since. Enough to know not only that you have powers, but that you must've been training for even longer." It's the reason I became so suspicious of him after what he did to Cody. The reason I was convinced what he was doing must've been intentional.

"Are you messing with me?" he asks.

"What you did to Cody. You got another explanation for that? Because I'd love to hear it." Real eager to hear how he tries to weasel his way around that.

"I just resisted what he was doing to me."

"Yeah, and he's been having the biggest fucking panic attacks since that day. He still can't get out of bed."

"I didn't do that, but you expect me to feel bad for him after what he brought up in me?"

I ball my hands into fists. I want to beat the shit out of him until he confesses, but I can feel those familiar sensations rising. Making my dick shift in my pants.

"Stop," I tell him.

"I told you—"

"I'm not talking about Cody." I take his hand and press it against my crotch, running it along the zipper so he can feel my girth. "You're doing this to me."

He grips my jeans and strokes, not like he's assessing it, but like he's playing with it again.

Pissed as I am with him right now, I fear this power he has over me. That all he has to do is ratchet it up enough and, like with that jerk-off session, he'll be free to make me do whatever the hell he wants.

He releases me, grabs my hand, and puts it on his crotch. "And what's this? Am I doing this to me too?" It's like he's got a stone in there.

"When I use my power on guys, it affects me too," I say. "I assume it works the same for you."

"Brad, I don't know how you got accepted to St. Lawrence if you can't get it around your thick skull that whatever's happening right now is clearly from whatever shit you and your friends are messing around with."

I take a few controlled breaths. I hate that he could have a point. It's not like we're experts in this. Although, what if this is just the part of me who wants to fuck around with him getting me to let my guard down?

Whatever it is, I can hear him out and reserve my judgment. What other choice do I have?

"Take me to the other guys," he says.

"Seth will fucking lose his mind right now. He's so on edge about Cody. We both are. Cody's very sensitive."

"Didn't seem all that sensitive when he was coming for me, weaponizing one of the hardest days of my life," Luke spits out.

I growl. "Since you're new around here, a little advice: don't fuck with Cody, or you're gonna get the wrath of the Sinners."

"The Sinners? Is that what you guys call yourselves?"

I nod. "Yeah. Cody's a good guy, and he was only doing what we had to do to scare you off."

"So that's your game plan? Getting rid of me? Fucking knew it."

He looks relieved to have some answers, and I wish I could enjoy the same catharsis.

"Why?" he presses.

"Because you being at St. Lawrence means some fucked-up shit is gonna happen."

"How could you possibly know that?"

"If you really are encountering this shit for the first time, then I'd think you'd throw out the window what you know about what's possible and start from scratch."

"Okay," he says. "I'll start from scratch if you'll start from scratch too and stop assuming you know what I'm thinking or doing here."

He reaches his hand out for a shake, and I eye it. "We both know me touching you more isn't gonna lead to anything good."

My gaze shifts to his lips.

And already I feel the impulse to lurch forward and take them.

He gulps, his Adam's apple shifting in a way that has another rush of energy sweeping through me.

Despite how distracting Straight Boy can be, I force myself to focus on the reason why I'm out here.

"Tomorrow," I say. "Meet me at the old church in the woods at eight. I'm not sure Cody will have the strength, but Seth and I will be there. A truce until then. And since shaking's a crap idea for you and me, let's just say you having my cum on you and me having yours in me will satisfy that requirement. Instead of with blood…a cum oath. Deal?"

He considers this before nodding. "Deal."

As soon as he says the word, I feel the impulse to move in for a lick…or a kiss… God, he has kissable lips.

Instead, I ball my hands into fists, and without another word, head back to the house.

There's a sting to walking away from him, but if I'd stuck around much longer, my body would've demanded another release.

And if we start something again, I'm not sure I'll be satisfied with jerking off or a quick blowjob.

7

LUKE

As I head out of the dorm on my way to the old church, my cock's already perking up, my body eager to be in Brad's presence again.

I wish my cock wouldn't betray me, that it'd be as frustrated as the rest of me with what an ass Brad's been. But after what he did to me last night, I can't blame my body. The sensations he stirred when he was right on me, his lips against my throat, then around my cock, his wet mouth promising an end to my suffering... And then when he swallowed my load, it felt like ever since he first saw me, he's been thinking about deep throating his Pretty Boy. Or his Straight Boy.

No, not *his*.

I'm not his.

I'm fucking straight, I remind myself. It'd be fine to be hot for him if I were queer, but what's happening between us doesn't have anything to do with my preference. Or does it? I was quick to deny being attracted to guys from the start, but I acknowledge there have been times I've thought guys were hot. Maybe I even felt attracted to them, and I just didn't realize that's what it was. What if this has always been in me and somehow Brad's bringing it out? Jury's still out on Brad orchestrating it with his powers, but even if he's not, it's possible this is because he and his idiot friends are playing with forces they don't understand, and maybe the way Brad and I are lusting after each other is an unintended consequence.

After our chat, Brad texted me directions to where we'd meet up. Didn't mention how he got my information. Was that in the background check too? Did he use magic to find it out? Or is there a more mundane explanation, like asking Alexei for it?

I follow the directions, taking one of the nature trails in the woods surrounding the school, using my phone light to guide me. This is about as stupid as following Brad into the woods, since the guys could jump me out here. Although, if Brad wanted to hurt me, he already had his chance when he had that blade on me.

I head along the path for a few minutes before it opens out to a clearing, where I spot a church. Just beyond it, the moonlight illuminates a few statues of saints and the Virgin Mary—a cemetery.

As I near the church, I notice the details in the dilapidated building—chipped white paint, rotting wood, boarded-up windows. It's not massive, but it likely catered to a few hundred congregants in its heyday—

maybe in the sixties or seventies, judging by the wear and tear. At the front, there's a gravel parking lot beside an old dirt road that I doubt has access to a main road anymore.

I head around to the other side of the church, where I discover a set of boards patching up a hole in the wall, which is where Brad's text said I should enter. I shift them, making space and heading inside. After resetting the boards behind me, I pan my phone around the room: old pews, a worn-out organ, and the expected church paraphernalia.

"You're late," a low growl comes from nearby, stirring fear, tension, and frustration in quick succession, all mixed with my undeniable arousal. Fortunately, the latter feels more manageable since we jerked off.

Brad's fist is clenched at his side, and unlike when he cornered me in the woods last night, I suspect this time it's not because he wants to hand my ass to me, but because he's got other ideas for my ass.

He guides me to a door, then down a set of steps to the basement. Candles are set up around the place, illuminating it in a soft orange glow. In the middle of the cement floor is the chalk pentagram I saw when Cody was fucking with my head. It's wild to have confirmation that it really exists outside my mind, and it helps my skeptical self accept that, despite any remaining doubts, this is real.

Seth rises from a desk on the other side of the room

and starts toward us. "What did you do to Codes?" He approaches fast, and I figure he's about to deck me, but he stops a few inches short and spits out, "Tell me the truth. Now."

I've felt his power. I know at least one of the tricks up his sleeve. He did it to me and I assume to Prof. Strauss too, so I wait to lose control of my will.

But nothing happens.

He grits his teeth, reaching into his shirt collar and retrieving a cross necklace like Brad's. "The truth. *Now.*"

Given how Brad's pulled that thing out at times, I suspect they're stronger when they hold the necklace…or maybe it helps them focus their power. Whatever it usually does, it's obviously not working on me.

Seth's gaze shifts to Brad. "You still believe a damn thing he says?"

"I didn't say I believed him. I said we should listen."

Seth grunts. "Look, you guys fucking around doesn't change shit."

I glare at Brad. "You told him?" Shouldn't surprise me, though. Maybe I was a fool for trusting him after all.

"No, no. I didn't," he insists.

"But *you* just did," Seth snaps. "See? Plenty of ways of getting the truth out of you, even without my goddamn powers."

"We didn't fuck," Brad clarifies.

"I don't give a shit." Seth moves quickly, snatching me by my jacket and shoving me against the corner by the stairwell entry. "Listen to me, you piece of shit."

"Seth!" Brad shouts.

But Seth disregards it and goes on, "You ever attack Cody again like that, you so much as give him a nasty look, and I won't need any powers because I will tear your navel through your goddamn skull. Do you hear me?"

Even in the dim lighting, I can see how red his face has turned and the tears in his eyes. Despite how he's treating me, there's something nice about seeing how much he cares about his friend. I've never had a friend willing to defend me like this. And as much of an ass as he's been to me, it's something I can respect.

But my appreciation of his loyalty doesn't distract me for long. "Cody attacked *me*," I say. "Like I told Brad, I was trying to clear my head of that shit he was dredging up. I didn't mean to hurt him."

He studies my expression. "If you're telling the truth, that's fucking worse." As I twist my face up, he says, "Which sounds worse to you: a psychopath who has his finger on a trigger to a bomb, or someone running around with a bomb, totally unaware of what they have in their hands?"

"Neither sounds like a great option."

"I'm struggling with the same thing." He gets right in my face. "If you come for someone, you come for me. Or I will end you. Are we understood?"

Brad grabs his shoulder and pulls him back, though

Seth keeps his hands firmly on my jacket.

"Seth, get your goddamn hands off him." The way Brad says it takes Seth by surprise, and even Brad flinches, like he wasn't expecting those words to come out so severely. They almost sounded like he's trying to protect me from Seth, but that can't be right. Not when he had a knife to my neck last night. Although, he said he was just trying to scare me, and after everything that's happened, I'm tempted to believe him.

Seth sneers at his friend. "You gonna tell me why you just said that, or should I urge you to tell me?"

"Seth, don't you fucking dare."

"I know it's hard with what's going on, but try not to think with your dick." Seth gives me a shove, and Brad tenses up like he's having to keep from going at his friend.

Given what just happened, maybe I shouldn't press, but considering how pissed Seth is, I'm too curious not to ask. "So how is he?"

Seth turns away from me. "Only time he stops crying is to sleep. One of us has to be there to make sure he eats. Cody's been down from using his powers before, but this is worse than normal."

"But he'll be okay?" I press, and Brad and Seth exchange a glance.

It reminds me of my conversation with Brad, who, despite his assumptions about me, obviously didn't have the answers for what's going on. But they have to know more than me, so I start asking the questions nagging at me since my chat with Brad. "You said you've had these powers since freshman year…"

"Yeah," Brad says. "Seth, me, and Cody would come out here to hang out—"

"Remember when we said the less we tell him, the better?" Seth snaps.

"So something in this old church is how you found out about your powers?" I persist, and Brad nods, which earns a groan from Seth.

"That's all you need to know about why we can do that," Brad says. "That better?"

Seth rolls his eyes.

"Now *you*," Brad says. "When was your first experience feeling like you could do something that you shouldn't have been able to do?"

"That thing with Cody."

"Bullshit," Seth says. "I know you did something when I pushed that suggestion on you and you resisted me."

Pushed? So that's what they call what he does.

"That first time," I say, "if I did something, I didn't know it. And I haven't done anything since I've been in here."

"I told you: he thought you hypnotized him," Brad explains.

"And Brad?" Seth asks. "What have you been doing to him?"

"Trust me, if I could stop it, I would." Now I'm lying. I never experienced anything like what we shared in the woods. Life's too short and too full of pain. Like hell I'd ever let anyone tear from me something that felt so fucking good.

"The thing with Cody was the first time I realized I'd done something," I clarify.

"So I guess we can just cut through the Q and A about all the dabbling into magic you've done in the past?" Seth asks.

"Outside of books, movies, and TV shows…no."

Seth's narrowed gaze suggests he's not buying it.

"Your turn again," I tell them. "Brad said you were trying to scare me off. That something terrible would happen if I stayed here."

"That's right," Seth says.

"Tell me what it is."

"I don't know that this is a good idea," Brad says.

"Oh, but I thought we were telling him shit. Why not this too? People will die." Seth looks me in the eyes. "Good people. Because of you."

In an instant, all the thoughts racing through my brain cease, and there's an unsettling quiet in my mind. When I look at Brad, he has his eyes closed, taking a deep breath. A question finally springs to mind. "How could you possibly know that?"

"Cody had a vision," Seth says. "You are connected to something wicked. Something evil that's about to be unleashed on Lawrenceville."

"Unleashed? What? From where?"

They exchange another look, tension thick in the air as neither chimes in to answer my question.

"*That* we're not willing to share," Seth says.

"Luke." As Brad says my name, a warm sensation stirs in my chest. "Cody has seen things in the past that have happened."

"Well, he didn't know I was gonna resist him the other day, did he? So he doesn't know everything. I've watched enough hack TV shows about psychics to know that he could be misunderstanding whatever he thinks he's seeing. You guys thought I had some kind of powers, so it's obvious you barely understand whatever you're messing around with. I can't throw away my future because of something you guys think *might* happen."

Seth says, "Now you see why we didn't just approach you, explain the situation, and ask you to please leave St. Lawrence."

"Luke, if you don't go," Brad says, "people will die. And you might too."

Unlike Seth, Brad is calm, measured, but I can hear the concern in his voice, and it's clear he believes that's what's gonna happen.

As I'm struggling to take it all in, Brad approaches me and rests his hand on my shoulder. I've worked up a shit ton of adrenaline since I got here, but his hand pressed against my jacket makes me relax.

"I think you've learned enough for now," he says. "Let's head back to the dorms. You don't have to figure everything out tonight."

I nod. Despite what a prick he's been to me since I arrived, he's right. I need time to process everything.

BRAD AND I walk along the path through the woods, back to the dorms, once again with my phone as a flashlight. Seth said he had some things to finish up at the church, but I have a feeling he just doesn't want to be around the bastard who hurt his friend.

I'm still trying to make sense of our conversation.

Powers? Visions?

What will be unleashed if I stay at St. Lawrence?

Despite everything I've experienced, it's hard for any of it to sink in.

"I guess now that we've gotten all that out of the way," Brad says, "I owe you an apology."

"For being an asshole to me, or for pulling a knife on me?"

"Yeah, maybe a few apologies."

"I'll consider accepting your apology," is as much as I'm willing to say, but truth is, since they started explaining what the hell's been going on, I'm discovering there's more to Brad than some asshole bully. If he and his friends really believe all that, then they had to find a way to scare me off to save people's lives...and mine too. Those aren't the actions of assholes.

I wonder if it's discovering this other side to him, or if it's being this close to him that activates all these powerful urges in me, but I want him to touch me so I can get another taste of that delicious rush.

I'm about to reach over to him, but I restrain myself. *Don't make it weird.*

We walk in silence for a few more moments before he pulls his hand out of his jacket pocket and reaches over, taking me by the wrist.

We stop, and I turn to him, enjoying the rush that pulses through me, exciting my nerves.

He releases my wrist quickly. "Sorry, I shouldn't have done that."

"Not a big deal. What did you want?"

"I didn't want anything. I just knew you wanted me to do that."

"You knew I wanted what?"

"Me to touch you."

My cheeks warm. I'm tempted to say it's not true, but my curiosity outweighs my embarrassment. "How did you know?"

"Not sure where it comes from, but it's like when we messed around at the house party and I sensed you wanted me to blow you."

That's right. I did think about wanting him on his

knees…and then he did just that.

"Are you reading my mind?"

"Not really." His gaze drifts off. "Have you ever had a dream where you run into someone you've never met in real life, but in the dream, you know all these things about them? Just, are certain of them? It's like that. Makes me a real good lay." He sports a cocky grin as his gaze meets mine, looking particularly adorable.

Jesus Christ, after the conversation we had, *that's* what's on my mind?

"A good lay and you know it? Sounds like a dangerous combination."

"Most people enjoy it."

My dick shifts in my pants as my thoughts wander.

I imagine him lurching forward and taking my mouth.

Maybe throwing me against a tree and showing me what else he can do with his mouth.

Maybe even with some other parts of his body so I don't have to think about all the wild shit he and Seth just told me.

His playful expression shifts to concern, and with one hand still on my wrist, he grabs my other arm with his free hand. "Stop," he warns.

Fuck, he wasn't kidding about his power.

"Well, touching me certainly isn't going to make me stop," I tell him, pulling away, and surely sounding more than a little resentful that he won't be making my fantasy come true.

"Sorry, yes, you're right." He shoves his hands in his jacket pockets, but that's not where I want them right now. "Speaking of which…I've been thinking a lot about what you said about me being a sexual predator."

I cringe at him even bringing up the conversation. "Brad, I'm starting to understand that you aren't doing this to me the way I thought."

"Yeah, but I'm sorry for messing around with you at Alpha Alpha Mu's party. I assumed you wanted it too, which is why I was feeling the way I was, but considering how much weird shit there is around you, and that I can't even control what I feel, we don't know what we're fucking with here. We don't ever have to bring it up again. And what's happening between us as far as what my powers are doing, we don't have to get into details with the guys about it if you're not comfortable with that."

Brad Henning is just full of surprises. In such a short span of time, he's gone from being douche extraordinaire to this thoughtful guy who's genuinely concerned about me.

"*I'm* not sorry about what happened at the party," I say. He tilts his head, and my cheeks are warm again. "It was pretty epic, actually."

He chuckles awkwardly. "It was, right?" But his expression turns serious again. "You're sure you're straight?"

I take a moment before replying. "Maybe I was too quick to say that. I've never done anything with a guy, and when it happened after the Seth thing, I assumed it was something you were doing to me. But maybe, like you mentioned with other guys, I have some bi-curious part you activated when we met."

"Maybe. I just don't know that we should fuck around like that again while we don't know what's going on."

My heart sinks. After all that, I'm not gonna be able to even feel that again? Fuck me.

"College is about experimenting, right?" I say as a half-joke.

He studies my expression. "You keep saying shit like that, and you're gonna make it real hard for me to keep my hands off you."

"*Shit like that*," I tease, which makes him smile before stepping closer to me, his gaze on my mouth.

I lick my lips, and he places his hand against my face, running his thumb across the bottom lip. Desire pulses through me, radiating through my body.

He pulls his hand back, leaving my body wanting so much more.

"I'm sorry for how we dumped all this on you tonight, Luke. I know it's a lot."

I was enjoying the distraction, but now he's brought it back to the thing that feels like too much to handle. "That's an understatement."

"I know we're asking a lot, telling you to leave your dream school, but we wouldn't be doing all this if we didn't think there was something to Cody's vision."

"I can appreciate that. But you see what I'm saying? What if you guys are wrong? I've been planning to come to St. Lawrence since I was a kid. This is a big ask."

He can't possibly understand how much this means to me. That this is one of the last connections I still have with my dad. But there's also the fear…what if they're right? What if my being at St. Lawrence could lead to something horrible happening?

He takes a moment before saying, "Yeah. I know it is."

I snicker.

"What's so funny?"

"I like this version of you a lot more than the ass you were being."

He grimaces. "Can we please forget that other stuff ever happened?"

"Oh, hell no. I fully intend on using this against you as much as possible. As a matter of fact, I think you should have to make it up to me."

I step closer, until I can feel his breath against my face. My nerves tingle with excitement as I think about how his face would feel against mine.

He gulps, surely sensing what's on my mind. "I think now would be a good time to get back to the dorms."

He's right. With all I need to consider, the last thing I should be thinking about is messing around with him.

But I know that's not gonna happen.

8

BRAD

"SO I GOT a bunch of Campbell's Chicken and Wild Rice because I know that's your favorite. And then I got some frozen pizzas..." Seth goes through the groceries we picked up at the store as he puts stuff away in the kitchenette cabinets. Most of the dorms don't have this luxury, but for the really wealthy kids like Seth and Cody, whose parents are willing to fork over money, or even better, donations to the school, they get the Delta One St. Lawrence experience.

As I sit on the edge of his bed, Cody grabs the remote and turns down the *Vanderpump Rules* episode he's watching. For the first time in a few days, his cheeks have some color in them again, and he can keep his eyes open, but he's got this glazed-over look in them.

After Luke's freak-out in the showers, Seth and I hurried over to the church to check on Cody. We found him lying still, both of us fearing the worst when we saw his unconscious body. He finally stirred, and once he recovered, he said he was just fatigued but too tired to get up, so Seth carried him back to the dorms. Since then, Seth has been diligent in his care of Cody, more so than usual.

"How you holding up, buddy?" I ask.

"Like I need to get off my ass and turn in some assignments so I'm not behind when I go back to class next week."

"Are you sure you're gonna be good by then?" Seth asks.

"I can get through it."

"How about we play it by ear?" Seth says. "You want me to throw some soup in the microwave? Or maybe just a bowl of Cinnamon Toast Crunch?"

Cody groans. "I wish you wouldn't go to all this trouble over me."

"You love when I go to the trouble."

Cody smirks. "In that case, Cinnamon Toast Crunch would be great."

Seth beams like knowing there's something he can do to cheer Cody up has made his day. He pours cereal into a bowl and joins us, plopping down on the opposite side of Cody's bed and passing Cody his dry-cereal snack.

"Thank you, Seth." Cody tosses a few crunches into his mouth, chews and swallows, then glances between Seth and me. "Okay, now that I'm feeling better, I'm ready to hear how it went."

Cody had asked about our meeting right after our chat with Luke, but he was still so depleted, Seth insisted we wait a few days, at least until he was coherent enough to hold a conversation. Now seems like the time, but considering how it went, neither of us is eager to share.

And unlike Seth, I don't blame Luke for his reaction.

Despite our pleasant conversation on our way back to the dorms, Luke hasn't talked to me since. Every time I've run into him, he's distant, distracted. But even worse, he doesn't look well, and I know it's because of the time we've spent apart. It's like I can feel his acute pain and want to comfort him. But I don't want to push when he clearly doesn't want to speak to me.

At least, not yet.

Seth and I tell Cody about the meeting at the old church, and when we're finished, Cody says, "I want to talk to him."

"You're not doing that," Seth says through his teeth.

"You're not the boss of me." It's the first time Cody's sounded like he has his strength back. "And just because this stuff hits me hard doesn't mean I'm this frail thing, so back off."

I know Cody appreciates the care Seth takes with him, but Cody never hesitates to let him know when he's overstepping.

Seth's jaw clenches.

"I can show him," Cody says, "like I did with you guys. If he sees, and really feels it the way we did, he'll have a harder time denying it."

Seth shakes his head. "Codes, he said he can't control

his powers. He admitted what happened was an accident. What if you try to show him and he resists, and you end up in the fucking ER?"

"Seth has a point," I admit.

"Don't either of you forget why we're doing this," Cody says. "It isn't about me or us. I know you think you're protecting me, but if I don't do this and people die, I have blood on my hands. And so do both of you."

"Codes also has a point," I say.

"He's a loose cannon," Seth insists. "And he clearly doesn't give a shit about who he's gonna hurt."

I'm not letting that slide. "That's not fair. If we didn't already have a year of experience with the stuff we encountered, do you really think you'd take everything we said at face value?"

"He's seen what we can do. And what he can do. What more does he need?"

"As he said, he also knows we've been wrong about things. And I'm sure he's wondering how we could know so much about the future but don't have a clue why he has these powers."

Seth glares at me. "You're not exactly impartial."

"What's that supposed to mean?"

"Ask your fucking dick."

"I can't help what's happening there. And since you brought it up, what's happening between us isn't making it easy for him to concentrate on what we talked about. I've seen Luke around campus, and he looks like he's got a bad hangover. Like the longer we go without touching, the harder it is on him."

"And how are you feeling?" Cody asks.

"It's not as bad for me, but every time I see him on campus, it definitely stings. Physically. Then there's this other part: seeing him hurting and knowing I can do something about it. He's avoiding me, though, which pisses me off. I don't like knowing he's suffering."

I get that he wants time to sort through all this, but fuck, it burns…more than I'm willing to share with Seth or Cody. So I can only imagine what it's doing to Luke, and with that on his mind, I don't know how the hell he's supposed to sort through this mess on his own.

"Nice to know you're so worried about your new boyfriend," Seth snipes.

I ball a fist and clench my jaw. "Back. The fuck. Off."

"Enough," Cody says. "I'm meeting with him. I should be fine by Friday. Brad, since I can't trust Seth to keep his cool, will you approach Luke and ask if he could meet us at the church then?"

Excitement courses through me, and Cody's gaze narrows. I don't doubt his intuitive powers have caught this, but he doesn't mention it, surely knowing it'll only piss Seth off that much more, since he's treating me like I'm sleeping with the enemy.

"I'll stop by his dorm. Now that he's had some time to mull things over, it'd be nice to have a chat."

I can tell Seth's stewing over this, which he confirms a moment later. "On the plus side, if he hurts Codes again, we won't have to worry about him being around anymore to be a danger to innocent people."

My nostrils flare, this protective instinct making me want to deck Seth for so much as uttering a threat against Luke.

"Oh, it's so cute having my straight bestie be all protective of me," Cody teases Seth, diffusing the tension. "Now I need another nap."

"Okay, I'll get out of your hair," Seth says.

"Uh-uh." Cody throws his arms around Seth and plants his head against his chest. "I need someone to stay and watch the new episode of *Vanderpump* with me."

Seth groans. "Only for you."

"You know I sleep best with my big straight pillow."

Seth and I share a laugh as Cody clings to him, and Seth visibly relaxes in his hold.

They have a unique friendship. It's deeper than the bond I share with either of them, but I tend to be more guarded anyway and not nearly as touchy-feely—unless I'm around Luke; I'd feel a lot better if I could just hold him in my arms until this pain lets up.

As Seth repositions so Cody has an easier time lying against him, I say, "In that case, I'm gonna head out. I'll text you after I talk to Luke about Friday."

I leave them to enjoy some reality TV, then head to Luke's dorm room. I knock and wait. Figure he might not even be in, but a sensation stirs in me, and I realize he's on the other side of the door even before it opens. My shoulders relax as I feel visceral relief at the sight of him. My dick constricts in the crotch of my jeans.

Luke doesn't make eye contact, and despite the ease of being this close to him, I still feel the sting, and he must feel it too. I just want to throw my arms around him and kiss him, take it all away.

Focus.

"You got a minute?" I ask.

He doesn't respond. Just steps back into his room, leaving the door open. I take that as an invitation and head in after him, closing the door behind me. His dorm's a standard two-bedroom unit, the side closest to the door adorned with Alexei's comic-book posters.

"Where's Alexei?"

"At the gym. He just left, so he'll be out for a bit." Luke heads over to his desk and sits on the edge, biting his bottom lip.

Quick scenes flash through my mind: I take his mouth, throwing him onto the bed, having my way with him. He wants me to take the lead, to show him how good it can feel.

I have my own fantasies about him, but I know these are his, and I hate myself for prying into what should be his secret thoughts.

I ball my hands into fists, steadying myself to keep from losing control and giving him exactly what he wants. What it feels like he *needs*.

"You're doing that thing again, aren't you?" he asks, cringing.

"I can't help it."

His cheeks turn the prettiest shade of pink. He really is Pretty Boy right now. "This is so awkward."

"I'm sorry."

"If you can't help it, no need to apologize."

As we stand in uncomfortable silence, I notice a picture frame on his desk. He's young, maybe nine or ten. I assume those are his parents standing on either side of him. It reminds me of other things I already know about the guy. His losses. His pain.

"Seems like you've been trying to avoid me for the past few days," I say. "Not that I blame you." Although, there's a primal part of me that's pissed, as though he's depriving me of something that's rightfully mine.

"Yeah," he says. "I needed to clear my head."

"What have your thoughts been since we talked?"

He places his palms behind him on the desk and leans back. "Depends on when you ask me. At times I think you, Cody, and Seth are out of your minds and that you've pulled me into your delusion. Other times, the longer I spend stressing out, the more I fear I'll be potentially responsible for causing other people's deaths. Then there's this selfish part to it…and trying to avoid you has been so…" His chin trembles and his eyes water. "Do you have any idea how fucking hard it's been to try and avoid seeing you?"

More than you know.

"How are you holding up?" I ask.

His jaw tightens as though I've only highlighted the pain he's experiencing.

"When I saw you in the hall at General Classroom the other day," I say, "it was like a spear to my chest. I had to run to the restroom and take a minute to recover." I'm hoping if I disclose my own experience, maybe he won't feel so uncomfortable sharing his.

He blinks a few times, glancing around his room. "I don't know... The image of razor blades lodged in my chest comes to mind." He chuckles, but the strain in his expression tells me it's not much of a joke. "Staying away has only fucked with my head even more. Feels like it about near killed me. Before I knew who was knocking, I was terrified it was just Alexei coming back for something he forgot, and then I would've started crying because I can't fucking stand this."

As much as it pains me to hear him say it, it's a relief too. "I promise it's painful for me too."

He smirks and finally looks at me. "Well, it does cheer me up to know it hurts you too. Some kind of fucked-up schadenfreude, right?"

I snicker.

"This is so strange," he goes on. "I shouldn't have this kind of feeling about someone I don't even know. And I'm supposed to be thinking about my future and if

I'm putting other people's lives at risk, and yet I can't get out of my mind what we did in the woods." He shakes his head. "Anyway, I'm guessing you didn't come over here to hear me bitch and moan about whatever messed-up chemistry we have."

"I know I may not seem like it from our initial interactions," I say, "but I can be a good listener."

He does a double take, like he's surprised by the comment.

"But as far as why I came over, I wanted to tell you that Cody wants to meet with you. He thinks it might help if you can see the vision and decide for yourself what you believe."

"Really?"

"He hopes he'll be strong enough by Friday."

"Seth must be so happy about this."

"Cody made it clear it's not Seth's decision."

"Even though he stirred up all that shit in my head, I think I'm already starting to like him," he says with a chuckle.

His lips look so adorable in that little smile, I'm tempted to—

No! Stop!

"I know it's hard to imagine," I say, "because of what a dick he was being to you, but Seth is a good guy. In the past, Cody dealt with a lot of issues that took him to some dark places, and Seth is just very protective of him. Like a brother. And he's that way about anyone who hurts Cody. He accidentally gave him Covid last year, and he wouldn't stop beating himself up over it."

Luke's gaze wanders. "I have an uncle who's like that."

"He's the one who took you in after..." I stop myself, but Luke's already looking at me. I've just reminded him of the other ways I've pried into his personal life.

"That's right. Background check. So you know about my parents." He's quiet for a few moments, surely hating me for violating his privacy. Then he turns to the picture on his desk, of him as a kid with his parents. "Yeah, my uncle took me in, and he's been good to me. He knew this was my dream, coming to St. Lawrence. My dad was always talking about it, and that kind of thing leaves an impression on you, you know? After his aneurysm, I knew this is where I'd go. I was accepted freshman year, but I was devastated when I didn't get a scholarship. Then when I made it for this year, it felt like fate. Being here makes me feel close to him. There's something about knowing he wandered these halls. Lived in these dorms. I think he'd be proud." He gulps.

"I'm sure he would be." I hesitate, consider stopping myself, but since I already know this shit about him, it feels right to share. "It's really beautiful that you care so much about your dad. Mine... The only reason he even fought for full custody was to fuck over my mom, who's great. But once he had me, he never treated me like a kid. Hell, he was barely even home."

"I'm sorry."

I shrug. "It's fine. It didn't kill me, right?"

"A lot of things don't kill us, but sometimes we wish they would."

It's a dark comment, one that resonates too deeply.

Seeing him sitting there, his lips frozen in a frown, impulses fire off within me. It'd be so easy to take all his pain away, to help him forget and give him relief. But since he's been avoiding me all week, I doubt it's what he wants right now.

"I should go," I say, starting for the door.

A knot in my chest constricts, tightening as I get closer, but suddenly, I feel Luke's hand against my wrist, and a rush shoots from my wrist to my shoulder.

That knot in my chest relaxes as I turn back to him.

His hand trembles against my wrist, a symptom of whatever withdrawal he's enduring.

"Please, Brad," he says, his voice full of desperation. "I'm trying to be strong right now because this is so fucking embarrassing. But if you walk out that door, it feels like I might die."

His wide eyes tug at something in me.

"Don't leave me like this," he begs.

I won't deny him.

That familiar sense kicks in, and I know exactly what he needs from me.

I place my free hand against his cheek, trailing my fingers across his flesh. He leans into my hold, taking a deep breath as the touch gives us both even more relief.

I guide him back until his shoulder blades are pressed against the wall between his and Alexei's desks. When he tilts his head back, exposing his throat to me, I run my thumb down to his chin, then to his Adam's apple, and around to his nape. His shaking subsides, as though his body is only content when it can revel in my touch.

Is it wrong how satisfying it is to know he needs this? Needs me?

I guide my hand farther down, probing the dip between his pecs and the rigid indentations in his abs. Then I lean close and offer a gentle bite against his throat.

He moans, and it's music to my ears, the sound of the release of so much of the pain he's been carrying around. It collides with my own relief, my belly vibrating with excitement, soaring because Luke and I are finally this close again.

Impulses I know aren't me kick in, and I drop my hands, grabbing the hem of his shirt and pulling it off over his head. I squat down and hook my arms around his thighs, lifting him and placing his ass on the desktop. I lean close so our mouths are only inches apart.

With his eyes closed, he waits, but I linger, enjoying the buzz of excitement making my lips tingle.

Luke opens his eyes. "I thought you knew what I wanted."

"I do. I'm just worried."

His forehead creases.

"Once I get a taste, I don't think that's gonna make being away from you any easier."

"That's smart thinking," he says. "Too bad I'm being a fucking idiot right now."

He moves quickly, placing his hand on the back of my head and mashing his lips against mine.

It's like a fire set in my mouth, spreading through my body, erupting through my flesh. I lose my concept of our bodies and time as we're just wet tongues, hot breaths, sensation, and smacking lips.

I'm still worried. We don't know what's happening between us. Giving in could be the worst thing we could do. But the selfish, primal animal in me doesn't give a flying fuck.

By the time I can think straight again, I discover we're on his bed. It's like I blacked out during the kiss, and now I have his wrists pinned down above his head. He's still dressed except for his shirt, and his legs are hooked around my waist, that ass tight against the crotch of my pants as I thrust, enjoying the sensation of our bodies urging us along.

9

LUKE

MAYBE I WAS a little overdramatic when I told Brad I might die if he left.

But it hurts so goddamn much, even worse once he got here.

Since our talk at the church, I thought distance would give me time to get my head around everything we'd discussed, but it's only made concentrating—on our conversation and schoolwork—that much more of a struggle.

As soon as I grabbed him, I felt soothed, and now that he's lying on top of me, his tongue sweeping across mine before he nibbles at my bottom lip, it feels like we're levitating.

Knowing he's not a total douchebag makes it easier to let him take control, but given how intense these sensations are, I suspect even if he was an ass, I'd still be begging him to end my agony, even if it meant complete and utter humiliation.

Each kiss morphs the shaking from my Brad withdrawal into trembling with excitement for what he'll do to me next. I run my fingers through the hairs along the back of his neck as his lips travel to my chin, which he bites at before kissing down my neck. He crawls back, continuing the trail of kisses down my body. When his mouth reaches my abs, my stomach vibrates with eagerness as he runs his nose against my navel, then offers a kiss and a lick beside it as he unfastens my fly. His movements demonstrate he's a fucking expert, the sex god I've heard about.

He pulls away from my body long enough to remove my jeans and boxers, discarding them beside the bed. Even though he's not touching me, the time we've spent locking lips has given my body enough assurance to quiet those painful sensations.

He strips off his shirt before resuming kissing, licking, nibbling at my abs, his hands gripping my sides, sliding across my flesh, exploring, every inch he covers offering my body the promise that it'll get what it needs and there's no reason to worry or fear.

He kisses up to my chest and licks around my nipple, stimulating the nerves so much, I arch my back.

"Fuck, yes, Brad."

He chuckles. "Does my Straight Boy like that?" he whispers against my flesh.

I blush. "Don't be mean." Feels ridiculous to think I was ever so adamant about being straight, considering how hungry I am for him to show me his secrets. All of them.

"Really? I think it's hot." He gazes up at me, a slick smile on his face. "My Straight Boy getting all hard for me." He crawls back down, pressing his lips against my shaft, then licking. "Throbbing for me."

"Fuck," I mutter, my lips practically buzzing with excitement.

He runs his tongue up and down my cock, which pulls off my abdomen, straining at an angle from how worked up he's got me. He finally takes me into his mouth, his lips and wet tongue sliding across my flesh as he works me up even more, reminding me of what we shared at Alpha Alpha Mu's party.

He releases my cock and says, "God, you taste so fucking good," then slides off the bed and removes his pants and underwear. He tosses his clothes aside before climbing back on top of me, straddling my leg so that his cock runs alongside mine. He relaxes his forearms at my sides, pushes his weight against me, this intense heat radiating off him.

I thrust up against his pelvis, reveling in the sensation of skin against skin, and soon we're both pushing against each other, finding our rhythm.

"You like that, Straight Boy?" he says, his smile spreading into a wide grin, clearly enjoying my little nickname.

"Fuck yeah."

As painful as it was before we started messing around, now I feel playful and alive. All that shit weighing so heavily on me has dissolved—it's impossible to think about it when I'm locked in this heightened state of excitement, eager to explore.

He leans down and kisses my throat again before grazing his teeth against it.

"How is it possible your mouth feels even more intense than when you touch me?" I ask. "Like it's got a direct line to my cock."

He lingers a while longer, his lips and tongue building that pressure in me so that I'm steadily thrusting, eager to get to release.

Being beneath him, his body a blanket over me, I feel sated, so far from the distressed headspace I was in when he first showed up to my room. With our bodies flush, his fat "magic cock" tight against me, I wonder what it would be like to take it. I'm not ready for it, but something in me—connected to the desire that draws me to him—assures me it'll be explosive. If he gave it to me, would I ever be able to manage without it again? Or would the rest of my life be agony, knowing I'd already experienced the greatest pleasure possible?

"You want me to fuck you, don't you?" Brad asks because he must have sensed it. Even if he didn't have this power, I doubt I could hide this from him. "You want to know if the rumors about me are true. If it's really that good. You want to know what it feels like to have a cock inside you. To have a man opening you up. No, not just a man, but *me*."

I should hate that he has access to my vulnerabilities and desires, but I'm so wrapped up in this moment, I don't give a fuck as long as he gives me what I need.

"I know it's too soon," he says, "but promise me your ass. Tell me you'll let me be the one. I promise I'll be good to it."

As his hot breath slams against my flesh, the combination of what he's doing to my body and the fantasies he stirs takes me higher and higher.

"Promise me it's mine," he begs.

My eyes water like I'm fucking relieved he wants me all to himself, and though I know this uncontrollable, overwhelming lust that's overtaken us is simply chemistry, I can't help myself. "It's yours, Brad. All yours."

He sighs and growls as his lips return to mine, his tongue rewarding me for my surrender. Then he pulls away and says, "You like the idea of me building you into it? Easing me into you?"

The images he's conjuring seize control of my thoughts. I can't imagine what it'll feel like to have a dick in me, but I'm fucking obsessed with the thought.

"Not sure how I'm gonna keep from blowing right into that virgin ass," he says against my lips, licking when he's done. His words are the promise of an adventure, but also torture because he's not doing it to me.

I roll my head back against my comforter as waves of sensation course through me. When I thrust up against him, my cock throbs. I've never been this painfully hard without shooting, but I can tell by our pace that we're both getting close. There's a rhythm to it, but also an erratic frenzy. Our bodies seizing control, demanding release.

God, I need fucking release.

"I'm so close," I warn him. My hands instinctively slide around his thick arms, caressing the smooth muscle before I grip them as though needing them to ground me before I take off.

He bites at my Adam's apple, then nuzzles his face into my throat. "Give it to me, Luke. It's *mine*."

He sounds so fucking possessive, and part of me thinks I should hate it or resist it, but suddenly, it's too fucking late for me. I gasp as the pressure mounts until the dam breaks.

Brad's all lips and tongue against my neck as I feel a warm rush across my abdomen, my hips thrusting beyond my control to milk out every last bit. Once again, I notice I'm trembling, but this time, it's obviously from the intensity of my orgasm.

Brad rises onto his knees, gripping his cock and jerking over me. His position, the way he pumps himself with a determined expression, makes it clear he knows what I want.

"All over me, Brad."

"With pleasure." He smirks before white streaks scatter, joining my cum on my abs. As it splatters against my flesh, it's like the final bit of relief I so desperately needed. My muscles relax as I catch my breath.

Brad covers me again, putting his weight on me so I can feel him mashing our cum between us. As he nuzzles his face against my throat, I hook my arms around him, my body screaming, *Fina-fucking-lly*. For the past few days I've been in so much pain and on edge, but in this moment, I'm clear-headed, blissed out.

It's even better than that first jerk-off together.

I'm utterly satisfied.

But as we lie there, breathing in sync, reveling in each other's scent and body heat, I become aware that we'll have to pry apart at some point, and that this magical moment will end.

I cling tighter because it doesn't have to end.

Not just yet.

Eventually Brad stirs, and I'm willing to release him so he can roll off me. When the nagging pain doesn't return, I breathe a sigh of relief. Thank fuck for that.

Brad lies beside me, still catching his breath.

It's amazing not being lost in the fog I was in the past few days, but with this clarity comes the awareness of how out of control that experience was. It must be the same for Brad because one minute he was telling me my ass was his, and now he won't even look me in the eyes.

Fair enough.

"Do you want a drink?" I ask.

"What you got?"

"Some of these canned margaritas. They're pretty good."

He nods. "I can do that."

As I roll out of bed, I feel the sticky mess across my torso, and though I feel so ridiculous for how much I needed it, I have zero intention of wiping it off. Having part of Brad on me right now might be the only thing making me feel normal again.

I grab the margaritas from our mini fridge by Alexei's desk.

Brad sits up on the bed, and I toss him a can before opening one for myself.

As awkward as he's acting, it's apparent, like I could have guessed by the way he prances around nude in the shower, that Brad may be awkward about some things, but his body isn't one of them. And definitely not that cock he's letting air out.

I take a sip of my drink before saying, "I kind of hate having to admit I finally get that those rumors about you aren't rumors."

He blushes. "Shut the fuck up."

"You're the one who brought it up," I tease. "Don't act shy now."

He laughs. "Frottage doesn't really count. Not like we've been fucking. And I only said that stuff because I knew you'd think it was hot."

"And you were right, even if you're not exactly playing fair."

His expression turns serious. "I told you, it's not something I'm trying to do."

"Jesus, Brad. Don't make this more stressful than it already is. If I can't make jokes, I'm gonna lose my damn mind."

"Well, I'm glad you brought up that stuff I was saying because obviously, that whole schtick about making you promise me your ass was just sex talk. I don't actually expect you to do that."

"You don't want this Straight Boy ass?" I ask, angling it toward him.

He glares at me before taking a sip of his drink. "I didn't say I didn't want it. I just don't feel like either of us is really in that much control when we're messing around, so I don't want you to feel like I'm holding you to anything we say in those moments."

I approach my bed. "What a gentleman. I wish I were as nice as you."

His brow creases.

"Because if you think after what we've done so far, I'm not holding you to it, then you are out of your fucking mind."

He chuckles, his gaze wandering. There's this nervous energy about him. It's a side of Brad that's surprising me. Kind of refreshing since it's such a contrast to the cocky bastard he made himself out to be during that first pickup game.

"I'm happy to hold up my end of that bargain," he says.

When I reach the bed, I flex my back and do a few

quick neck stretches before settling on the edge. "Christ, it's wild how different it feels compared to when you got here tonight."

"Tell me about it."

"When I was thirteen and figured out what masturbation was, I thought it was this horrible thing I needed to stop doing, but the more I tried to stop, the more I had to rub one out. This reminds me of that experience but on steroids. Like the more I try to not think about it, the worse it gets."

"You don't have to tell me," Brad says.

"So, lesson learned: not doing anything isn't an option."

"I mean, it's an *option*. A very painful one."

It shouldn't make me feel good knowing how much it hurts for him too, but I don't even think it's schadenfreude as much as assurance that the more it hurts for him, the less likely he is to deny me this thing I need. Now that I'm thinking rationally again, it's clear the answer is simple: "While we figure out Cody's visions, how about we agree to mess around, like, I don't know, once a day? See if that makes things more tolerable?" I study his expression carefully, trying to read his answer, but he just stares at me. "Well?"

"You think I'm gonna say no to doing that once a day, Straight Boy?"

As I laugh, a smile plays across his lips.

"Then I'll talk to Cody," I tell him, "and we'll sort

this shit out, and then…go from there." That's the best I got right now. As he nods, he sets his drink between his legs, and I find myself resenting a fucking can for obscuring a part of his dick from me.

"That sounds like a plan I can get behind."

"Please tell me that pun was intended."

"Very much so." He winks like he thinks he's so goddamn clever, and I chuckle. It's nice to be playful after spending the past few days struggling with pain and anxiety.

Although, I have a horrible feeling there's plenty of pain and anxiety to come.

10

BRAD

FUCKING AROUND WITH Luke is intoxicating.

This isn't like what I'm used to experiencing. Yeah, it can get hot and steamy, but what Luke and I do…that's just us.

Wild, feral lust.

As though our bodies were designed for each other.

When Cody first warned us about Luke, I thought it would be easy to get rid of the guy, but with each taste he gives me, I realize how hard it's gonna be for me if he leaves St. Lawrence.

As I take another sip of margarita, Luke's gaze drifts to my necklace.

"What's the story behind that? I've seen you grab it a few times, like you're using it to access or enhance your powers. Seth has one too, and Cody was holding his when he was doing that thing to me."

The guys won't be happy if I start revealing all our secrets, but it's not fair to expect Luke to uproot his whole life and future without anything.

"They help us control our powers. It's one of the reasons Seth and I had a hard time believing you were doing these things without any knowledge or experience. Without these, we can still use our powers, but it's much easier when we're wearing them."

"How do they help? Where did you get them from?"

I tense. "That's starting to get into areas I should probably chat with the guys about before I answer."

"So maybe this has something to do with where these powers come from. Something to do with the old church…?"

"At the rate you're going, you'll probably get to the answer on your own."

"What are you worried about telling me?"

I choose my words carefully. "When we discovered this stuff, it was like playing with a Ouija board. I don't know that any of us grasped how serious it was. But the more we messed around with our powers, the better we got, and the more we realized how powerful this is. How dangerous it could be in the wrong hands. So it's something we'd rather keep to the people we trust. Not that I don't trust you, but…"

He shrugs. "You don't really know me, so I don't take it personally." He takes a sip of his drink, then sets it on the nightstand. "Surprised not all of you went with walking-sex-god as your power."

I chuckle. "Doesn't really work like that. We each sort of stumbled into our particular powers. And they relate to each of us for…reasons."

The way he raises his brow, it's clear that caught his interest.

"Okay, you're gonna make it sound that intriguing and expect me not to be interested?"

"I guess I'm not really giving anything away by sharing this, maybe other than risking you knowing about the most embarrassing shit from my life. I never had any sex appeal. Was awkward and I'd get flustered when I was hitting on a guy. Couldn't have told you who was gay or bi or straight to save my life, which led to some uncomfortable situations. My first sexual experience was freshman year, and I got performance anxiety. Guy started telling people how I couldn't get it up, and a bunch of his friends started calling me Soft Serve."

My cheeks burn, my chest constricting as I remember the painful humiliation. I don't understand why I'm even sharing this, but like with that stuff about my dad, it comes right out.

I'm waiting for Luke to laugh or poke fun, but he doesn't look amused. He's listening, and I find myself wanting to share more. "After I discovered my powers, I ended up having sex with that guy and some of the other guys who talked shit about me, and I haven't heard the word *soft* from any of those fuckers."

"Guess you showed them."

"Yeah. Revenge sex seemed like a good idea at the time, but it's a hollow victory. Wish I could have been confident enough to let them keep saying shit like that and just lived my life, you know?"

Now that I've shared that story, I'm wondering what he must be thinking. Surely, he's judging me for being so damn petty.

But Luke's expression isn't judgmental. He twists his mouth up and rests his hand on my thigh, offering me a sensation that's like warm flowing water across my flesh. "I dealt with my share of bullies," he says. "Kids who thought it was fun to pick on the quiet, strange guy in class. I wish I could say I always handled it the way I should have, taken the higher road and not let it get to me or lash out when it was too much. But it doesn't always work that way."

I study his expression, see the sadness of a guy who must've been in so much pain and had kids being even worse to him after everything he'd already been through.

"It sucks that people can be so shitty," I say as we sit with the cruel memories from our pasts. "Anyway, I should probably get out of your hair before I make this even more awkward."

Because surely, I don't need to start sharing any more embarrassing-ass stories or bring to mind any more shit from his past.

I slide off the bed, letting Luke's hand slip off my thigh, my gut tightening as my body already resists the idea of parting with him. "Mind if I take the drink on the road?" I ask, holding my can up.

Luke scrunches up his forehead and crawls across the bed toward me. "Actually," he says, rising onto his knees, "if you're still thirsty, I had another idea before you run off."

As he glances at the nightstand, I notice his cock expanding quickly, and it's got mine doing the same.

"Alexei should be gone for another thirty minutes, so how about we get this done in twenty? And if you keep my lips busy enough, you're not gonna have to worry about me asking any more questions."

He cocks a brow, and eagerness pulses through me.

He doesn't have to ask me twice.

OVER THE NEXT few days, Luke and I discover his plan for messing around once a day works.

Better than works. Not only do I not feel the agony I went through when depriving myself of him, but I have more energy than usual throughout my day.

He obviously benefits from it too—I don't see the tired, strained Luke I'd seen when he'd tried to deprive us before.

Neither of us brings up the heavy shit.

Cody's vision.

The Sinners and our powers.

Can't tell if he just wants to enjoy our cum sessions without the added stress, or if he doesn't see the point in getting into it until he's seen Cody's vision for himself. But even though we don't discuss it, it's always hanging over us, this ominous threat that makes us take advantage of this time that may soon be stripped away from us.

And who knows what the hell that will do to us?

When Friday evening finally arrives, I head to the old church to find Luke already in the cellar, alone. He's leaning against the wall, his arms folded. He gazes at me but stays put.

I'm balled up with tension. It's hard to know which way this will go. Maybe he'll see Cody's vision and won't be nearly as impressed as Seth and me. Or maybe it'll freak him out so much, he'll be on the first plane home.

I don't want him to go.

But he must.

"This is strange," I acknowledge, heading toward him. "First time I've seen you that you haven't jumped my bones."

He smirks. "Kind of nice not needing to for a change."

"I prefer it the other way," I tease, but really, I'm glad neither of us is suffering like before.

Luke smiles, unfolds his arms, and approaches. "Maybe we have time to rub one out real quick before they get here."

One eyebrow arches slightly higher than the other, and in no time, his lips are mashed against mine as he shoves me against the wall, his hands working my fly, unfastening me like it's become second nature.

I cherish every kiss and lick, knowing after Cody arrives, we'll have to keep our distance throughout the meeting…and Luke might not want to mess around for a while after Cody shares the vision.

He reaches under my briefs, wraps his hand around my cock, offering firm strokes. It's such an effortless move for him, suggesting how far we've come in such a short time since those first bumbling jerk-off sessions.

I place my hands on either side of his face, firming our kiss.

"Just as…hard as…usual," he says between kisses.

"Don't act…like you…know me…already."

"In that case…I figure you…don't want to…suck me off?"

"Now you're just being mean."

The familiar sound of boards being moved comes from upstairs, and I growl like an irritated dog as I look toward the stairs.

Luke licks my cheek, making my head and eyes roll back. "It'll make it hotter when we're done," he whispers, pushing off my arms.

I redo my fly, finishing right before Cody and Seth start downstairs.

"Hi, Luke," Cody says, taking the lead.

He's looking much healthier than he did at the start of the week. Mostly I've seen him in bed, so he's been in a tank or shirtless, his hair a mess. Tonight he's in slacks and a button-up. His bangs are gelled into his signature blond wave. The only sign that anything might still be off is how he uses the rail for support as he heads down.

While he offers a warm smile, surely to make Luke feel more at ease, behind him, Seth scowls.

"Nice to finally meet the guy who was fucking with my head," Luke says as Cody reaches the bottom of the steps.

Cody's expression twists up. "Sorry for our strange introduction." He stops a few feet short of Luke. "I wanted to explain in person. I was trying to affect your mood, not tap into that particular incident in your life. It sort of sucked me in without warning. And then you really knocked me down after that."

"From what I understand, you learned your lesson," Luke says, "but I appreciate the apology."

Cody inspects his own arms, then turns to me. "Ooh, this energy between the two of you is intense. You guys have been going at it like fucking dogs."

"Fucking knew it," Seth mutters, shooting me a look, his disapproval loud and clear.

But I'm too pissed about what Cody just did to give a damn. "Cody, the hell? Don't read him without his consent! I don't go around making you hard for me, so—"

"I'd have to be attracted to you for you to make me hard for you," he says. "And you're not really my type, beefcake. Maybe give me the benefit of the doubt. He's practically shooting this at me right now."

That makes more sense. There were a few times when Cody slipped into my head when he was first learning how to use his powers, but he's always been respectful of boundaries.

Luke looks at me with wide eyes. "I'm not doing anything."

"This is our issue," Cody says. "You are, but you don't realize it."

Cody turns his palms to face Luke, who steps back, turning to me. "What's he doing?"

"Relax," Cody says. "You're radiating energy. I'm just trying to get a feel for it."

"You can trust him," I assure Luke, who takes a breath, relaxing his shoulders.

Cody closes his eyes, moving his hands back and forth in the air, and I wish I could tell him to stop acting like a freak. We need Luke to trust us, but Cody doesn't seem to give a shit how weird he looks as he persists until he opens his eyes and rests his arms at his sides. "I noticed it when I saw you at the field that day, before I tried to influence your mood. But it's gotten stronger since then."

"What are you talking about?"

"Have you heard of auras? It's not exactly that, but this energy around you... I can't see it, but I can feel it. It's like the air is a little thicker here, harder for my hands to pass through. Sorry, I'm making you anxious.

Would you like to sit down?"

"I'm fine standing."

I don't need Cody's intuitive abilities to detect how defensive Luke sounds.

"Look, can we cut it with the bullshit?" Luke says. "I didn't come here to hear about auras or talk about how thick the air is. I want answers."

"Just show him," I tell Cody, who glances between us, then nods.

"Okay," he says. "I was trying to make this less awkward, but that's obviously not working, so let's get to it. Luke, you mind taking off your clothes?"

Luke's jaw drops.

Hope he's ready for shit to get weird.

11

LUKE

TAKE OFF MY clothes?

The hell?

"Just do it," Cody says. "I'm not perving on you, dude."

An odd request, for sure, but now Cody and I are seated in the center of the pentagram, cross-legged and facing one another, in just our underwear. Part of me is convinced that any minute now one of their other buddies will jump out from somewhere, displaying a phone as they record the ridiculous bullshit I fell for. Brad will hunch over laughing that his little Straight Boy was such a fucking sucker, and I'll go viral for what would go down in history as one of the most epic cases of bullying ever.

But maybe that's wishful thinking—that I would prefer an ordinary explanation over an extraordinary one, even if it meant my complete and utter humiliation.

With his eyes closed, hands resting on his knees, Cody takes deep, steady breaths.

"Seth, if you could come here," he says. "I might need to borrow some energy."

Seth doesn't question his friend, just moves closer before Cody goes on, "And, Brad—"

Brad starts toward us, but Cody raises his hand. "Back the fuck up because your energy is interfering."

"Maybe he should leave," Seth says.

"That's not fucking happening," Brad replies through his teeth, and he and Seth exchange tense looks.

For guys who seemed pretty damn chummy when I first arrived at St. Lawrence, now they seem a few choice words away from a fight. I'm sure I have plenty to do with that, but I'm glad Brad's sticking around for whatever the hell Cody's about to do. I've only just barely started to trust Brad since he opened up the other night. But I definitely trust him more than his two buddies, who I don't know shit about.

Cody takes a few more breaths before opening his eyes. "Okay. Now we're gonna rise on our knees and move closer, until our bodies are touching, and you'll lock hands with me."

"Why does this keep getting more pervy?"

"All this stuff is kinda pervy," Brad mumbles.

"Trust me, Luke," Cody says. "It will make it easier for me to pass the vision on to you. I've tried touching with my fingertips and—"

"It's like fire," Seth interjects. "Doing it like this, you'll feel the heat, but it won't be as intense since it's spread out."

The guys really aren't selling this to me, but I accept it's what I have to do if we're gonna follow through with this, so I rise on my knees, and Cody does the same. Unlike with Brad, I don't feel this intense, inescapable lust as I move closer to him. We push against each other, and it all feels clinical.

I raise my hands.

There's a sound, like a growl. I recognize it from sexier moments and turn to see Brad, nostrils flaring.

Cody must have picked up on it too, since he shoots Brad a look. "I'm not going under until you calm your ass down."

"I can't fucking help it," Brad says.

"Don't worry," Seth chimes in. "He comes over here, and he won't have a dick to fuck anyone with. Got it?"

Cody rolls his eyes. "Boys, boys." He smirks, clearly not entirely hating their sparring.

And I must admit, there's something comforting about knowing Brad's getting jealous over whatever the hell we're doing. If for no other reason than knowing he'll keep me safe just to ensure he can fuck around with me again.

Cody rests his palms against mine. "Okay, so I know I said it's not like a sex thing…" he says in an uneasy tone.

"This seems a little late for a warning."

"When we're done, there's gonna be a bit of a mess."

"A mess?"

Cody tilts his head, quirking his brow in a way that's plenty suggestive.

I pull my hands away. "What the hell? Maybe someone should have told me about this."

Brad shrugs. "If I'd said that, would that have changed what you had to do?"

"I don't have a fucking clue, but God forbid I get a heads-up about any of this."

"The guy's wasting our fucking time," Seth says.

I grunt. "It's fine. Let's get it over with."

"Relax," Cody says. "I have tissues and moist towelettes in my bag."

The way he says *moist* makes me think he's trying to guarantee this will be the least erotic experience of my life.

"Can you please just start?" Brad asks, and when I look at him, I notice his fist clenched at his side like he's having to restrain himself, and Seth has his eyes on him like if Brad makes a move, blows will be exchanged.

"Okay, okay," Cody says. "I'm gonna count backward from ten, and just listen to me and pay attention to how you're feeling in your body."

I nod as he presses firmly up against me. He interlocks his fingers with mine, and I wrap my fingers over his hand. I can't help thinking that for a guy who considered himself totally straight, I've sure been doing a lot of gay shit the past few weeks.

I close my eyes and try to focus on my breathing, but I'm fixated on this heat Cody warned me about and wondering how and why this is gonna end up messy.

I don't have to wonder for long before I feel a sensation, but it's not heat; it's like someone took a baseball bat to my chest.

"Fuck," I say, the wind knocked out of me.

When I open my eyes, I'm not in the church cellar anymore. I'm running through the woods, racing behind someone who screams, "Help! Somebody help me!" I move like an animal, lurching forward on all fours. An overwhelming sensation grips me. Hunger—no, starvation.

Before I know it, I've caught up with my prey. Then suddenly I'm right on top of…a man, who stares up at me and screams in terror. As that horror-struck face burns into my brain, a rush pulses through me, sating my intense hunger before everything changes.

What feels like memories come in flashes.

Yellow vision…crawling from some kind of thick film, covered in goo.

I can see my hands, but they aren't human. They look almost like branches that have formed the shape of a hand, with long fingernails at the ends.

There's a deep hunger within me that must be sated.

I claw through some kind of sac, the yellow fluid spilling out around me.

In a moment, I'm transported elsewhere. I'm not on

top of the man or fixated on the strange memories. I'm in a crowd of people, and there's a deep pain I can't identify for a moment, but then I realize what it is—I'm starving again.

I move so fast, I can barely process my surroundings as shrill cries fill the air around me. There's some kind of statue—an animal, maybe a rat, no, a squirrel in a cap—before those clawed hands move in front of me, and then all I see is blood spraying through the air.

So much fucking blood!

"Cody!" I cry out in a panic, closing my eyes, trying to will myself out of this nightmarish place. My eyes pop open, and I try to scream, but it catches in my throat.

Cody lies on top of me, trembling, as I feel a sensation burst...release.

Sweet fucking release.

Cody moans as his hips thrust against me for a few moments until Seth grabs him and pulls him off me. As he removes Cody, I feel arms hook around me. Brad's got me, holding me as I search around, struggling to reorient myself to being back in the church, away from those haunting images.

Brad pulls down my boxers and wipes me with a towelette. He's asking questions, and once I can make out what he's saying, he's asking Seth, "How's Codes?"

"How the fuck do you think?" Seth snaps. "I told you this was a crap idea."

"It's okay," Cody says. "Seth, I'm fine. It's not like

the other times."

As I struggle to get oxygen back in my lungs, I'm reminded of the day Cody attacked me, albeit unintentionally, with those thoughts about my dad's death while I was in the shower.

I finally manage to force some air into my lungs. "That's...the...vision?" I ask, heaving as soon as I get the words out.

"What did you see?" Cody asks.

"What do you mean, what did he see?" Seth asks.

"It wasn't like when I did it with you guys. It was like I got kicked out of it."

It takes me a few moments to regulate my breathing. Brad hands me a pair of briefs he must've brought for me, and I slide them on, noticing the bulge in the crotch where he's stretched the fabric. He grabs my clothes, and as Cody and I get dressed, I collect my thoughts enough to walk them through the different images, sharing what I witnessed. By the time I'm done, they're all looking at me like I'm out of my fucking mind.

Cody shakes his head. "That's not the vision I had. Not the way you described it, at least. I saw several bodies. One impaled. One charred from fire. Others covered in blood."

"How the fuck did you conclude that you had to get rid of me so that this wouldn't happen?"

"Before the deaths, I saw a silhouette of a guy. His face was blurry, and it was like flashes between him and this creature that looked like a fetus before it was birthed. Its genesis. I could sense a connection between the figure and the monster, so I asked the Guides—"

"The what?" I ask.

"The Guides are entities from another world—or dimension," Cody explains. "There's a sort of tear between our world and theirs. We call it the Rift. When I reach a certain mental state, I can connect with these Guides. It's very difficult to manage, but I can channel information from them. In one session, I received the message: *He must go. It's time for him to go. Go now.* So I had another session, and they gave me your name."

Guides? Other dimensions? Channeled messages?

If I hadn't seen their powers for myself, I'd be wondering what kind of drugs they're on.

"Well," I say, "for guys who were trying to keep me alive, it sure didn't seem like it."

Brad interjects, "It was only when we realized you had powers that we started thinking the Guides might have meant something else. Before that, we believed we just needed to get you away from St. Lawrence, hoping we could deal with it before it had a chance to get to you."

"But since discovering you had powers," Cody adds, "we thought the Guides might have been trying to tell us something else. That maybe you were somehow responsible for why this thing gets birthed into our world."

"And I'm just supposed to believe these imaginary friends in your head from another world?"

"The Guides worked with the original Sinners. Helped them fight creatures like this, so we know their information is reliable."

Before coming to St. Lawrence, I would have called BS on all this. But here I am, seriously considering the shit Cody's saying, which is wild as fuck. "So..." I drag out, "this thing you saw that's about to be 'birthed' and go on a killing spree...what is it even?"

Cody retrieves his phone from the pants he discarded on the floor. He scrolls through it before passing it to me, revealing a drawing—a hunched creature with long, sharp, clawlike hands and wide eyes. "I sketched it after the first vision. This is what it looked like after it was born from the sac, but you didn't see my version because you experienced everything through its eyes."

I shudder. "Well, none of this tells us very much, does it?"

"It tells us, at least according to your vision, that this thing is still gonna get loose."

But I have a bad feeling about that already. And something fresh is on my mind. "This monster...it'll start here, right, if it's breaking free from—what did you call it? The Rift?"

"The Guides call the places they escape from *gates*—like open doorways from the Rift into our world."

"And it'll be hungry," I add, "so it'll need a victim

right away." I pull my phone out of my pants and key away.

"What are you doing?" Seth asks.

"Will you shut the fuck up for five seconds so I can think?" I search "missing" + "Lawrenceville, GA" + "news." Sure enough, an article from yesterday pops up, with a face I recognize. "George Farrow hasn't been seen since Monday, October twenty-first. Fuck," I mutter, handing my phone to Brad. "That's who I saw. That's who I was chasing. This thing is already out, so clearly, my leaving isn't gonna do shit."

"Then something's changed since my last vision," Cody says. "Something's happened that's affected the outcome."

"Or you read it wrong," I insist.

"It's possible," Cody says. "We've just never had this happen before."

"You've really fucked with everything since you got here," Seth adds.

"So whatever the hell this thing is," I say, ignoring Seth, "we know it's out there and hunting people. I know with everything in me that it killed that guy. You have no idea how much it needs to kill. I could feel its hunger, and it was so intense both times I saw it attack. It's like it's not even just feeding off their bodies, but—and this sounds so fucked—feeding on their fear of it."

"Their fear?" Cody asks.

"Yes, it's like I was feeling satisfied even before eating

121

them. Fuck, I don't even know how I know that."

Brad says, "You remember when I made that comment about it being like a dream where you just know certain things? You felt it about the guy it killed and about the place it came from, but you don't have the other part that's connected to you. We know you're the reason this is all happening."

"And I'm just supposed to trust that?"

Brad holds his hands up like he wants me to calm the hell down for a minute, but he didn't have to see what I just saw.

I feel like a fucking monster myself.

"I'm not saying you guys are making this up, but you can understand why you bringing me here, telling me I'm gonna see one thing, then seeing something totally different, would make me suspect you have no idea what the hell you're seeing."

"That's fine," Brad says. "We all need to be skeptical, but it doesn't have to turn into a fight about everything."

I take a breath. He's right. "Sorry, this stuff is fucking with my head."

"It's okay," Cody says. "It's a lot. But it clearly doesn't knock you down the way it does me, which is a good sign."

"Good sign? Did you hear what I said? There's a monster on the loose and already killing people...and apparently will kill more people. We have to do something."

"No, no," Seth says. "Me, Cody, and Brad have to do something. You aren't a part of this."

"Seth…" Brad says. "You're not being honest there."

Seth's jaw clenches. "Don't do this. Don't you dare fucking do this now."

Brad gives Seth a stern look; a warning. "It's time to tell him. He needs to know."

"I need to know what?"

"We all agreed to this!" Seth insists.

"Brad's right," Cody says. "It's too late to stop whatever's coming. And maybe Luke could help us. I mean, you can feel the power radiating off him."

"Powerful, but a loose cannon," Seth reminds them. "All this shit he's been doing to our powers and with the powers he has that he doesn't understand might even be the reason why this thing is out already."

"That might be true," Cody says, "but it's irrelevant at the moment. We need to move forward with these new insights."

I agree with Cody and am fast becoming beyond exasperated with Seth. "I get it, Seth. You don't like me. I don't like you. Now whatever the fuck secrets you guys are keeping, you need to be out with them because I'm getting tired of this crap."

Cody nods. "Seth, would you grab the book?"

Seth doesn't look happy about it, but he heads back to the stairs and grabs Cody's backpack, retrieving an old leather-bound book. He eyes me as he returns to his friend and passes it to him.

"When I first came to St. Lawrence," Cody says, "I stumbled upon this place. I was having a lot of depressive episodes and anxiety. I found when I came here that they eased up. One day, I felt this impulse to head toward the floorboards over in the corner there. It intensified the closer I got, this powerful urge to shift the boards around until I discovered this. Like it was calling me to it." He flips to the first page and passes it to me.

At the top, in cursive writing, it says: *The Sinners*. And beneath it, two names:

Josh Dobbers
Mark Waters

Seeing my father's name, in his handwriting, soothes some of my tension from that fucked-up vision.

"Dad," I mutter, running my hand across the ink. But just as quickly as I feel ease, the tension returns, but this time, it's rage. I turn to Brad. "You were keeping this from me?"

He doesn't make eye contact. "I thought we were doing the right thing."

"Well, that was a fucking mistake." I stare him down. If I have some fucking powers, I wish I could blast him with all my anger right now. But whatever's going on with me, that's clearly not a thing, since nothing happens.

I head to the desk and snatch my bag, shoving the book inside.

"Hey, you can't take that," Seth says.

I don't respond, just hurry toward the stairs.

Seth starts for me, but Cody stands in his way. "Let him. This is a lot."

"Luke…" Brad calls after me, but I'm rushing up the stairwell. I'm so pissed.

I want to get away from these guys and get my fucking thoughts around the vision and our subsequent conversation.

12

BRAD

"THE FUCK HAPPENED to you? You look like someone stomped on your heart."

My roommate, Matteo, lies across his bed, phone in hand as I close the door behind me.

"You think someone rejected me?" I ask skeptically, and he rolls his eyes.

"I was only telling you what you looked like. But you're awfully defensive for a guy who didn't get his heart broken. So what's up?"

Matteo's a decent guy. I don't want to take out my anger on him, but my emotions are all over the fucking place, and while Luke didn't stomp on my heart, I'm terrified that what just happened in the old church will lead to something happening to him, something with worse consequences than depriving me of what I need now.

"It's nothing." I head to my side of our room and collapse in bed.

I keep thinking I should have chased after Luke, tried

to reason with him, but after stopping Seth, Cody stopped me too. *"He needs time to process this. Give him a minute, guys."*

Cody's right, but giving Luke space isn't easy. Since he hurried out of the church in a huff, I've felt this searing pain. *His* pain. And yet it swells in *my* goddamn chest, brought about by this connection neither of us can explain or escape.

"You want to play a video game?" I ask because the distraction might do me some good.

"Can't. Meeting with that girl I was telling you about—Steph. We're gonna hang at that pizza place down the street."

"You need me to be gone when you get back?" Matteo has had my back plenty of times, so I'm always happy to give him his space when he has a girl over.

"That's sweet of you, Brad, but naw. She already let me know her roommate is out for the night with her boyfriend. So pop on Grindr and line 'em up while you can." He winks.

If only he knew that for the past few weeks, only one guy has occupied my thoughts.

Matteo gets ready and heads out, leaving me to stress about Luke.

I knew he would blow up. I knew he might fucking hate me for what we'd withheld. But it was time for him to know the truth. The whole truth. No more Sinners' secrets. No more sticking to oaths we made when we still had no clue what we were dealing with.

It's clear from everything that's happened since Luke arrived that none of us really know what's going on, and if what Luke said is true—and I believe it is, that this monster is already out and killing people in Lawrenceville—then getting rid of Luke won't fix our problem. We must work together.

In a desperate attempt at distracting myself, I sit at my desk, trying to focus on my homework. Not much of a chance of that happening, but as long as I can keep myself from hurrying out the door and down the hall to his room, I should be fine.

But the longer I try to distract myself, the more challenging it becomes. My chest twists in knots. Anxiety bubbles in my belly. And just when I think I'm about to cave, there's a knock at the door.

I hop to my feet, hoping, wishing it's him. As I near the door, I become more confident that I'm right. It's like I can fucking smell him through it.

When I open the door, he's standing outside, giving me those same dagger eyes he cut me with less than two hours ago. His hair's disheveled, like he's been running his hand through it. And he's holding the Sinners' bible.

"Luke," I say, ready to apologize, but before I can get another word out, he shoves me back into my room. His lips clamp down against mine. It's like some of the times we've met up before this evening, and given what happened, that throws me, but as my back slams against the wall and Luke's tongue invades my mouth, I'm not fucking complaining.

Despite all the stress, despite all the bullshit that's going on, as he buries his face against mine, all teeth, tongue, and lips, everything is right in the world.

He growls and pulls away. "I can't believe all the times we've messed around and you were keeping this from me." His words are hot with fury before he pushes another kiss on me.

"You...have every...right to be mad," I manage between kisses.

"Damn...right...I do."

What is fucking happening to us? It's like it's even harder for us to keep our hands off each other because he's upset.

I guide him to my side of the room, and we collapse on the bed, our kiss missing as our jaws clash from the desperate attempt to keep ourselves invested in the moment.

Soon, Luke's on top of me. He manages to pull away long enough to place the Sinners' bible on my nightstand.

"Don't...think this means...we're cool right now," he says between more kisses.

"I...know...I'm sorry...Luke."

He licks up the middle of my lips, then grunts. "Fuck. I told myself a thousand times I wasn't gonna come over here tonight. That I would fucking chain myself to the bed if I had to. And then suddenly, I was lying to Alexei about hitting the gym, and on my way here."

"It was hard for me too," I assure him.

"It's supposed to be hard for you after what you did."

He sizes me up before rising on his knees on either side of my leg. He works my belt, then my fly, so focused, like he's having to keep from looking at me, otherwise he'll never get the job done.

Once he gets my pants undone, I help him pull them down with my briefs. He pushes them just past my balls, then leans down and presses his face against my abs, near my navel, licking and nibbling at my flesh. My cock is a brick as he trails kisses toward it.

"Luke, are you sure you want to do that?" We've messed around plenty, and he's let me suck him off, but he's never put my cock in his mouth.

"Shut up," he says, running his nose alongside my shaft.

I curse as I roll my head back, enjoying the sensation of his soft skin against me. He moves around my crotch, the tip of his nose and his breath leaving me in suspense. Is he really about to do this while he fucking hates me?

"Does it hurt, wanting me to pop it in my mouth?" he asks. "Do you wish I would just do it to end your agony?"

He's a fucking sadist! But he has every right to punish me.

He rubs his lips along my girth, like he wants me to know he could so easily take all this pain away.

"Fuck, Luke, please…"

As he continues his vengeance, my cock bounces off my abs, like it has a mind of its own and just wants to push into Luke's mouth. Feel that warm, wet tongue against it.

He snickers, the sadist enjoying what he's doing to me.

"Yeah, it does hurt you too," he says, "doesn't it?"

"You know it does."

"I was doing fine before I got mad at you tonight. Like I could have gone a day or two without messing around, but then all this anger is fucking twisted up and turned against me."

"Somehow tonight made things worse. Maybe something to do with the vision."

"Whatever it is, it's so fucking cruel," he says before sliding his tongue from the base of my shaft up to the head. "God, you taste good," he confesses, pushing his face against my cock and taking deep breaths. "I hate you for not telling me the truth. And I hate you for being so irresistible that I can't stand to be apart from your body. And I hate that as much as I'm enjoying torturing you, it's fucking killing me too. That all I want is your cock in my mouth right now. That I just want you fucking my face until you come in me, and then I can devour you like you've devoured me. I hate that this is all I can think of when I should be focusing on that book and what any of it means."

As he speaks, his wet mouth is pushed up right against my cock, and it's tearing at my soul how close he is to bringing me some goddamn relief.

"We'll make it quick, Luke, and then we can talk it out. I'll tell you anything you want to know."

"Anything?" He licks up my shaft, slowly, deliberately.

I gaze down as my Straight Boy teases me, gripping my hips like he's having to push to restrain himself.

"I didn't want to keep it from you, Luke. I wanted to tell you, but I promised them. Jesus, please don't be mean."

He spits in his palm and wraps it around my shaft, gazing up as he offers me a few gentle pumps. "Tell me why you haven't fucked my ass yet."

"What?" Not where I was expecting him to go with this. Like...at all.

"You said you'd tell me *anything*," he presses. "You know how fucking badly I've wanted it, so what are you waiting for? For me to fucking beg?" He sounds as pissed as he is about the secret Cody revealed. When I don't answer right away, he says, "*Tell me.*"

"I don't want the reason I fuck you to be this thing that's controlling us," I confess.

He slows his stroke. "Go on."

"I want you to really want it. Of your own free will."

He runs his fingers under the head of my cock, then back down to the base, making me gasp. With each movement, my hips shift subtly as my body begs for the release he's teasing me with. His eyes narrow, and he leans close, sticking out his tongue and running it against the head.

"Oh fuck, Luke."

He licks his lips. "This is what it feels like for me. You keep giving me something so close, but then you leave me hanging. If you're gonna make me suffer, then I'm gonna make you suffer too."

"I am suffering, Luke. You think I don't want to take that ass every time we're together? You think it's not all I think about, especially the way you're sticking it up right now?"

My dick firms in his grip, and he gives it a squeeze as his lips curl into a wicked smirk. A jolt of awareness ripples through me as vivid images crowd my thoughts.

I'm kissing him, then pushing him onto his stomach.

Without undoing his fly, I yank his pants down, creating red marks along his hips as I expose his ass before burying my face against it. I open him up with my fingers, then push the head of my cock against him, watching him writhe beneath me as he begs for it.

Hard. Fast. Raw.

It's his desire, one I've seen before now, one that's become my desire too.

"If you really need it now, I can," I say. "I just…"

"No," he snaps. "You don't get that. Not after what went down today. Now, even if it fucking kills me, I'm willing to die to deprive you of it."

He pumps me a few more times, my muscles twitching as I'm totally submissive to his movements.

"What do you want from me, then?" I ask.

As he continues working me up, he considers this carefully, as though crafting a torture designed just for me because of my betrayal.

"I want you to tell me what you want to do to my ass. I want you to confess all the filthy secrets you've kept from me. It's only right, since you already know mine without my consent."

He's right; this hasn't been fair to him. Not that I want it to be this way, but even now, I can feel how bad he wants it. Even if he's trying to hide it, it's not something he can keep from me.

"You don't just want me to give it to you, you want me to take it," I say, and his cheeks flush red. "You want me to be forceful but tender. Want me to take my time opening you up, making you ready to take me. You're scared of how big I am, but you want to give it a try because now that it's in your head, you're too curious not to know."

He scowls. "I said tell me what *you* want."

"I'm getting to that. You want me to start with my tongue first and then use my fingers, until you're lifting your ass, pushing me deeper so I can show you what all the prostate hype is about. Then you want my cock."

He bites his bottom lip.

"I want all that too, Luke. I want to see every shift in your expression as you take me. Want to see your eyes get big when I hit your prostate just right. Want to hear you begging for it harder and faster, making me really put in the work to serve your needs." My cock throbs in his hold. God, I can't bear this. "And then I want you begging me to come. I want you to need my cum fucking seeding up inside you. I want to feel it in my fucking soul how badly you need that. And then when you shoot, and only when you shoot, I want to empty my balls inside you."

My hips jerk again, but he's stopped pumping me, leaving my body desperate to play out the fantasy I just expressed.

"There," I say. "Now we're even. I know what you want, and you know what I want."

For the first time since we started this, he doesn't look pissed or angry. He looks satisfied.

But as he keeps his hand around my cock, this wish has built up so much pressure without any promise of relief.

"Fuck, Luke, you're killing me. Please just let me jerk it off."

I know that's not what he wants, but a guy can only bear so much.

He grins before shaking his head, and my eyes water.

"Please, Luke. I—"

He licks the head of my cock, and I roll my head back, appreciating the sensation of his warm tongue once again.

"Now at least I know as I'm blowing you...you're still gonna be hurting as much as I am." He gives another lick, starting at the base, then trailing up to the head before inhaling deeply. "Why do you taste so good?" he asks with a growl before sliding my cock into his mouth. His lips glide down my shaft without hesitation as he goes for it like he doesn't have any reservations about taking a cock.

Fin-a-fucking-lly.

I revel in the sensation as Luke bobs his head up and down. The pressure in me mounts, but it doesn't have that sting to it, not now that the end to the pain is in sight. It may not be the hole I want, but after how he tortured me, I'll take anything he gives me.

With each slide down my shaft, his wet tongue welcomes me back to his throat. He's more and more ambitious until I hear him gag.

"Jesus, Luke. Don't fucking choke yourself."

But I'd be lying if I said it didn't make me even harder hearing how determined he is to get as much of me in his mouth as he can.

He pulls off my cock briefly. "Don't tell me what to do." Then he's right back at it.

I know he's just playing out fantasies he's already had

of this. In those times when we messed around, I could tell he wanted to deep throat me, but like with anal, he was nervous about taking that next step. He sure as hell isn't nervous tonight as he surrenders to his desires, which become my desire with every slide and gentle suck.

I feel a nudge, as though he psychically projected it to me, and I lower my hand to his head, encouraging him as I stroke my thumb along his temple.

"Good, Straight Boy. That's real good."

He moves faster, like he's trying to suck the cum out of my balls. If so, it's working.

"I'm not gonna last much longer," I warn him, which makes him pull off.

"Fuck my face," he says, leaning back, and I roll off the bed, my legs still trapped in my jeans, which I push down to my ankles. But I can't bother with more than that. I need to end this.

"Lie on your back," I tell him, "and put your head over the edge of the mattress."

He obeys, and as I move closer, he says, "Just know, after you come in my mouth, I'll still fucking hate you."

"Come in your mouth? Are you sure? While you fucking hate me this much?"

"Shut your fucking mouth and put your dick in me." I doubt he could sound any more annoyed if he tried, and I'm so delirious from everything he's done to me, I just follow instructions, sliding my cock between his willing lips.

He grabs my ass cheeks, guiding me in, and again, he's ambitious with how deep he takes me.

I admire how he takes what he needs from me.

I want him to use me like a fuck toy.

As I increase my pace, I grab either side of his head. "Fuuuuck," I groan, and it's too fucking late for me as the final rush of energy springs through me. "Luke, I'm coming, I'm coming," I call out as he takes me like a champ. Drinks me up as I continue thrusting into his face. His greedy hands pull me close, my cock jammed back, and I can feel his throat.

I gasp with relief as his body relaxes beneath me. He pulls my cock partly out of his mouth, his tongue still going wild like he needs to make sure he's got it all.

As I pull the rest of the way out, I notice some of my cum drip onto his lip, but it's not there long before his tongue collects it and he takes a deep breath.

"Fuck yeah," he says as though he's just run a fucking marathon.

"Please, Luke. Can I suck you off?"

After how he's punished me, I'm expecting him to refuse me just to piss me off, but he says, "Please," like even he can't resist this anymore.

I kick out of my pants while Luke undoes his and pulls them down to his knees with his boxers. Then I climb into bed, helping him out of his shoes, pants, and boxers. As soon as his clothes are off the bed, I hook my arms around his thighs and go right for his hard cock.

I'm desperate to have him in my mouth, to bring him the relief he craves. Maybe because I think, in some fucked-up way, that if I get him off, it might make up for all the other shit.

I know that's not how it works, but I don't care.

My mouth is here for him.

I cling to his thighs, taking him to the hilt as I breathe in his scent.

"Fuck," he groans, and I feel his hips jerk. "Pull off. You don't get to enjoy me. This is your fucking punishment."

He might as well have stabbed me in the gut. The ache sears through me as I surrender, pulling off his cock and swapping it out with my hand. His body twitches and trembles as he shoots onto his abs. *A fucking waste* is all I can think as I watch it collect on his skin, wishing for a little taste.

"Can I just—"

"No!"

I push my face against his thigh, struggling with Luke's most cruel punishment. Not just because I want it, but because I know he wants it too.

My chest continues to burn as I jerk him off, emptying him of what's left of his load.

"Look at it," he demands. "Look at it and suffer."

As good as I am at reading him, clearly he's getting good at it too because as I look, he must see the pain in my expression as he denies me what feels as necessary to me as food or water.

My gaze shifts to him, and his tension relaxes. "Go ahead," he says with a nod.

Thank fuck.

It's like I black out, can't remember the moments between him giving me permission and when my face is mashed against his skin, my tongue going wild as I lap him up like a dog.

"Take it all," he says.

And I do, beyond grateful.

13

LUKE

THAT WAS VINDICTIVE of me.

I'm just so fucking angry.

Not only because Brad didn't tell me about my dad's involvement, but because of this lack of control over my feelings. I should've been able to take a moment with the book and figure out what the hell I was looking at, but when I got back to my dorm room, I was so worked up that I could barely concentrate on the words on the page.

And it seemed the more I hated Brad for his betrayal, the more I needed to see him, to the point where I finally broke down, submitting to these sick impulses within me that have me lusting after a guy I can't even stand.

Although, fucked up as this may be, after helping each other release all that tension, I'm relaxed once again. Now that Brad's given me so much peace of mind, it's easy to grant him some forgiveness.

I lie on his bed, breathing deeply, reveling in those moments of bliss, when Brad says, "Here." He stands beside the bed and passes me a towel.

"I'm assuming this is to clean up your saliva because I think you took care of the rest."

"Wasn't gonna leave a damn drop," Brad says, and a warm sensation stirs in my chest.

I pat myself down with the towel as he sits on the edge of the bed. "How are you feeling?" he asks, like he really gives a shit, which only makes me feel that much worse for how I treated him.

I remind myself that I have a right to be pissed. "You should have told me."

"As I said before, I made an oath to the guys that we would keep these secrets between us. And I was the one who pushed them to tell you."

It's true, I know it. But it doesn't make me feel any better.

"I'm not just angry with you," I confess. "I'm so messed up since I saw Dad's name in there. A part of it flared up missing him. And then another part of me wonders how he could have kept something like this a secret."

"It's okay. It's confusing-ass shit. I can't imagine how I'd react if I were you. And not an excuse, but one of the reasons I didn't push the guys to mention it sooner was that from what you mentioned about your dad, I worried it would only add more stress. But I was wrong. That wasn't fair to you."

Damn you, Brad Henning, for being so fucking considerate. "Can't you go back to being the douchebag you were when I first got here?" I joke, maybe to bring some levity to the conversation. Neither of us is laughing, though.

"I have plenty of time to be a douchebag later," Brad says, leaning over to the nightstand and retrieving the book. "So how about, for now, we start going over the Sinners' bible. I'm sure part of why you were so upset when you got here was because it's not exactly user-friendly."

I scoff. "Fucking understatement. Some made sense, like their meeting minutes. And I could tell some of the pages were spells or incantations or such, but a lot of that was gibberish." That's what really set me off. I thought I could get some answers, only to get stuck with what looked like garbled nonsense.

"The book was meant only for the original Sinners—Josh Dobbers and your dad. Dobbers recorded how he and your dad came upon this stuff—this place, their powers—and what they learned about it. They wrote down the information Dobbers channeled from the Guides—like how to make amulets and use them with their powers. They didn't want anyone to stumble upon the book and know what they were up to, which is why it's encoded. Cody cracked it, hence his nickname Codes. That's how we learned to experiment with our powers. Most of what we know about the Rift and our powers comes from this book."

It's nice to finally start getting some direct answers.

"So why did they call themselves the Sinners and not like, the Saints?"

"They explain in the bible it was just something they came up with while dicking around. Both were raised to be good Catholic boys, here at a major Catholic institution, but wound up playing with magic."

"And this Rift you guys keep talking about? What is it exactly?"

Brad flips to a page, displaying a sketch of darkness and eyes and teeth.

"What am I looking at?"

"Another world. Dobbers was like Cody. He could feel the presence of the Rift, this tear between our world and another. And his powers gave him the ability to probe into that world."

"What kind of world? Like ours?"

"The Sinners did a lot of occult and New Age reading to come up with their jargon, and they use the phrase *sentient thought forms* to describe it."

"Ghosts?"

"Not the best descriptor. *Ghost* usually refers to something that has lived at some point, but a lot of what's in this other world has never been corporeal. Some ghosts do end up there, but our understanding is that's almost an accident—a spirit wanders into the Rift by mistake and gets trapped there. It's not what I'm describing, though."

"Are there more Rifts in the world? And others who

knew about this before Dobbers and Dad?"

"The Guides have worked with others in the past to close gates and prevent monsters from wreaking havoc on our world. They told Dobbers this is where a lot of myths originated—creatures that escaped and entered our world. Some are still out in the world now, though most of them aren't as dangerous as the ones the Guides have helped others stop. In that way, Dobbers and your dad were the original Sinners for this Rift, here in Lawrenceville."

"So what does all this have to do with these powers you guys have? And with whatever I'm able to do?"

"From what we've gleaned from the book and our experiments, this alternate world creates an energy around Lawrenceville that we can manipulate."

He flips a few more pages before displaying one with a cross necklace and some more gibberish. Then he removes his necklace and hands it to me. "These amulets have copper in them, which for whatever reason, this energy from the Rift is drawn to, and it can build up in there like a battery, which helps us use it whenever we choose. We've experimented with other metals, trying to improve them, but copper does the trick best."

So many fucking questions… "This energy is around Lawrenceville, so what happens to your powers when you go home?"

"The energy is everywhere, but it's stronger here. I can still use it when I'm away, but it's nothing like when

I'm here. Same goes for Codes and Seth."

"That makes sense, I guess, but Jesus fucking Christ, how do you guys know that it's okay to be fucking around with energy from another world? I mean, there must be a reason my dad and Dobbers stopped playing around with it, right? At least, I'm assuming they did and that's why they hid their notebook. Have you even talked to Josh Dobbers?"

He shakes his head. "Dobbers passed before your dad, from cancer."

That hits me like a brick. "And that doesn't sound disturbing to you?" I start to consider that maybe my parents' deaths had something to do with all this.

"I don't want to be insensitive, Luke, but their causes of death were nothing alike. And as far as we know, your mom wasn't a part of any of this. Sometimes people just die."

He's not wrong. They could have discovered this and, unrelated, died of various causes years later, but…I don't like coincidences. "So why did they leave behind this book with all their secrets, without any explanation?"

"Back when your father and Josh Dobbers went here, when the Guides in the Rift called to them, it was because there was a tear in the Rift—like Cody mentioned, a gate—that allowed evil entities to escape into this world. The Guides showed them how to use their powers so they could protect our world from things that might escape."

"If that's true, then why did they stop?"

"They eventually closed the gate, but the Guides had them leave this book behind in case another gate opened, which we believe it has now."

"This has bad idea written all over it. You guys are playing with fire."

"I hear your frustration, and we've had our own discussions around this, but we've had positive experiences with the Rift. And what were we supposed to do—lock this book back up and pretend nothing was happening if a monster escaped and started killing people?"

But for someone who's been so forthcoming, I can tell he's holding something back. "I can understand wanting to protect this world from monsters, but I still don't know that you should be trusting some book. What did you mean by positive experiences with the Rift? Is that about being good at getting laid?"

His gaze drifts, his jaw tightening. "That's not what I'm talking about, but I have my reason, just like Seth and Cody have theirs. They're all deeply personal, so I'd never share theirs, and the most I'm willing to say about mine right now is that it's a good fucking reason."

"But you won't tell me what it is?"

He shakes his head. "Not tonight, no."

His entire body language has changed. His shoulders tensed, and he's not looking at me. Even though he's not willing to share what it is, I'm tempted to believe that, whatever it is, it's a damn good reason.

Still, there's a flaw in his logic. "You're saying you had good experiences with the Rift, but now there's this thing that came through and already killed someone."

"Okay, maybe I should have worded that better. We hadn't had any bad experiences until those visions started up. But like I said, once that happened, knowing what the original Sinners faced, we knew we couldn't walk away from this."

Can't really fault them for that, not when I'm not willing to walk away now that I know what I know.

I glance at the Sinners' bible, running my thumb across the page. "I appreciate your sharing all that with me." He's holding something back, but I accept he's done his best to help me understand this wild world I find myself in.

And really, though his answers only created more questions, I have to say, "I think that's all I can handle for one night."

"Yeah. I understand that."

We're maybe a foot away from each other, but I find myself resenting the space. Like if we could just close it again, then maybe some of this confusion and frustration would dissipate.

But now that I'm being pulled out of our conversation, back into the moment, I notice I'm naked. "Maybe I should put some clothes on."

"Really? I prefer you like this," Brad says, doing a

once-over as a smug smirk slips across his face.

My dick shifts, which doesn't escape his attention.

"You don't need to put your clothes on right away," he adds.

"Shut up."

He chuckles, and as I reposition, he gets up and heads around the bed, picking up my boxers and pants and passing them to me. I thank him, and when I slide into them, a rush of disappointment pulses through me—my body's disapproval of my decision not to have another go.

"Guess I'll head back to my room now. Figure I can text you if I have anything I'm dying to get an answer to."

"Yeah, that works." He pulls on his briefs, which cling to his thighs and ass, reminding me that he is head to toe one hot motherfucker. He pulls his pants up and buttons his fly. "This is probably going to be awkward, but…that thing you brought up about why I haven't fucked you yet."

My chest tightens up. "Fucking kill me now. Can we not get into this?"

"You brought it up."

"I can't control half the shit I'm saying when we start messing around."

"But that's what you want. I *know* that's what you want."

Of course he'd know—it's all I can think about when

we mess around, so I'd be surprised if he'd even need powers to pick up on it. "Don't rub it in."

"I'm only mentioning it because I think it would be wise to have a conversation about it rather than get lost in the moment next time."

Next time. I know there's gonna be a next time, but damn, it feels good to hear him say it.

"You sounded upset that I haven't done anything to your ass."

"*Upset* seems a generous word for it." More like hot rage, especially since it feels like he's denying me something he knows I need.

"Luke, I wasn't being entirely honest with you while we were messing around."

"What?"

"I do want you to want that of your own free will. And each time I mess around with you, it feels like we have our wits about us a bit more. I was hoping that at some point you'd know it's you wanting that, not just this all-consuming lust driving you to make that call."

Damn him for being thoughtful again.

"But there's more to it than that," he says. "Truth is, it scares me. Terrifies me might be a better way of putting it. When I think about that…fantasize about it all day…then dream about it as it haunts me in my sleep, I just know that once we go there…I'm not ever gonna be the same. Like I'm going to need that ass…a lot. Even more than I do now. And that it'll be even more difficult for you too. That's frightening."

It's wild to hear him say something I've felt too. That once we pass that point, for whatever reason, it's over and this ass really is just his. It should scare me too, but it doesn't. Maybe because this lust has overridden the part of me that should give some fucks.

"Just so we're clear, you're saying you're terrified of my ass," I joke, which earns a glare.

"Don't tease me."

"Really? Teasing's helping me not think about all the other shit."

"All right. In that case, tease away."

We share an awkward laugh before I say, "I should probably get back to my room before your roommate gets back."

He nods, and I grab the Sinners' bible off the bed. "You think the guys mind me borrowing it?"

Not because I understand any of it, but because it makes me feel closer to my dad.

"I'm sure Seth is thrilled," Brad teases.

We share a much more natural laugh, and he follows me to the door.

My cheeks warm since it's like I can sense he's checking out my ass, and I love knowing what that does to him.

When I reach the door, I grab the handle, then stop and turn back to him. "I'm sorry. I should have talked to you before getting so worked up. I have a bit of a temper, and what I did was mean."

"I appreciate the apology, but if anyone has a right to be upset, it's the guy who had to deal with all this crap the first few weeks of his sophomore year."

I snicker. It is wild to think that we're still just in those first few weeks when so much has happened.

"If you have any questions about the book, feel free to text me."

"Will do. In the meantime, enjoy a last look for the night." I pull my pants down, flashing him my ass.

I meant to be silly, but he rushes up against me, pushing me against the door. We're stuck together, our bodies magnetized. By the time I can make sense of the quick movement, I feel his girth behind his boxers, rubbing between my cheeks. He pushes it up against me, and his hands slide under my shirt, one tight against my hip, the other sliding up to my chest as he kisses the back of my neck. I reach my hand behind me, resting it on his head, my eyes rolling back as he offers a low, rumbling growl against my skin.

My body's alive with sensation, but there's also this emptiness in me that I know can only be filled with him, and as he thrusts his cock against my ass, I push back. Doesn't even feel like I'm in control. Like my body's just begging for him to end my suffering.

He grips me, biting at my neck gently. "Luke...we have to stop," he breathes into my flesh.

"Why?"

"Luke!"

No, he's right. It's too much, and especially with all the other shit going on, we don't have time to be consumed by the sort of fucking I feel like we'll need once we go there.

I grit my teeth as I spin around, pulling my pants back up. He pulls his hands from under my shirt and places them on either side of the wall, steadying himself as he glares at me, taking deep breaths.

"Maybe don't tease me *like that*," he says.

"I have a little fun, don't I?"

"You fucker."

"Night, Brad." I lean close and offer a kiss. It lingers for both of us, but I finally manage to get out the door and head down the hall.

He closes the door behind me, and as I walk toward my dorm with the Sinners' bible tucked under my arm, my mind's spinning with everything that went down tonight.

As complicated and fucked up as this all is, knowing what Brad and I are inevitably moving toward somehow makes the wildest parts easier to bear.

That's what this sick lust does to me, at least.

14

BRAD

"YOU TALK TO Luke?" Seth asks as he lets me into his and Cody's room.

I push past him and find Cody in only trunk boxers and socks at the espresso machine in the kitchenette. He glances between Seth and me, concern on his face, like he's ready for a fight.

"He came by my dorm last night."

Seth closes the door. "And you didn't text us?"

To what? Tell you how Luke drove me insane?

How he blew my mind yet again?

How he sucked the cum out of me? And then, after I begged, let me drink his up?

Or does Seth want to hear about how Luke teased me with his ass and I shoved him against the door and started dry-humping him? How I could taste how much he wanted me as I licked his flesh? How I could hear the desire when he moaned, and how he ran his hand through my hair, like his entire body, his every move, was beckoning me to take what was rightfully mine?

Of course that's not what Seth's asking about, but it's hard to think about much else, even when I know there are more important things to get to.

"I figured neither of you is planning to run away from St. Lawrence, so I didn't see the harm in waiting a few hours." I can't disguise my irritation.

"Okay, okay," Cody says. "We're all stressed. Brad, I'm making chocolate shakes with espresso for Seth and me. How about I make you one too and then we'll get into this?"

Unsurprisingly, Cody has a better grasp of what I need right now.

"I'm in," I say, settling on the love seat in the main part of the dorm room.

Seth joins me, sitting on the arm.

Neither of us speaks as Cody runs the blender for a minute, but every time Seth glances my direction, I can feel his curiosity burning into my skin.

"He obviously couldn't read most of the book," I say, "so he came by to ask me what it said."

"And you told him," Seth says. It's not a question; it's an accusation.

"Of course I told him. He has a right to know."

Seth spits out, "Maybe we should have discussed that or at least decided what you could tell him, you know, as a group."

"As far as I'm concerned, he's in the group already, whether he chose to be or not."

"That's not how this works."

"Seth," Cody says from the kitchenette. "What did we talk about?"

Seth grunts. "Brad, I'm sorry. I know it seems like I'm not listening to you right now, but it feels like you aren't listening to us either."

Sounds like Cody attempted to get ahead of a fight, but I doubt Seth is going along with whatever script Cody gave him, since Cody would have worded this in a way that didn't leave me annoyed as fuck.

"My issue, Seth, is that you aren't listening to Luke. Just because he wasn't a member with us from the beginning doesn't mean he doesn't have feelings or that this isn't affecting him."

"Oh God. This is that stupid lust thing you've been dealing with."

"And *now* you're not listening to *me*. You can't dismiss me every time I advocate for him. That's not fair to either of us."

Cody steps around the island with two travel mugs in hand and hands one to each of us. "You two make all men look like a bunch of antagonistic asshats. Seth, why don't you tell him the concerns you shared with me earlier, without criticizing or accusing?"

Sometimes I find Cody using his psych courses annoying, but in this case, it might actually help.

"This is exactly what Luke's dad and Josh Dobbers were concerned would happen," Seth says. "The wrong person getting their hands on this stuff."

"Luke isn't the wrong person," I insist.

"How could you possibly know that? How can you be sure when he's the reason this thing has already killed at least one person? We don't know Luke. We don't know what he could do now that he knows he has this power."

"But you said it yourself: as long as he has all this power and doesn't realize it, he's dangerous. If we explain this to him, help him control his powers, maybe he won't be."

Seth's gaze wanders, like for the first time, he's seriously considering something I've said. I'm sure it's at least in part because of Cody's intervention.

"So which is more dangerous?" I press. "Him doing this stuff without knowing what it is, or him doing it on purpose?"

"It's not just that," Cody says. "Luke can obviously see things without getting wiped out like I do. That could be an advantage against the Slasher."

This is the first I've heard Cody give it a nickname. "Is that what we're calling it?"

"It's how the original Sinners referred to it. At least, I think this is similar to something else they encountered."

"And you're just telling us this now?" I ask.

"He doesn't know for sure," Seth says.

"After Luke mentioned the creature was feeding on blood and fear, I remembered some of the monsters the original Sinners profiled and checked my notes."

Since discovering the Sinners' bible, Cody has been working his way through it. He's got a binder full of translations, which we've relied on as we learned how to use our powers and connect with the Guides. It's also how we know about the history of the Sinners.

Even though Cody shares everything he's translated, there's too much for me to remember all of it, and clearly, even Cody needs to occasionally refer back to it to refresh his memory.

Cody heads over to his desk, retrieves some papers, and passes them to me. "They called this type a Slasher. They can appear in different forms, but they are similar in nature. Feed off blood and fear—those are the elements they need to grow and become stronger. When Waters and Dobbers encountered the first one, they used their powers to trap it and a shotgun to blow its head off, so we know it can be affected by the laws of our world and the spells we have."

"There's more," Seth says. "We think something about Luke's power is what it's after. That's what the Guides were trying to tell us."

"Because it feeds off energy?"

"Exactly," Cody replies. "Maybe they were warning that if it gets Luke, that will make it far stronger, which in turn…"

"Means it can kill even more people," I conclude.

"There's another fact about the Slasher," Cody adds.

"The way it murders its victims helps it extract more power. The first kill was quick because it needed to feed, but as it gets stronger, it can slow down, take its time to torture its victim to extract as much energy as it can from them."

"Like setting someone on fire or impaling them."

"All seems to fit together," Cody says.

"More reason to get rid of Luke," Seth adds, and I glare at him before he snaps, "I told you how I feel about this."

"Yeah, and what happened to 'we decide those things as a group'?" Cody retorts, making Seth huff.

"Seth only wants to do things when they work for the plan he already has in his head. Maybe we need to remind you that life's different when you can't just push what you want on people."

Cody's eyes narrow. "Did you really feel that was constructive?"

"No," I confess.

He disregards it, saying, "Is there anything else anyone wants to bring up? Anything that maybe you feel like the other hasn't been hearing?"

"I've said what I need to," I reply.

Seth takes a moment before he adds, "I'm a little annoyed at Brad right now because I feel like, since Luke got here, he's been keeping secrets about this...whatever we're gonna call it. *The Lust.*"

The Lust. That's apt.

Seth goes on, "You don't talk about it or tell us what you're going through. And when we ask, you get real defensive."

"You keep giving me hell about it, but then expect me to share something this personal?"

"That's a fair criticism," Seth concedes. "I've been pressing you about that because you are so secretive. But we need to understand what you're experiencing. It could help us make sense of what the hell is going on."

I grunt. "I don't like this."

"Okay," Cody says in a gentle way, like he knows Seth hit a nerve. "Brad, do you have anything you want to say about that?"

"Can you not talk to me like I'm one of your future clients?"

"I'm just trying to get to the bottom of this."

It doesn't make this shit any less weird. "It's not the kind of thing I want to talk about. It's embarrassing, and deeply personal. And then it's not just me. I can't speak for Luke—"

"We're back to you putting him first," Seth says.

"Seth, we're listening now," Cody presses, which makes Seth take a breath.

I go on. "What if I was probing you about things you could only share by also sharing things Cody might not want me to know?"

"Don't play like you know this guy like I know Codes."

"Seth, can you understand what he was trying to say?" Cody asks.

Seth considers the question. "I do, but my point stands: I don't get why he's being loyal to someone who hasn't earned that."

"I don't feel like I'm being loyal as much as seeing Luke as another person who deserves consideration."

Seth's gaze meets mine, and his expression relaxes. "Okay. I hear that."

About fucking time.

I take my first sip of Cody's shake, cherishing the mix of ice cream and espresso—two of my favorite things. Between Seth actually fucking listening to me and the taste, my defenses are starting to come down.

"Okay," Cody says. "Now that we've gotten all that out of the way, there's more."

"*More?* Fuck."

Cody heads to his desk and takes out a spiral-bound notebook. He opens it as he approaches me, and I can see it's notes about Luke's vision.

"He mentioned a statue he thought might be a squir-rel with a hat," he says.

"I remember."

"We think he got it wrong. The animal, at least. The mascot for the winter festival."

"Bucktooth Beaver?" I'm surprised I didn't make the connection from Luke's description.

"We'll have to check with Luke," Seth says, "but you

wouldn't necessarily know the animal unless you're familiar with Lawrenceville. The fair doesn't open until November twenty-first, so we think another murder will take place after the twenty-first."

"You *think* but don't actually know. Based on what he described, he seemed to be jumping around in time."

"It's something to go off of, at least," Seth mumbles before Cody interjects, I assume to keep Seth and me from spinning around in our frustration.

"The original Sinners said the Slashers need to take breaks after they feed—at least in their early development. It's a physical creature, an animal, so it grows and evolves like any other. If we're right, we have some time to sort this out. I say we all meet with Luke again. This time, we have a more open dialogue about everything, including the Lust you two are experiencing, if you're both comfortable sharing that. And then we start acquainting Luke with some of the tricks we've used. Help him figure out his powers the way we learned how to figure out ours. Luke's powers seem to allow him to get inside this Slasher's head. If he can find a way to control that, maybe we can find out where it's hiding."

"What if we don't have time for that?" I ask.

"I'm not strong enough to go back under yet," Cody says. "I do wonder if there's a way I could piggyback off what Luke's doing and maybe use that, but that's gonna take time to figure out."

"I don't like that," Seth says. "It sounds dangerous."

"It's all dangerous," Cody says. "But with that thing out there, we're gonna have to take risks. We also have to hope I'm right and that we have some time to try and make sense of this."

"And if we're wrong?" I ask.

Cody's gaze sinks. "Then at least one more person will die."

So like with so much of this shit, what choice do any of us have?

15

LUKE

"YOU CAN'T KEEP doing this," I say.

Brad messaged me this morning to let me know the guys were meeting at the church again. He didn't push, but I agreed to meet them. We were gonna have to deal with all the shit that came up on Friday sooner or later.

Once there, Cody took the lead, telling me about their interpretations of the visions, about a monster called the Slasher that the original Sinners discussed, and about their plan.

"Keep doing what?" Seth asks. I don't know if this guy can talk without sounding like an asshat.

"You clearly had another of your secret club meetings and reached all these conclusions without running any of this by me."

"We actually know what we're dealing with here," Seth says. "You don't."

"If I've learned anything, it's that you don't know all that much about what's going on. And as long as you keep having secret meetings, I'm always gonna be in the dark."

"Luke has a valid point," Cody says, glaring at Seth. "I understand why you feel that way, but we were trying to give you some space, and we had some insightful discussions that included how we need to involve you more."

His words set me at ease. Given how pissed I was when I rushed out last time, I hardly expected them to text me to brainstorm about our next steps. But they did ask me here, and at least Brad and Cody sound like they're trying to involve me in the process.

"That's fair," I say. "But I don't think you guys appreciate how shitty it is to always be the last to know what's going on, and on top of that, getting curveballs like finding out my dad was in this group and none of you bothered to mention it. It makes me feel like you're probably not telling me other things that are gonna rear their head and fuck with me later."

"I get that," Brad says. "But that's not how we're moving forward. You said it yourself: we have to work together if we're gonna find and kill this thing. And the plan Cody was describing isn't set in stone. You can interject if you have a better idea or if you think of a way of looking at this that we haven't considered."

I'm waiting for Seth to chime in with some asshole remark, but he just stands there, arms folded, silent.

Even though the guys sound much more reasonable

than on Friday, it doesn't change that they kept that secret about my dad from me. It's the sort of thing that'll make it hard for me to trust them, but knowing Dad was part of the original Sinners when he went to St. Lawrence is one of the reasons I'm standing here today. As much as these guys may have tried to fuck me over when I first got here, there's an important connection here, one I have to explore.

"Okay," I say. "So based on what I described, we have some time to see if we can find this Slasher—if that's what we have to call it."

"It's what the original Sinners called it," Cody clarifies. "I feel like if I'd been around, we would have come up with more scientific-sounding names. Do you mind if I see the Sinners' bible?"

I fish into my backpack and retrieve it, handing it over. Cody flips through until he gets to a sketch of…a creature without hands but with elongated, sharp-looking arms.

"This is the Slasher they encountered," Cody says.

"Doesn't look like the sketch you showed me of what you saw in your vision."

"From what Dobbers and your father say in here, they don't have to manifest in the same form, but from what you described, it works the same as this creature as far as feeding off blood and fear, so even if we're not spot-on, it seems safe to assume these creatures are similar enough, at least to find and kill."

"How did they find it?"

"The Guides offered Dobbers a similar vision, which they apparently had an easier time interpreting. I think because he had a better connection to the Guides than I do. Sort of innate, like your ability. It's the difference between a singer with natural talent and someone with skill. Both in combination are ideal, but separately there are weaknesses. You seem to have a lot of innate talent, but the rest of us have acquired what we have through training. Dobbers was more of a mix."

Of course it wouldn't be so easy for us. "Okay...so if we don't know where it is, what do we know?"

Seth replies, "I did some research on the victims Dobbers and your dad listed. There were four. It looks like it was a month and a half from the first disappearance to the next victims, which confirms our timeline for the attack on the fairgrounds."

"Taking time because it's gaining strength from the first victim," I say.

"And acclimating to a physical body," Cody adds. "The next three victims were killed on the same night, so it clearly just needs to recover from its first meal."

With this new information in mind, I go through everything we've discussed. "So this thing goes on a killing spree to feed off more blood and fear, which there'll be plenty of at a frat party."

"Exactly," Cody says. "If we're right, there's no telling what it'll be able to do after. Hell, it might kill everyone and have the strength to come and take you right away, like a snowball of energy that can keep going without stopping."

"Fuck, I hope we're wrong," I mutter, then try to refocus on what's important. "These supposed Guides warned you that it's after me, possibly because it might be able to use my powers to help it on its killing spree, right? That's our working assumption?"

"At least we know he's a good listener," Seth says.

I ignore him. "So the plan is to meet here every day, you teach me some of these things you've learned how to do, and we find this thing and kill it before it has a chance to kill again so it doesn't become this murder machine?"

"That about sums it up, yes," Brad says.

"I don't love the idea of waiting around while this thing is on the loose, but if we're lucky and the Slasher doesn't attack again until late November—big if—I guess that raises my next question: how long did it take you guys to figure out how to use your powers?"

"It was different for each of us," Brad explains. "Cody had a more intuitive sense about it right away. Took me a few weeks. Seth a little longer than that. And then some time to figure out our…specialties."

I'm curious how that played out, particularly given what his relates to, but I figure now's not the time to ask.

"But we weren't like you," Cody says. "None of us had whatever it is that allows you to tap into the power without having these secrets from the Sinners' bible, which makes me wonder how quickly you'll catch on."

"I wish I were that optimistic, but it's not like I walk around doing the kinds of things you guys do. It's simply happened, whether I wanted it to or not."

"Speaking of powers you don't understand," Seth says, "that brings us to the next aspect of all this that we should discuss."

"Seth," Brad says, shooting his friend a glare.

"Seth means," Cody adds, "we think it might help if we knew more about the Lust."

My cheeks warm. "What did you tell them?" I ask Brad. Did he betray me?

Cody chimes in, "He hasn't told us anything since he first started experiencing it after you arrived. The whole reason we're bringing it up now is because Brad doesn't want to talk about anything you're uncomfortable with."

Even though my defenses are up, it's nice to know Brad hasn't been sharing such intimate information with his friends. Although, this raises yet another issue. "I don't know that it's something I want to talk about."

Cody nods. "We understand it's a sensitive subject, but we're not perving on you guys. We wonder if something about what you're experiencing might help us understand this connection you share."

"Not sure *connection*'s the right word," I say. "We just get hard for each other."

I'm full of shit and I know it because it's much more

than that. Each time I get together with Brad, I see new aspects of him. As abrasive and intimidating as he was initially, I realize that was for show. The real Brad is sensitive and kind. Hell, if he wasn't here advocating for me, I wonder if Seth and Cody would've even been willing to share all these secrets with me.

"It would help to understand what the Lust is doing to each of you," Cody says. "Maybe by sharing, we can gain some insight into your powers. Like…is it that your specialty is also something sexual, and that since you came here, Brad maybe activated something in you?"

"I can see how that might help, but really, I'd rather keep it private. For now, at least."

Seth scoffs. "So you want us to bring you into our secrets, but yours are off-limits?"

Before I have a chance to clap back, Brad says, "There's nothing wrong with Luke setting a healthy boundary. Maybe as we work together and gain your trust, you'll feel more comfortable sharing. And if not, we'll work around that."

Again, just as quickly as Seth put me on defense, Brad sets me at ease.

"Sounds like a plan," Cody says, and Seth hesitates before nodding, maybe just to keep himself from making another snide jab.

"Okay." I can work with this as long as they're willing to include me and not push me to share anything I'm uncomfortable with. "So where do we start?"

Cody grabs his backpack and retrieves a small box. He approaches me and opens it, revealing a necklace like the ones they wear. Picking it up by the chain, he raises it to display the cross. "I made this one for you. Consider it your official invitation into the Sinners."

"I'm not much of a joiner," I say, but despite my resistance, the fact that it connects to the original Sinners feels like it's bringing me closer to the man I lost.

"Then consider it a gift from the Sinners," Cody says with a warm smile.

Man, I really like this guy a hell of a lot more than Seth.

I reach out, and he places the necklace in the palm of my hand.

"We did a quick spell on it before you arrived to infuse it with energy, but it'll take time, and you need to keep it on you so that it can become stronger."

As I grip the necklace, I feel something—I wonder if it's just in my head because he told me they'd performed a spell on it, or if I'm actually sensing this thing's power.

My gaze shifts to Brad, who's watching me. A rush of goose bumps pricks my flesh, but I try to play it off so the guys won't notice.

"So lesson one," Brad says. He flips through the pages of the Sinners' bible, showing me a few diagrams. "This is what we started with. You're gonna have to bear with some of these being kind of dumb, but it's better to start small and build your confidence. Think of it like weight training."

I study how his muscles help him fill out his thermal. "I'm more into running," I say.

"Right?" he says with a smile. "So like building up to a marathon."

"We gonna do 'light as a feather, stiff as a board'?" I tease.

"Sounds like someone's been watching *The Craft*," Brad says, his smile expanding.

"I started it last night, but it seemed a little close to home for my taste."

Brad takes my hand and guides me to the pentagram. "Kneel in the center here."

"Oh, don't worry, I've seen this one before," I say, shooting Cody a look.

He cringes. "Sorry about that. Again."

I assume the position, facing the full-length mirror leaning against the wall. Brad gets on his knees behind me.

With him so close, I notice I feel more than just the familiar Lust. He's the person I'd prefer to guide me through this, since I know him best.

Maybe that's something they discussed before I showed up, knowing Seth sure as fuck wasn't gonna be the one to help me.

"Okay," he says, "now place the necklace around your middle finger and let the cross hang in front of you. Good. Just like that. Imagine it moving in circles. Try not to do it with your hand. Just in your mind."

Wow. He wasn't kidding when he said they'd be dumb, but I follow his instructions, and unsurprisingly, in less than thirty seconds, it's spinning. "You know there's a word for this, right?"

"Ideomotor effect," Cody replies.

"It's something *I'm* doing to it, not magic, so is this step really helpful?"

Brad snickers. "Okay. You want to jump to the next part? Fine. Give it here." I hand it to him, and he walks on his knees in front of me, blocking the mirror. Facing me, he assumes the same pose I was in, the necklace dangling from his finger. "*Now* do it," he says.

"What?"

"It's the same idea, but now instead of doing it on your finger, you need to make it move in circles while it hangs from mine."

"That's impossible," I blurt out. Of course, after everything I've seen, I know better, but it was one thing when Seth and Cody were influencing my mind, another to think telekinesis is real.

But the necklace begins spinning, slowly at first, then much more dramatically. I inspect Brad's hand and arm, both stiff, unmoving. I'm not totally convinced this isn't just the ideomotor effect again and physics, but then the necklace starts spinning so fast, I can't even make out the cross. Then it abruptly moves side to side.

"Okay, Seth," Brad says. "Stop showing off."

The cross comes to a sudden halt to the side of Brad's hand, hanging midair, before dropping to its original position, dangling from Brad's finger.

I turn to Seth, who grips his necklace as he sports a cocky grin. "Just trying to help," he says.

"Not so impossible now, is it?" Brad asks, quirking a brow.

"I—wait, you guys can levitate shit with your minds?"

Brad's forehead creases. "We can do little tricks. Mainly because of the energy already in these amulets. On a good day, we can get a pen to roll off a desk, but we can't like, throw bricks across a room or anything like that."

Still, even just what he showed me is beyond what should be possible.

But... "Even if I can do this, if you can't do something bigger, I don't get what this helps."

"You have to use your powers," Seth says. "It's the only way you become more attuned to them. A lot of this is based on feelings and instincts, and you have to get in touch with those."

Finally, he says something useful!

"So let's go again," Brad says.

I feel like such a fucking moron, on my knees in front of Brad, focusing on a necklace, trying to get it to spin. But after what I saw in my mind and then the missing and certainly dead guy, I know I must take this seriously.

I study the cross.

"Just imagine it moving in a circle," Brad says. "Spinning and spinning."

I follow his instructions. It reminds me of being a kid and trying to use the Force like I saw in *Star Wars*, but like when I was a kid, nothing happens.

"It can take a while," Cody says. "Don't be hard on yourself."

"I mean, it's not that hard," Seth adds.

"Keep that up, and I'll tell him how long it took you," Brad says, which shuts Seth up.

"Why don't you let him wear your amulet?" Cody says. "That's how we got Seth to move his."

"That's not a bad idea." Brad removes his necklace and places it around my neck. There's a warmth to it as it rests against my chest. *His* warmth.

I close my eyes, enjoying a swirling sensation, as though he placed his finger where the cross rests. A soft gasp escapes my lips as I open my eyes, and Brad's gaze shifts to my mouth. He smirks, like it pleases him to see my reaction, and when I glance at his crotch, I notice just how much he enjoyed it.

"Focus," Brad says in a stern voice, but he's still smirking. "You can touch it if you want."

I reach for his crotch, and he glares at me. "Not what I meant."

"Gross," Seth groans. "You guys have plenty of time

to do this outside of training."

But Brad's still chuckling, and blushing a little, so fuck what Seth thinks.

I grip Brad's necklace, imitating the way I've seen him hold it. Then I stare at my necklace, dangling from his finger, imagining it spinning the way Seth had it going.

I wait.

And wait.

And wait some more.

"Don't get so tense," Brad says, and only then I realize my face is all tensed up. "It works better if you're at ease. You're not forcing it with your body. That's what I meant before when I said you have to build up confidence. You're not accessing anything physical. It's something deep within you."

I try again, but still, nothing happens.

"I told you," Seth spits out, and Brad's nostrils flare.

"Told him what?" I ask.

Brad sighs. "Nothing. He's just being a dick."

I glare at him. "I thought you guys were including me now."

Brad bites his bottom lip, and I have the urge to lurch forward and kiss him, but I stop myself.

"We hoped because of all the power we'd seen from you already that you'd take to it faster than we did. But if you had done it already, that would have been ridiculously fast. It took Cody days, and that was hours and hours of trying. A few minutes is nothing. Here. Let's go back to you doing it on your hand. I'll let you know when you're moving it, and once you get better at that, we'll come back to this, okay?"

He's so patient with me. So attentive.

"And I think it would be better if Luke and I did this alone," he adds. "It might help Luke relax a little bit."

"Fine," Seth says. "I have a group project to work on anyway."

"Yeah, that works," Cody says. "Do you mind if I take the Sinners' bible back? You can totally hang on to it for longer if you want. I just prefer to keep it safe."

"I would like to look at it some more," I say. "And I'd like to see what you've translated too."

Cody and Seth eye one another uneasily, and Cody says, "Luke, it's not that we don't understand why you'd want to see it."

"But we can't just hand over basically all our secrets to someone we barely know."

I turn to Brad, wondering if he feels the same. "Maybe just not now. But once we've all become better acquainted, and everyone's comfortable, except maybe Seth…"

"Ha…ha…" Seth drags out, sneering.

I can't really blame them, considering they don't know me or really understand my connection to the Slasher. But it sucks knowing there's this connection to my dad I don't have access to.

"I can pull out some pages that are just about the historical parts—Dobbers writing about your dad. I'll give you those tomorrow, if that works."

I feel tears stir—that's very considerate of him. "That would be nice. Thank you, Cody."

Cody and I swap information before he and Seth head out. As soon as the door at the top of the stairs closes, Brad sets his hand against my cheek, running his thumb across my bottom lip. My body relaxes as I tilt my head, taking his thumb into my mouth and biting gently.

"You know how hard it was to keep my hands off you that whole time?" he asks, sending a surge of energy coursing through me.

"Well, nothing's stopping you now," I say, and he moves quickly, pushing his lips against mine, our tongues colliding as he drags me to the floor so that I'm under him.

"Brad, you're gonna fuck up the pentagram."

"I'll fix it later," he says before kissing down to my chin, offering a quick bite, then trailing kisses down my neck. "How about we get off real fast before getting back to this?"

A wave of heat overtakes me. "Doesn't have to be that fast."

He laughs into my neck before nibbling again.

And if this is part of what these lessons involve, I'm all in.

16

BRAD

OVER THE COURSE of the next week, I continue working with Luke on overcoming this first, basic hurdle.

Just like when we tried to scare him off, he's no quitter. It's one of the qualities I admire about him.

Hell, the fact that he saw those images of the Slasher and immediately wanted to stop it rather than getting on a plane back home says a lot about him.

Since Sunday, every evening we've met up at the old church and gotten right to work.

Maybe not *right* to work. We've been guilty of some good fun. We tell each other it helps us focus on his lesson, but it doesn't make keeping our hands off each other that much easier, especially when he looks so damn cute when he's serious and trying to focus on using his powers. We usually have to end our sessions the same way we start them, which makes his teacher very happy.

On Thursday, Luke is as focused and determined as ever, but despite an hour of attempts, he grunts, and not for any of the fun reasons.

"My arm's going to sleep again. Are you sure I'm gonna be able to do this?" he asks, relaxing it at his side.

"I know it's frustrating, but anytime it feels like you can't, maybe just think that even Seth figured it out."

"If you think I haven't been motivating myself with that, you're out of your goddamn mind."

I chuckle and check the time on my phone. "It's almost nine. How about we get out of here? I assume you're heading to Alpha Alpha Mu's Halloween party?"

His expression twists up. "Alexei told me about it, but the last thing that's been on my mind is a fucking party. I've been reading those pages Cody gave me."

"How does that feel?" In some ways I'm sure it's a relief, in others a painful reminder of what he's lost.

His gaze wanders. "It's...a lot. Dobbers is talking about Dad learning to use his telekinetic abilities, which evidently, he had a better handle on than me, whereas Dobbers was better with telepathy. I guess you know all this already?"

I nod.

"It's not just about getting my mind around what Dad was doing. My whole perspective of reality has shifted. It's overwhelming."

He takes a breath, and in it, I hear how exhausted he is. Between everything we've expected him to come to terms with and pushing him to use his powers, it's simply too much.

"We both need a break," I say. "We're going to that party, and you're gonna have a great time."

He tilts his head and shoots me a cross look. "While I know there's some monster I need to help you guys find and kill?"

"If that doesn't warrant a break, I don't know what does."

"It's okay. I might stay here and try some more."

"No way. And I'm not leaving you out in the woods with a monster on the loose."

He smirks. "Aren't you bossy tonight? Don't you want me to get this?"

"Yeah, and you know why Seth took so long to figure it out? He's too in his head, and that's what you're doing right now. You're getting in your own way. If you can cut loose a little, then maybe when we come back to it, you'll do better."

"That's a real clever pitch to get me to go to a party." His gaze wavers as he thinks it over. "I don't have anything to wear. I don't really do parties. That first one I went to, I was just there to see you."

"Guess you're lucky I do party. And hard. I have some old costumes and a few options for different events for this year, so we'll swing by my place and see what I've got."

"If we're gonna be at your place for a bit anyway, maybe we can have a quick jerk-off session before we head out." There's a familiar, determined expression on his face.

I shake my head. "Uh-uh."

He pouts. "But I tried so hard, and I always get a little something when we finish up."

It's true, and I can feel that he wants it, but unlike some of those early times when we messed around, we've done plenty this week, so it's not the ache of the Lust pulling us together. And as much as I wouldn't mind claiming him right here and now, I have a better plan.

"How about you be a good Straight Boy and come to the party, and if you're good…" I lean close to him so that my mouth is inches from his. "…then I'll make sure to satisfy all those naughty fantasies running through your pretty head."

"All of them?" he asks with a raised eyebrow.

I know he means he wants me to fuck him.

"If you're *real* good, you never know," I say.

Now that it doesn't feel so primal and uncontrolla-ble, it's a tempting thought, one I'm surprised I'm so willing to entertain.

He winces. "If this is all a trick to get me to go to the party, then I want you to know it's a very mean one."

I laugh, then reach out and cup his cheek, running my thumb across his bottom lip. "But I still make you hard, don't I?" I say, and he smirks subtly before I claim his mouth.

A few tongue-filled kisses later, we pack up and re-turn to the dorms. We shower first, then head to my room, where I go through my costume bin. Among the options, I notice two pairs of wings, one white and one black. I figured best be ready if I needed to be an angel or a demon, depending on the occasion, which comes in handy now. I bought pairs of spandex shorts to go with them, and I'm pleased with how good Luke fills out his.

"You couldn't have picked out an outfit with more clothes?" Luke asks as he assesses himself in the full-length mirror. He tugs his shorts down.

"You try to cover those thighs, you're gonna end up showing dick, right?"

As he laughs, I adjust the straps on his wings, then fix the chain on his necklace so the link is behind his neck. I take a step back, studying his gorgeous body—the lines in his abdomen, that defined chest that's just the right size. Fuck, this guy has the perfect body.

He glances himself over before saying, "I have a pair of white sneakers I can grab on our way out."

"I doubt anyone's gonna be looking at your shoes, but that sounds good."

He takes another look in the mirror. "We look like sexy strippers."

"We look hot as sin, and trust me, if you wore more than that to Alpha Alpha Mu's Halloween party, you'd stick out like a sore thumb. But you don't have to wear it if you don't want to."

He shrugs. "I like it. But going to the party together as an angel and a demon, people might think we're an item."

"If we're wearing similar costumes, they'll think we're friends. When I have my tongue down your throat on the dance floor, *then* they'll think we're an item."

He grins like he wouldn't mind fulfilling that fantasy.

"But obviously," I add, "if you don't want them to think anything, I—"

"I don't give a fuck what anyone thinks." He moves close, hooking an arm around me so that his abs are tight against mine. "Now give me a kiss, demon."

I do as told, and as we embrace, a rush of energy moves through me. Luke grabs my crotch, stroking my firm cock. "Oh, no." I force away from our kiss. "I'm not letting you trick me into fucking around so you can get out of this party."

"Trick you?" he says, playing shocked as he tugs my body closer, my hard-on rubbing along his abs with just the thin costume fabric between us. "But I'm an angel."

"A very naughty angel." I take his mouth again, and as I pull away, I say, "Which gives me an idea."

I grab some glitter markers from my desk drawer. With the white, I write SINNER on his right pec, and on mine, in the black, he writes SAINT.

Luke smiles. "The perfect touch." We do a quick check, then grab his sneakers from his room.

It's a bit of a walk to Alpha Alpha Mu, but it's a nice enough night that we don't need a jacket. And being

Halloween, we're hardly the only bare-chested guys en route to the frat, which looks more like a stripper convention when we get there.

Luke and I head inside and throw back Jell-O shots before grabbing drinks. I text Codes to see if he and Seth have arrived and discover they're already out back. When we find them, Seth is in tight pants, pads, and a football jersey, his abs on full display. I have no doubt this was Cody's handiwork.

As we approach him, I'm waiting for him to make some clever remark or say we look like boyfriends because of the matching costumes, but he nods and says, "Nice work."

"You did a good job with yours too," Luke says.

"*Cody* did a good job with mine. I don't really give a fuck about these things, but he enjoys dressing his straight friend up, and I've learned he loves him a jock."

He points, and we turn to see Cody flirting with Gage Lorde, tight end for the school team.

"He dressed you up as a football player and now he's ditching you for a real one," I tease, shaking my head with feigned disapproval.

He laughs. "I know, right? So sick."

"But for some reason, I have a feeling you'll still wind up waking in Cody's bed."

He smiles. "Only if Gage doesn't push me out of it."

We share a laugh, and Luke looks a little confused. I get it. You have to know Cody and Seth to understand their friendship, but surely if there was even a hint of sexual feelings, those would have been dealt with already.

"Seriously, though," Seth says. "I just got Shira Maron's number and a text to meet her upstairs in five, so at this point, where I wake up isn't really what's on my mind."

I laugh. "Nice work, stud. Maybe if you're lucky, Cody'll be in the next room over and you can hear Gage running drills on his ass."

His jaw tenses, catching me by surprise. Then he shrugs. "Well, as far as I know, Gage is straight, but I guess it'd be great if we're both having fun."

For the first time since he and Luke have been within a few feet of each other, neither looks pissed. I can't help wondering if it's at least in part because Seth's already gotten a few drinks in him...or maybe the promise of what he'll be doing with Shira upstairs later.

"Luke fucking Waters," I hear behind me, and Luke and I turn to see Alexei approaching, in jeans and a black cape, wearing vampire makeup. "You blew me off when I told you about this party."

"Yeah..." Luke drags out. "I didn't want to bother to get a costume, but Brad had an extra one, so..."

Alexei eyes him skeptically. "Don't lie. Brad clearly only had an extra third of a costume."

We share a laugh, but Alexei keeps glancing between Luke and me. Given what he'd seen of us in the past, I'm sure he's shocked to see us not only hanging out at a party together, but wearing matching costumes.

"I'm about to head inside, and I better see both your sexy asses on the dance floor in ten or I'm gonna come find you."

Seth watches Alexei go, like he's waiting for him to be out of earshot before he says, "So how was this evening?"

Luke shrugs. "Same as usual."

"Are you moving the necklace a little bit, at least?"

"I don't even think I can summon the ideomotor effect at this point," Luke says.

I can tell it's weighing on Seth, and any confidence he was wearing from his success with Shira is gone.

"Hey, hey, man," I say. "Can we drop it for tonight? I brought him so we could have a good time."

"Yeah," Seth says. "I would also like to have a totally normal night and pretend that everything's fine, so I'm gonna go find another Jell-O shot."

He gives me a hug before heading off, at which point Luke says, "Alexei's being awfully friendly tonight."

I shrug. "Is he? You know him better than I do. But he was right about one thing. We need to get your sexy ass on the dance floor, so let's finish these drinks and get out there."

We take a few swigs before heading back inside, to the living room, and as we enter, we can hear the music rather than the intense thud of the bass. I get a few glances from guys I've hooked up with in the past—the sort of looks that tell me they wouldn't mind having another go. I struggle between moving closer to Luke to let them know I'm not available for any ass other than his at the moment, and keeping my distance because he doesn't need to know I feel like a clingy boyfriend. We've barely known each other a month. It's partly the Lust that makes me feel that way, but it's something else too. Something more than raw sexual desire.

As we find an open space in the middle of the crowd of our scantily clad peers, Luke spins around to me. "Let me know if I'm about to smack anybody with these wings," he jokes.

I don't recognize the song, but it's a decent beat, so I don't hesitate, partly because I want to impress Luke. Meanwhile, he does a little bob, glancing around uncomfortably as we keep about a foot between us.

"That's cute." I move closer.

"I'm not much of a dancer. Can you tell?"

"We can fix that." I step even closer, pushing up against him. I'm waiting to see if he'll pull away, if maybe he was acting cooler with being seen out with me than he really is, but he doesn't resist, and I can't help grinning as I squat down and grind up against him, crotch to crotch. "Come on. Just follow me."

He snickers as I hook my arm around him, pressing against the small of his back as he starts to move along with me.

But the awkwardness doesn't last long. Soon his

movements expertly mirror mine, our cocks like rocks, our bodies as in sync as when we mess around. When his gaze sinks to my lips, I steal a kiss. Luke places one hand against my back, the other cupping my ass as we dance. Doesn't feel like we're at a party anymore—it's just me and him and our bodies reveling in the sensation of being close.

Luke tears his lips away and spins around, his ass gravitating to my pelvis. I slide my hand around his waist, caressing his abs as I kiss his neck. His hand relaxes against the back of my head as I nibble, lick, and kiss.

Now I'm following his movements, this guy who was so awkward only moments before but who's suddenly so fucking in tune with the music.

I've surrendered to him. He's surrendered to me.

We've both surrendered to this thing that's taken control of us.

He turns his head, at the perfect angle for my mouth to move from his neck to his mouth. I'm delirious with sensation, trapped in the moment, making it hard to tell how much time passes—a minute, thirty minutes, an hour. All I know is that when I come to, we have an audience cheering us on and Alexei's at our side.

"Look at you guys go," he says.

Luke pulls away, though he doesn't look bothered by the fact that his roomie just caught what we were doing.

"Aren't you full of surprises?" Alexei teases. "Mind if I steal this stud away from you real quick?" He drapes an arm over my shoulder.

"Uh, sure," Luke barely has a chance to say before Alexei pulls me aside.

"I knew you guys must have made up since that initial pickup game, but I didn't realize how close you'd gotten." He leans back and looks me dead in the eye. "So I just wanted to let you know, if I find out you're fucking with him, I'm coming for you."

Alexei's normally cool and chill, but I get why he'd be suspicious about my interest in Luke after the way I've treated him since he first arrived. But there's something in his gaze...like he might be talking about something else. Something he shouldn't know.

That's wild, though.

There's no way.

"What do you mean?" I ask.

"What do you think I mean?" His stare doesn't let up. "Don't play games with him. I'm watching you." He pats my shoulder condescendingly before he's off, hurrying back through the crowd.

The warning leaves me a little shaken, but I remind myself that Alexei doesn't know about the Sinners or the Rift or Cody's visions.

I return to Luke, who's standing by the wall, gazing off. As I approach him, he doesn't look like he did only moments ago.

"Luke?"

"Sorry, I'm not feeling very good."

"Is this about Alexei seeing us?"

"Huh? No. I—I'm feeling a little lightheaded."

I assess his face. He looks pale. And though he's saying it's not about Alexei, considering the timing, I wonder if he's struggling with being out to his friend before he was ready.

"Here, let's get you some water." I lead him to the kitchen and grab two bottles, then take him to a room upstairs. "We can lie down in here."

"I think the guy whose room this is might mind."

"Preston's his name. And I found him in the bushes near the dorms one morning after a party, naked, and lent him clothes so he could get back to the frat in one piece, so he owes me. Just lie down. You look like you're about to be sick."

Luke takes a seat on the edge of the bed and drinks a sip of water. "Sorry. I was having a good time. I didn't mean to fuck it up."

"You have nothing to be sorry about. And you didn't fuck anything up."

I sit beside him as he takes a few breaths. Finally, he says, "It's so dumb. It's why I shouldn't have come out tonight."

"What do you mean?"

He closes his eyes and says, "I was really enjoying dancing with you. Like really enjoying it, and I got lost in the moment, and then when we stopped and you stepped away, this memory fucking hit me. I mean, I've thought about it plenty, especially today, but it was so vivid. I couldn't push it back. And then I felt so fucking guilty for enjoying myself."

"Guilty?"

"Mom and Dad were big on holidays. At Halloween, we'd spend time decorating the house and making cookies. They made a game of figuring out what costumes we'd wear when we went trick-or-treating. We'd watch scary movies together." He chuckles. "Nothing really scary, mostly black-and-white movies. Anyway, I was just thinking how it's not the same without them."

I notice a tear stirring in his eye, and he turns away from me.

"Fuck, Luke. That's why you didn't want to come out tonight."

He nods.

"I'm such an asshole."

"No," he says, resting his hand on my thigh. "I wanted to come. I thought it could be fun, and it was...until I fucked it up."

I rest my hand on top of his. "I don't think that counts as you fucking it up, Straight Boy."

He snickers at his nickname, and I'm glad because I was hoping to ease some of this weight he's carrying.

"I appreciate your sharing that with me, Luke. I wish I'd been more considerate and asked why you didn't want to come."

"No way you could have guessed that."

"Maybe you're right. I'm glad to hear both your parents were so involved in your childhood, though. My mom was great. Dad...not so much."

"Your dad didn't do anything with you for Halloween?"

I chuckle, but as soon as I do, I realize how fucked up it is to be amused at the thought of him giving that many shits about me. I shake my head. "Let's not talk about my bullshit for now. This is about you."

He turns to me, his gaze boring into mine, as though he can see my deepest, darkest secrets. Instinctively, I look away.

"What is it?" he asks, assuring me he hasn't seen this darkness within me. "Brad?"

Luke's ruminations on his past have activated mine, and I find myself sifting through memories I prefer to keep buried...and regrets I couldn't bury if I tried. Luke would hate me if he saw this side of me. He would see me for the selfish coward I really am.

But as he sits here, being so vulnerable with me, all I want is to protect him. From me.

Maybe it's my conscience or this connection between us, but even wishing I could keep the words down, they slip past my lips. "You might have guessed from what I told you already that Dad's a controlling man. He was that way with my mom. Kept her like a doll. She was one of those people who believed you were supposed to make a marriage work, no matter how hard. He wasn't physically abusive. Just a dick. Both Mom and I knew when he was coming home late that he was seeing someone else. How fucked up is it that a child knows his dad is cheating on his mom?

"When I was eight, she'd finally had enough and called him out on it. She wanted a divorce…and so he made her life a living hell. Dad was the one with the money, so he dragged her through it. Incredible, the case a rich man can make with lawyers who are experts at redactions and objections and filing bullshit motions to get the opposition to run out of cash. Mom wound up in a mental-health facility, that's how bad it was, and he won sole custody."

Tension knots up in my chest at the flashes of being questioned by social workers and attorneys.

"Before they divorced, we celebrated holidays, but it always seemed to annoy Dad. After he got custody and we moved in with his new girlfriend, there wasn't anything. Not even my birthday. Then she got pregnant, they got married, and it was clear he finally had the child he really wanted. I was the mistake. I was nothing and nobody to him."

"Brad," Luke says, his voice full of concern as he grips my hand tighter.

For once in my fucking life, it feels like a relief to talk about this shit. Maybe that's why I can't fucking stop. "I tried to get out of that house. I snuck away to see Mom from time to time, and each time, he got worse. Told me

I was her child and just as worthless. That I'd never amount to anything. I could see the disdain in his eyes every time he looked at me, wishing he could get rid of me, but keeping me from Mom was a cruel torture for both of us."

"I'm so sorry, Brad," Luke says, turning his hand and interlocking his fingers with mine.

I was so lost in the telling of my past that I hardly noticed the blur in my eyes and the warmth sliding down my cheeks. I consider turning away from him, but now that I've shared so much, I don't want to. Wild to think I didn't want him to know any of this, and suddenly, I want him to see me. All of me.

But as I see the warmth in his expression, I spit out, "Don't look at me like that."

"Like what?"

"I don't deserve sympathy, Luke. Not after what I've done."

"What you've done?"

My chin trembles. "Yes. Luke, I've done something terrible."

He tilts his head, seeming surprised to hear this.

Maybe that's because I've gotten so good at hiding my sin, even from myself.

I don't have to tell him more. I could leave it there with him feeling sympathy for me, but I don't want to lie.

Not to him.

Not anymore.

17

LUKE

A SEARING PAIN burns like fire within me. I can't believe what Brad just shared. I cringe when he uses the word *dad* to describe this bastard. But just as soon as Brad pulled at my heartstrings, now I can't help but be suspicious. Done something horrible? What has he done?

He doesn't leave me in suspense, getting right to the point. "After I graduated from high school, I connected with Mom again. And she's the same woman she's always been. Loving, caring. She welcomed me back into her life effortlessly, and my dad refused to see me after my 'betrayal.' But life has a real fucked-up way of giving you so much only to take something else away because Mom had been diagnosed with MS...multiple sclerosis."

As if his tragic past wasn't bad enough.

"You know what that is?"

I nod. "A little."

"Shaking. Seizures. Terrible, crippling pain. Mom's progressed quickly. And it's hard knowing that the person you finally have back in your life is already slipping from your grasp."

As he says the words, it's hard to imagine how he could think any of this means something terrible about him. But I'm quiet, wait for him to go on.

"Remember when I told you we each had our reasons for fucking around with our powers from the Rift?"

"Yeah."

"When we found out about the Sinners, and Cody convinced me this stuff actually worked, I thought I could find a way to use it to help her. A spell or something. Cody has some healing abilities, but we've learned those have their limitations. Then a few months after realizing what my own powers were, I discovered that if I visited Mom, her pain and symptoms would be gone for weeks. When she would go to the doctors, they would be shocked by things they saw, like parts of her brain healing that shouldn't be. It's not some miracle cure. Only gives her a few weeks of relief before she gets symptoms again, but if I make a quick visit, she's fine again. It's not something I can control. It just happens. Either from her being around me or maybe because it's something I want so deeply, part of me is doing it without consciously being aware of how, like what happens with you."

I would have expected him to share that with enthusiasm or hope, but his words are filled with dread.

"That's good, right?" Even as I say it, I fear I know where this is going.

His gaze narrows as he glances at me. "It gave me hope that I could cure her. The Sinners' bible mentions the Guides who helped them unlock the Rift's secrets. I thought if we contacted them, maybe they could help my mom. Permanently. The bible mentions evil beings we might encounter in the Rift, and that we'd need to be able to guard against them. I knew we weren't ready, but I pushed. When we went under, we came across one of those beings. We all felt it. And we had to stop. It lurked near the opening of the Rift. We didn't expect something would get through, but then Cody started having visions, and we discovered something was going to break into our world and hunt people. That's why initially we thought you were going to be one of its victims…before we knew about your powers."

"How could you know that you're the reason this monster was going to enter our world?"

"It's hard to explain…but the better you get at this, the more you can feel the Rift, become in sync with it. You can feel when what you're doing is working with it, honoring its power, and when you're overstepping. It's the same as your conscience when you do something right or wrong. You fucking know in your soul. I knew we weren't ready to go in, but I pushed anyway because I was more concerned with being with my mom who'd been taken from me. I didn't give a fuck about the consequences. And now a man's dead. And others may die because of what we've done." He turns away from me. "Don't you see? I'm a monster. Fucking around with this stuff is why this thing got out, and now we're paying the price of my sin."

There it is.

This was why he didn't want to share his reason for playing with this stuff. Because he feels guilty about what's gotten out.

"When I left my dad at eighteen, I'd finally started to believe he was wrong about me. Even came to the same school as him with my inheritance from my grandfather to prove him wrong, to show him I could be somebody. But now I've just proven that every time he looked at me with scorn and disdain, every time I could see him hating me for reasons I didn't understand, maybe it was because he could see me for what I really am."

It's a chilling confession. "Brad—"

Another tear breaks away from his eye, streaming down a familiar path.

He pushes to his feet. "I should go," he says, but I grip his hand. "Please, just let me leave, Luke. I don't want you to see me like this."

I rise from the bed, keeping my hand tight against his and resting my other on his shoulder. "Brad, please don't go. Please don't shut down."

He refuses to look at me. This is less like the guy I've come to know and more like a child trying to avoid his asshole dad's cruel gaze.

"Please look at me, Brad," I whisper because I want

him to see how I'm really looking at him, without the judgment he fears.

He gulps and takes a breath before his gaze meets mine.

"I don't know if what you did is the reason for all this, but knowing how painful it is to lose someone you love, if I thought there was a chance to keep my mom or dad around for a minute longer, I can't say I wouldn't have done the same. Maybe it's selfish. Maybe it's wrong. But fuck, we're only human. Your dad wasn't right about you. And I can see how fucking wrong he is when I look at you."

His expression relaxes, and I feel his tension easing as he feels my support.

I move close, until I can feel his breath against my lips. I don't just want him to see and hear my words, I want him to feel them in his fucking soul.

As I kiss him softly, there's a vibration in my lips. His tongue slips into my mouth, and he hooks his arm around me, tugging me close as he takes out all his pain on our kiss.

I draw him back onto the bed, our lips parting only long enough so we can get positioned, him lying on top of me, his arms hooked around my neck. His warm tears slip onto my face as we thrust our hard cocks into each other.

I just want to relieve all the tension from that conversation, not just for myself, but for him. I want to help him escape, the way he helped me on the dance floor.

When his lips finally pull away from mine, he kisses down a familiar path to my throat, his tongue and teeth worshipping my flesh.

A powerful desire moves through me. It's not as painful as it usually is. It feels...inevitable.

"Yes," he whispers into my neck. "Yes, I'll fuck you, Luke."

I roll my head back as his assurance has my nerves on edge, eagerly anticipating this desire that's plagued me since the seed was first planted weeks ago...since it became not just a fantasy, but an obsession.

His lips travel down my throat, to my chest. He explores my body with his mouth, tongue, and teeth as he makes his way down to my shorts, pulling them back to expose my stiff cock.

He rubs his face against it, teasing the head with his tongue before growling. He pries himself back, rising onto his knees. "These shorts are hot, but right now, they're pissing me off." Like the expert fuckboy he is, he tends to my shoes and socks first, tossing them off the bed before grabbing either side of my shorts and pulling them down my legs. Only then do I notice he's already kicked off his shoes—when the fuck did that happen?

He gets my shorts off, then tosses them aside before removing his socks and sliding his shorts down. After he gets them off, he reaches into a pocket and retrieves two packets.

"Did you know this was gonna happen?" I ask.

A smile plays across his face. It's like I've helped him shake those dark thoughts off, and I see the Brad I was so desperate to get back. Not the guilt-ridden kid, beaten down by his father's cruelty, but the confident guy I've come to know.

"You think I'd let myself get anywhere near you without being prepared?" he asks, and my cheeks warm. "I've been carrying around a condom since you first wanted my dick in you. And a little packet of lube I got from the clinic 'cause I'm thoughtful like that."

I grab the strap of my wings. "We should take these off."

He shakes his head. "Uh-uh. You're hotter with them on."

He wears a cocky smile, and I must admit, I'd rather him keep his on too, so I leave them.

He tosses the condom and lube on the sheets at my side before crawling back over me. He puts his weight on me, his lips returning to mine, our cocks beside each other as we find our way back into our familiar pattern of thrusts.

"Oh, Luke, I'm gonna take so much pleasure being inside you," he whispers, and the heat in my face intensifies. He nibbles at my jaw before he says, "You mind if I try something?"

"Huh?"

"It involves using my powers."

I tense up. "I'm not sure that's smart. Should you be fucking with this stuff?"

"The power around us is here whether we do anything with it or not. It's not harmful in and of itself, and messing with it won't affect the Rift. Trying to mess with the Rift itself is what's dangerous. Does that make sense? Once you get a better grasp of the Rift, you won't be afraid of it or the Guides. At least, not find them a threat or the cause of any of the shit we're dealing with."

Given what he shared earlier, I have a better understanding of why he's confident that using their powers isn't what freed this monster, but it's all so new and strange, it's hard not to be frightened of it.

He quiets. "Do you trust me?"

"Yes," I say, shocked by how quickly I answer him.

He smiles. "You'll like it."

"You say it like that, and you can do whatever the fuck you want to me."

Despite my apprehension, I surrender to him. He slides his hand between us, gripping his cross before kissing my neck again. It's like that first time he touched me, sensation shooting through me, every nerve in my body electrified as his tongue sweeps across my flesh, and I gasp at the intensity of the sensation pulsing through me in waves. My heart races. My thoughts scramble.

"Holy fuck," I mutter.

He chuckles. "You like that?"

"You know I did."

"Of course I know," he says, crawling down my body and kissing my nipple.

"Ah," I moan as another surge races through me. I've only just adjusted to the first, but now he's taking me even higher.

He takes his time at my nipple. It feels like pooling energy into me as he runs his free hand across my torso, leaving where he touches swirling with heat.

After working me up, he continues down, trailing kisses, each one sending those same powerful impulses soaring through me. My head rolls against the bed as I call out, "Yes, Brad. Yes, I need it." Even though it's what I want, I don't even feel in control of the words I'm saying. What he's doing pulls them right from me.

Soon, he's crouched down, hooking his arms under my legs, positioning me so that my ass is on display for him. After what his mouth has done to the rest of my body, I'm curious what it'll do there, but he doesn't leave me in suspense. He offers a lick, his arm around my thigh, his hand still gripping his cross.

It's a fireworks show, going off and making the pressure swell. I arch my back, enjoying each explosion, as he continues licking and kissing. If it didn't feel so damn good, I'd be pissed at him right now for not giving it to me sooner, but lost in these sensations, it's impossible to be anything but appreciative of his skilled tongue as he slides it around my hole.

He relaxes his arm and pulls it back around my

thigh, shoving his index finger in his mouth before tracing it along the rim.

"Please put it in, Brad. I can't take much more. I need to know."

He doesn't disappoint me. He slips his finger in, easing his way in so expertly, navigating—

I notice my nipples, my abdomen, my cock, and behind my ears radiate with sensation, much stronger than the rest of me. And then...then the fireworks start again as his finger pushes up against what I can only assume by the explosive waves of sensation is my prostate. I moan as he stimulates it. My eyes are closed, but I know he must still be clutching his necklace because of the heat that overtakes my body, pooling at my face.

The sensations are so intense—they're bright colors, flashes of blue like lightning, and they tingle at my tongue like a delicious taste. It almost feels overwhelming, so much so that I have to force myself to ease into it.

He must've sensed my wish because there's a subtle pressure before I feel him push another finger in me. Brad seems so abrasive and forceful, but in this moment, he's tender, the seasoned pro showing me the ropes.

When his second finger hits my prostate too, I gasp in ecstasy as I enjoy another flash of this inner color and taste. My flesh feels alive, each nerve thanking Brad for the pleasure he's bringing me.

I'm sure he already knows, but I have to tell him,

"Please fuck me. I'm ready. I promise I'm ready."

"I love how hungry you are to have my cock inside you."

Even his voice is turning me on differently than normal, but unlike the other times when I've craved, wished, that he would end my agony of wanting to know, he pulls his fingers out of me. I glance down to see him slide on the condom and tear open the packet of lube. He lubes himself first, then generously applies some to my ass. He needs to be generous with how hard I want him to fuck me.

"Get on your knees," he orders, reminding me of how much he can read my every sexual wish.

I obey his command, rolling over and getting on my knees, placing my hands on the mattress in front of me. His hand rests on my ass cheek, caressing before he offers a firm grip and a low, rumbling growl. Just hearing his feral desire for me makes me arch my back, my body's plea for him to take me.

"Is my Straight Boy ready for cock?"

I have to laugh. "Your Straight Boy's desperate for it."

I blush, though how is it embarrassing to confess that when he already knows it in his fucking soul?

I feel the wet lube as he lines his cock up with my hole, then a little pressure...sweet, delicious pressure that makes my flesh prick with anticipation. As he eases in, my body welcomes him, and I push my ass back. I know the spot I need him against.

But the pressure mounts too quickly.

"Be patient," he says, gripping my ass. "I want it too, but you gotta be patient."

I relax, trusting his expertise as he takes his time, opening me up with that fat cock. Once my body has eased up and I can feel he's getting close to that spot, I'm too greedy, though, and I force myself back farther until he finally hits.

I close my eyes. I know it's only in my mind, but I'd swear I see bursts of flashing lights as my body erupts once again in tingling. Even where he's touching my ass is hypersensitive, somehow making his simple caress that much more intoxicating.

"Fuck," he moans as his hand slides from my ass, around my waist, to my abs. "How does that feel?"

"You know damn well how it feels."

He chuckles as he leans down, resting a hand on the bed as he relaxes his chest against my shoulder blades.

"Well, even if I didn't have the power to tell what you wanted from me, I can tell by how hard your ass is gripping on, like it's never gonna let me go." He kisses the back of my neck, then licks. "Tight. Virgin. Straight Boy. Ass. And it's all mine." He's so fucking greedy for me. I love it.

"Yes, it is." I breathe in and out, adjusting to him as his cock pushes against my prostate, my body reeling in sensation. After a few moments, he must feel my demand for more because he pulls back and offers a subtle thrust.

Then another.

And another.

With each rub against the spot, he gives me more pleasure than it feels like I've ever experienced in my goddamn life.

He takes my earlobe between his teeth and tugs gently. "Thank you for letting me be the one," he whispers, and I can feel his appreciation in another gentle thrust.

I twist my head back and he leans closer, taking my mouth, his tongue sliding between my lips as he grips my abs and continues his subtle movements. I can tell I'm loosening up, which helps him pick up his pace until there's a frenzy to our movements.

As he thrusts, I push my ass back. Then we pull away together and go again, creating a rhythm. I'm not even sure I'm in control of my movements anymore. Just following the inspiration of my muscles and this desperate craving that has us sweating and panting, speeding up, faster and faster, as that explosive energy seems to build to my chest.

He follows the guidance of my imagination as we change positions several times, showing me how good each angle feels. Helps me explore this part of myself in a dance of eagerness, excitement, and pressure.

I lose the idea of being separate from Brad as we tangle up in our pleasure, fully exploring the experience we've been so desperate for.

I'm trying to catch my breath from the workout when he urges me onto my back, pushing back into me. It's clear how far we've come now that he's able to drill me, each thrust clapping so loudly, it echoes off the goddamn walls.

His sweat drips onto my body. I throw my hands over my head, and his hands clamp down on my wrists, his body pushing against mine, my cock hard against his abs as he continues fucking me.

"I'm so fucking close, Brad," I warn as his flesh against my cock works me up that much more.

Suddenly, his cock feels different inside me, a smoother sensation against the walls of my ass. I revel in the sensation when Brad stops.

"Fuck," he mutters. "I think the condom just broke."

"What?" I ask, barely understanding the words.

He takes his hands off my wrists and starts to pull away, and instinctively, I hook my arms around him. "Brad, no—"

He smirks. "I love that you want me to fuck you so much, but, Luke—"

"We've both been tested, and I haven't had sex with anyone since we started messing around. I told you this ass is yours. Please. I want it." No, that's not enough. "I *need* it."

I knew how badly I wanted his cock, but I couldn't have imagined how much I'd crave his cum being inside me until this moment. Now that the opportunity has arrived, the thought of him pulling out of me feels like a cruel abandonment.

"Don't stop," I say. "Don't make me beg."

"As long as this ass is mine, then this cock is all yours," he says as his lips return to mine.

He drills me, his submission to my request.

I keep my arms around him as he kisses me some more.

He grips his necklace once again, and I gasp into his mouth as the intense heat overtakes me. I feel as though my body's radiating pleasure.

It's the sensation of flesh against flesh.

The Lust that overtakes us.

And whatever the hell he's doing to me with his necklace.

It's a wild combination. I'm fucking flying, soaring, eyes sealed shut as I disappear in the sea of sensation, ripples becoming waves of pleasure crashing into me. It's so powerful, I have to wonder if a person can die from too much pleasure.

But just as I feel like I'm about to explode with it, I know it's too fucking late for me. I cling to his body as a thrust sends the cum shooting out.

"Good Straight Boy. Here you go. Here it is."

His body jerks and twists as he bites against my jaw, grunting, and it's as if I have that knowledge he has of me, this awareness of his release inside me, feeling it fully to the core of my being.

In that moment, as his mouth returns to mine, I kiss him, cherishing every last second of this experience, knowing that just like when we danced, at some point I'll have to come back to reality. But not yet. Not as long as he keeps kissing me like this.

18

BRAD

I DON'T THINK I even knew what it meant to be blissed out until I fucked Luke Waters.

I love the way he needs my cock.

That he trusted me with his heavenly ass.

How he let me show him how amazing it could feel to be inside him.

I would've thought after finishing I'd be able to let him go, but no, not yet.

He's still as addicted to my taste and touch as I am to his.

We're both clinging to these last remnants of the high of the experience, one I'm so grateful for, and not only because of how it helped me get away from all those things that came up before we started going at it like this. Because at the same time, it reminded me that what's between us is more than the Lust and our desire to quench this unbearable thirst.

We stay clinging to each other for a few more moments before I slide out of him, kissing from his mouth, then to his throat. Luke rolls his head back, allowing himself to revel in everything I have to give him.

"Thank you, Brad."

"Thank *you*," I whisper—and something bumps my chin. Feels like my necklace. I push it away, but it swings back and hits me in the face.

The hell?

I pry myself away from his warm flesh, and that's when I see his necklace isn't flat against his chest, as it should be; the cross is floating over his chin, the necklace as erect as our cocks were during our fuck.

My jaw drops, and as I'm trying to wrap my head around that, I notice the room looks different. No, not the room. The perspective. The ceiling's lower, the overhanging fan only inches from my head. My gaze shoots to the floor, now several feet beneath us. But while it feels like my legs are supported by something, it's not the mattress.

"Brad?"

I refocus on Luke, who's tilting his head toward me. He wears a smirk, his eyes still closed. As he opens his eyes, he looks to me before zeroing in on the cross floating above his chin. His forehead creases, he glances around, and his eyes widen in panic.

"Holy fucking—"

It's like an invisible trapdoor opens beneath us, and we collapse onto the bed. My knees hit the mattress, but Luke bounces and I crash down on him, our jaws clanging together as the headboard slams against the wall.

"Fuck!" Luke groans as I crush him beneath my weight.

As soon as I regain my senses, I pull off him. "Luke, are you okay?"

Drenched in sweat and his own cum, he grabs at his jaw, where we collided, his face tensing up. He curses again, then chuckles, searching around like he's trying to figure out what the fuck just happened.

Seeing he's okay allows me a moment to feel my own tender jaw.

"Did I—Was that—"

We share a smile.

"Okay, eager to see this supposed progress," Seth says with a sigh as he reaches the bottom of the cellar stairs.

After discovering what Luke did when we fucked at the Alpha Alpha Mu Halloween party, we experimented through the weekend. Matteo had texted me that he'd be staying with a girl Halloween night and through the weekend, so we had my dorm room to ourselves. Neither of us is shy about experimenting. We skipped classes on Friday, and I've spent most of the weekend with my cock buried inside him. During this time, we fucked and messed around to gauge the extent of Luke's powers.

I fucked him in my bed. Up against every wall. On my desk. On the window seat. In my closet at one point, maybe because we were running out of places. The dorm showers, twice. Although that last wasn't testing his powers. That was just good fun.

On Monday, I called a meeting at the old church, and now I'm buzzing with excitement, eager to share our discovery.

"About time you got here," Cody tells Seth. He sits at the desk, keying away at a game on his phone. "They wouldn't show me until you got here."

Seth tosses his bag in the corner.

"It's weird," I say, "and I figured we should get through the awkwardness once, rather than dealing with shit from both of you."

"Awkwardness?" Seth asks, his eyebrows tugging closer together.

"It's something you'll have to see," Luke says, chuckling. He must find this as amusing as I do.

Cody keys on his phone a bit more before setting it down on the desk and rising to his feet. "Okay. Let's get this show on the road. The sooner we can get him onto the next task, the better."

"Let's not rush things until we see for ourselves," Seth says. "I'm not gonna be happy if you've been this cryptic and he can just do a few spins, you know?"

I snicker. "A few spins...yeah."

Luke glares at me. We said we wouldn't give them

any clues—we wanted this to be a total surprise, but it's hard to sit on such a big-ass secret around my closest friends, the guys I've trusted with some of my darkest secrets since we met last year.

"Let's do it." Luke kneels in the center of the pentagram.

As I step behind him, Cody's and Seth's expressions are rife with confusion. "Trust me on this," I say, getting on my knees behind Luke, sliding close so that his ass is tucked against my crotch. Even with my friends watching, I'm stiff as a board.

Luke's never had an issue with getting me hard, but now that I know what it's like to be inside him, my cock pulses with desire. I know what it wishes we could do right now, and the best I can do is enjoy the fantasies, assuring myself I'll be drilling this ass as soon as we're done with show-and-tell.

Luke watches himself in the mirror as he holds out the necklace, letting it dangle from his finger. He eyes me as I push my chest against his back, hooking my arms around him. I kiss his neck, and Luke tilts his head, inviting me to explore a little more.

I hesitate, only because this isn't the kind of thing I'd ever normally do in front of Seth and Cody, but I remind myself why we must. I open my mouth and given him a wide, tongue-filled kiss, then a nibble. Despite how strange it is, it's easy to get lost in his flesh, to lose myself entirely, until I hear Seth say, "Um...this is…"

"Kinda hot," Cody chimes in.

"That wasn't what I was thinking."

I keep up my work, opening my eyes briefly to check the mirror and see the amulet starting to spin in front of Luke. It's not spinning much, though, so I give him a few more kisses.

"Okay, just stop it, you guys," Seth says. "Brad, you think I don't know what you're doing?" He approaches, standing behind us so I can see him in the mirror. "You can't trick us into thinking he's already figured it out, when—"

His necklace pops up from his chest, the cross hitting him square in the forehead.

"The fuck!" Seth exclaims, which makes Luke chuckle. "Did he just—"

I get back to work on Luke's neck, helping him show the guys what I've already discovered he's capable of.

"Okay, that's a cute trick," Seth adds, "but that doesn't make you some kind of wiz—"

The sound of scraping against the cement floor catches my attention, and I see Seth's bag drag across it before flying through the air, slamming against the wall, then plummeting to the floor.

"Straight Boy's showing off," I whisper before granting a tender kiss as a reward.

Seth opens his mouth to speak, but nothing comes out.

"Holy. Fucking. Hell," Cody finally manages.

"What was that?" Seth follows.

"That's what we wanted to show you," Luke says.

As Luke and I get on our feet, Seth's still staring at his bag.

"When the hell did you find out he could do that?" he asks.

"At Alpha Alpha Mu's party last week. We were messing around, and this weird thing happened."

"And you waited through the weekend to tell us this?"

"We figured it was something I did," Luke says, "but we weren't sure if I could control it."

"So something about your chemistry together lets him use his powers," Cody says, his gaze narrowing as he considers this.

"Yeah, and it's stronger when I'm—" I stop myself.

"What?" Seth asks.

"That's very thoughtful of you," Luke says, clearly appreciating my attempt at discretion. "It's stronger when we're fucking. Technically, when he's inside me. But as you can see, even if we just fool around, I can still do more than anything I could have imagined."

"You seem to have a lot of control over it," Seth says.

"It took a lot to do that with the bag."

"It takes us a lot just to play around with our necklaces," I say.

"If you have access to this much power already,"

Cody says, "that's a good sign."

"It suggests he'll be able to manage it at some point," is as much as Seth concedes, but I can tell by Cody's wandering gaze that his thoughts are elsewhere.

"So you can do more than just what you showed us?" Cody asks.

"The night we figured it out, we were levitating," Luke says. "Brad's head was so close to the ceiling fan, I'm surprised it didn't clip him."

"But since then," I add, "we've tried, and he can levitate us consciously while we do stuff."

Cody's lips twist up as he considers this. "Can you do any of it when you're not messing around with Brad?"

Luke shakes his head. "I can't do what you just saw, but I can do some things."

"So you can only use all this power when you're fucking?" Cody asks Luke.

"That's how it seems so far."

Seth looks at Cody, who's pressing his lips together, his gaze narrow.

"What are you thinking?" Seth asks.

"If he has this much control while they're messing around, maybe if I tried to give him the vision again, he'd have more control in there too."

Seth cringes. "How would you even do that? Are you gonna like, lie on top of Luke while Brad fucks him?"

Cody's lips twist up, and he seems to actually be considering this, so I shut it down. "Not gonna happen."

"Cody, why are you even thinking of that?" Seth asks.

"If he can control it," Cody says, "he can get more information. He might even be able to find out where the Slasher's at."

"Again, you're not lying on top of Luke while I'm inside him," I say, "if that's what you're suggesting."

Cody rolls his eyes. "Will everyone stop making it sound like I'm trying to instigate a threesome? If Luke has this power and can focus it while he's under, then if we can find a way to get the vision to him, you know what that means he'll be able to do."

It's a fair point, one I don't like but have to consider.

"No," Seth snaps. "He's only known he can do this for a few days. It's way too soon to be talking about something like this."

"I'm not saying they need to strip down and get to it," Cody says, "but you know I'm right."

"It's too soon."

"For a conversation?"

Seth huffs.

Cody presses, "If Luke can manage this kind of control while he's under without the consequences I experience—"

"He kicked you out, which we didn't know was going to happen, and that was before he'd tapped into all this power."

"People's lives are at stake here, Seth."

"Exactly! Who the hell knows what might happen if you do this too soon? He could fucking kill you. Hell, if Brad's fucking him, then he could kill both of you, and then it's just me and the guy who doesn't know what he's doing. What am I going to do? Push on the monster to stop and go back into the Rift? No. I let you guys rush that shit before, and look where it got us."

He's not wrong.

The room quiets.

Cody bites his bottom lip. "I know it sucks, but we can't sit around and do nothing because it's dangerous."

Seth's gaze wavers. "I get that, and I'm assuming he can breeze through the first three tasks now without issue." He looks to me, and I nod, having already tested them during our fuck-fest over the weekend. "So he needs to have the Moment."

Cody eyes me, and I figure we're thinking the same thing even before he says, "That took me months. And you guys even longer."

"Wait. What's a moment?" Luke asks.

"Not a moment. *The* Moment," I explain. "Remember when I told you about the way we're in sync with the Rift? We each remember that distinct moment when it happened. Think of it as an epiphany. It's like you suddenly have another sense. It's hard to explain beyond that, except to say you'll know when it happens."

Luke's narrowed eyes suggest he doesn't really get it, which I understand, since I doubt any of us would have before it happened.

"Cody couldn't navigate his visions until then," Seth explains. Seems like the first time he's talked to Luke without being a total ass to him. He turns his attention to Cody. "Once he has the Moment, we'll know he can at least do that, and then maybe it's worth the risk."

Now I'm getting pissed. "Are you even going to ask us how *we* feel about it?"

Seth and Cody seem taken aback.

"As I mentioned before, Cody, you're not gonna sit on Luke's face while we're doing that."

"No, that would be too dangerous," Cody says, clearly missing the point. "What if because he's so strong, I won't have to touch him like I do with you guys? What if I did it from here, on the pentagram, like that day after the pickup game? I mean, he could blow me away from the dorm showers, so it might be enough to give him the vision."

"Worth a try." That's an experiment I'm far more comfortable with than Cody trying to sit in on one of our fuck sessions.

Seth's jaw tenses. He's not sold, and I don't blame him. This *is* dangerous. And it'd be foolish to jump the gun. But given the stakes, can we simply sit around and do nothing when people's lives are at risk?

"It's definitely the safest way to go about it," Seth concedes. "And I'll feel better once I know he's had his Moment. It'll convince me he has some control over this."

"Yeah..." Cody drags out. "But we need a backup plan, in case it doesn't happen in say, the next week or so."

"What do you mean?" I ask.

"The vision suggests someone will be dead by the week of the twenty-first. We don't have a lot of time. And considering the first vision changed..." He trails off, clearly unwilling to state what we already know—that someone could die at any moment.

"We can burn that bridge later," Seth says. "Right now, let's show Luke how to perform the ritual to connect to the Rift. And hope for the best."

Hardly anything in the way of a plan, but it's something.

Luke's quiet, his expression tense. This is a lot of pressure on him.

"How do you feel, Luke?" I ask, since he should get a say in all this.

"What choice do we have, right?"

Fuck.

This must've been a lot to hear, but I have to believe, given everything we've already seen he's capable of, that the Moment will come easier to him than it did any of us.

At least, I have to hope.

19

LUKE

"IN…AND OUT…" BRAD says.

With my eyes shut, my legs crossed in a meditation pose, I focus on my breathing.

After the meeting, Seth and Cody headed out, leaving Brad and me alone in the cellar. Considering the shit we've done throughout the weekend—moving objects with my mind, levitating, though not as impressively as I did the first time we fucked—I was expecting the next task to be something a little more interesting than a guided meditation.

"In and out…"

How does he think I'm supposed to concentrate on my breathing when I have so much on my mind? And it's not just the meeting and the chatter about the Moment and the changing visions that are spinning around in my head, but everything I've learned I can now do by messing around with Brad.

As he starts to prompt me again, I open my eyes. He's sitting cross-legged between me and the mirror.

"Brad…please tell me there's more to this than concentrating on my breaths."

"You want me to lie?"

"That's what causes this big moment? Some dumb meditation?"

"You seem skeptical, but it really does work. It's how all of us were able to quiet enough to have the experience."

"Can you stop acting like *the Moment* is an actual thing?"

"Okay, this was why I thought we shouldn't jump right into it."

I hate that he's reminding me I was the one who pushed.

"You're upset, Luke. I get it. You have a lot to think about. Now you know what you need to do, so let's take a break."

"Take a break? I have to try and stop people from getting murdered. I need to figure this out ASAP."

"You won't be able to as long as you're frustrated. I promise you that. And considering we were able to get there with a fraction of your power, you're gonna be fine. I promise you that too."

I grunt. Fuck him for being right.

"Hey." He reaches out, rests his hand on my thigh. "I understand this is a lot."

His words set me off. "No, you fucking don't. You guys were dicking around with this shit when you started. And I got dropped in the middle of it during what could become a killing spree, so it's a little more stressful."

"That was bad wording on my part. I'm sorry. You're right. I *can't* understand what you're going through."

Now I'm even more pissed. "And you won't fight with me, so I can't even chew you out to get some of this stress off my chest."

He shrugs. "If you need someone to argue with, I can text Seth and get him to come back."

He starts like he's about to get up, but I grab his hand. "Don't you fucking dare," I say, and as he shoots me a sneaky look, I can't help smiling.

"Damn you for being so charming."

"You like when I'm charming."

We lean toward each other, and when our lips meet, some of my tension dissipates.

Brad growls before shifting, getting on his knees and guiding me onto my back for a quick make-out session, which unlike my attempts at quieting my mind, helps dissolve all my confusion and frustration.

When he pulls his lips away, he trails kisses along my jaw.

"I like training like this a lot better," I confess.

He chuckles, his warm breath tingling against my skin before he relaxes on his side, gazing at me. "Better?"

"Much better." Which gives me an idea. "Maybe you could fuck me real quick and then we get back to it."

"Our fucking is taking a toll on your life. You thought you were gonna have to get an extension on that homework assignment. And then you had that deadline today for the group project—"

"Both of which I managed to get done."

As on top of my work as I usually am, this has been more than a little distracting.

"Oh, I remember. I was watching you at the end of the bed last night while you were keying away on that laptop, toying with me with that hint of ass crack slipping out of your boxers."

The way he looks at me, it's like he knows I'd tucked it down just for him. To keep it on his mind. So he'd be good and ready for me when I finished.

"Guess we've learned a little bit more about each other these past few days," I say.

"What have you learned about me?"

"On top of being a very generous lover, you're a diligent flosser. A big fan of Dua Lipa. And you always make sure to respond to texts when they're from your mom."

His gaze narrows. "Aren't you observant?"

Or obsessed. I blame the Lust, but I know that's not entirely the case.

"Hard not to pick up on a few things when we spent all that time together this weekend."

"Like how I couldn't help noticing that you watch too many funny TikToks and have your alarm tunes set to Taylor Swift and Zach Bryan."

There's something exciting about hearing the little things he's picked up on. Knowing he gives enough fucks to have paid attention.

"Look who's also observant," I tease before planting another kiss on him.

His hand gravitates to my ass, gripping firmly. "I guess the next question is: how does my Straight Boy want to be fucked right now?"

A few ideas spring to mind, but one in particular catches me by surprise. "Actually…I have a better idea."

His brows shift. "Does it end with my dick in your ass, because that's probably the only way I'm gonna be okay with it."

I grin. I love that he's just as obsessed with our fucks as I am. "It definitely ends with your dick in my ass, but it doesn't start there."

"I'm listening…"

"You hungry?"

"If you think I've been eating regular meals since all this started, you don't know me at all."

"Then I guess I do know you because we were messing around as soon as we got out of classes at four, and between that and coming here, I know the only thing you've had to eat, and I don't think it's enough calories to keep a person alive."

"At least it's a snack for me," he says. "But it can't be any use where I'm putting it away."

I chuckle. "I wanna make a joke about how you can get it in my mouth too, but if I told you that's where I wanted it, you'd know I was lying, wouldn't you?"

A grin sweeps across his face. "You know damn well I'd know."

It's annoying that he knows, but I love it too.

"You ever been to that pizza place off Breznel?" I ask.

"A few times."

"They happen to have calzones?"

"I wouldn't go if they didn't."

I smile. "Well, good. Then I guess you can take me there."

He winces, then moves closer, until his lips are inches from mine. "Luke Waters, you asking me out on a date?"

"I asked if you knew that pizza place. But I wasn't asking you on a date."

He eyes me suspiciously.

"I was *telling* you we're going on a date."

He laughs. "You dork."

"Hey, I'm not the one who likes a sexy dork."

He blushes, and God, this is one of only a handful of times I've seen Brad Henning blush about something. It's adorable.

"I'll go on a date with you, Straight Boy."

Now I'm the one blushing.

We get off the floor and grab our things. Brad leads me on a shortcut through the woods to the main road, and we wind up a few blocks from the pizza place. Once there, we order at the front, then settle in a booth, placing the coiled stand with our numbers displayed for the server.

The place is pretty busy, which isn't surprising. I recognize some kids from St. Lawrence, and there are older couples and some families I imagine live in downtown Lawrenceville.

"You like a lot of meat in your calzone," I note, since he got steak and sausage in his.

Is it weird that I like finding out shit like this about him?

"And you prefer to keep it simple with pepperoni and cheese."

"With all that's going on in my life, I love the idea of playing it safe with my calzone."

He raises his hands in surrender. "Fair point." He sizes me up. "So how are you feeling? From today's meeting, I mean."

"Feels better now that everyone's talking."

"I figured."

"But it was also frustrating that I didn't have much to contribute to a conversation that was about me. Made me feel like a tool you guys are using rather than someone who can actively help."

His brow creases. "We just happen to know more about what's going on. Hell, you're picking up more about this than any of us did back when we first stumbled upon it."

It doesn't cheer me up. Although, knowing that every moment that passes could lead to us seeing another missing person report in the news, wondering if it's connected to that creature, doesn't help either.

"We're all figuring this out as we go," Brad says, and I nod. "Anyway, forget I brought it up. How about we pretend for the next hour that we don't know anything about the Sinners' bible or the Rift or powers or the Moment?"

"I don't know how good I'll be at this game," I confess. I doubt I'll be able to stop thinking about those things. Feels like there's a weight on me; like it's hard to breathe.

Brad reaches across the table, sets his hand on mine, gripping gently. His touch feels so supportive, so comforting. It's different than how we usually spend our time together, when we let raw, wild passion possess us.

It's nice.

I rub my thumb along his finger, and our gazes meet before he smirks.

"This is...uh...weird for me," he says. "Putting my hand on yours like this."

But he doesn't pull away.

"Weird like you're wondering why you did it, or weird like you're surprised you like it?"

"Both, maybe," he says with a chuckle. "I don't really date. Just have fun. Prefer to keep it that way. Because of the shit with my family, I have a hard time getting close to people."

"That makes sense."

"You've had girlfriends, so I guess this is something you're used to."

"The last girlfriend I had was freshman year of high school. That was before Mom passed." I cringe. "I can't believe I just said that. I fucking hate when people say 'passed.' Died. She fucking died."

Brad's eyes widen.

"Sorry, after my parents died, people kept saying things like how they 'passed' or 'moved on.' I was ten when Dad had the aneurysm. It was hard to let it sink in, and words like that didn't help me grasp what was going on. That he was never coming back. I was fourteen when Mom died, and I kept repeating to myself that she was dead so that it'd get through. I didn't want to have any fantasy that she was going to walk through the door and give me a hug because no matter how many times I wished or prayed for it with Dad, it never worked."

Brad tightens his hold. I can feel his support and compassion, but I want to blow past this awkward moment I created.

"Anyway, after she died, I broke it off with the girl I was seeing. I needed time to myself. I would mess around with girls, but not go on dates or anything. I guess…I guess I just had this feeling that if I did get close to someone else, then…" I don't finish my sentence; he can fill in the blanks.

"I can understand that," he says, but then his expression twists up. "Fuck, I ran right into that same mistake as earlier. I *can't* understand what you went through—"

"I get what you're saying, Brad. It was thoughtful of you. I'm sorry I jumped on you earlier."

"You get to pay me back for how we started off…maybe for another week or two," he jokes, rubbing his thumb against my hand again. "I know I said it was weird, but it also feels right."

As I roll my hand over, he loosens his grip, and when the back of my hand's on the table, he grips it again.

"*Really* right," he whispers, so low it's almost like he didn't intend for me to hear. He gulps, then his breath hitches, his gaze wavering before he says, "Luke, I like you."

"If I couldn't tell that from this weekend, I'd be pretty dense."

"No, beyond that stuff. Certainly doesn't hurt that we have fun in the bedroom, but I like getting to know you. I like when you talk to me about your past and share things that don't have anything to do with the Sinners. Back when we started messing around, I knew it was the Lust drawing me to you, and maybe that's still true physically, but what I'm interested in now is beyond that."

Since he's confessed what he's experiencing, I don't hold back either. "It's that way for me too."

He continues running his thumb back and forth

across my skin, gazing into my eyes, when the server arrives with our calzones.

We release each other to grab our silverware and start eating.

"Cut me off a piece of yours," I tell Brad.

"Really? I thought you were sticking to playing it safe tonight."

"Eh, I was thinking I've had a good time experimenting recently." I wink at him, and a smile sweeps across his face.

Yes, I've had very good experiences. And looking forward to many more.

THE NEXT TWO days, Brad and I don't meet up just to fuck around.

Or, not *only* to fuck around.

As this Sinners stuff becomes more involved, I realize I have to find a way to make it work with school, so we schedule a study hour at the library, and if I'm real good and get all my work done, Brad shows me a good time in the fourth-floor bathroom.

Since our date, things have been different between us. We've been more playful in bed. There's been more jokiness and teasing between all that. I can let my guard down around him. Be myself.

Of course, if only the days were just about fucking,

school, and spending time together. Unfortunately, I still have to make my attempts at meditating to receive this magical Moment that…doesn't seem to be happening, and with each day that passes, I become increasingly concerned.

On Thursday, Brad and I are in the church cellar, in our familiar seated positions. I've gotten better about steadying my breathing, concentrating, but my thoughts are as cluttered as ever. There's so much to think about.

All the interactions I had with the guys initially.

The bizarre conversations we've shared.

The horrifying vision and seeing that monster hunting that poor guy.

Not for the first time since we started meditating, a familiar image springs to mind.

Dark hair.

Sharp jawline.

Kind eyes.

Dad's face.

Not the one I was used to seeing growing up, but from pictures I saw of him taken when he was around my age. I can see him, vividly, as he sits down in the cellar with the Sinners' bible in his hands, studying the information Dobbers received from the Guides.

What did he think about all this? What was his experience? I get why he never mentioned it to his kid, but did he tell Mom?

Then suddenly, the images shift to my past.

"Daddy's not okay, sweetie," Mom says.

And I know in an instant what she means, but I still ask, "He'll be okay, though, right?"

But even then, I knew better.

A tightness twists in my chest before it burns like a fire. Tears slide from my eyes. "No," I whisper. Please, not that.

"Luke?"

As I feel Brad's hand on my thigh, I force my eyes open. My body trembles, and I break out in a cold sweat. "I need a moment," I confess.

He sizes me up. "What's wrong, Luke? What happened?"

"That stuff Cody picked at in the shower? It came up again. The same memory of the day my mom told me my dad wasn't going to be okay. It was…rough."

And I can't shake that shit. It lingers, tormenting me, cruelly, with one of the more horrifying days of my life.

"Of course it was." Brad gazes at me for a few moments before scooting closer and hooking an arm around me. Despite how soothing his hold is, there's a searing pain in my chest, one that doesn't get better.

And the tears come again.

I turn to Brad, wrapping my arm around him and pulling him close.

He rubs my back. "I'm here. It's okay."

As comforting as his hold is, I know it's not okay.

Nothing about losing them will ever be okay.

20

BRAD

O N TUESDAY THE following week, after my second class, I head to the courtyard and FaceTime with Mom. It's her day off, and I reach her while she's catching up on some *Real Housewives of Salt Lake City*. I check in, asking about her symptoms. I keep waiting to hear about the tingling and fatigue, the usual signs that I need to make another trip home, but based on what she says, her MS hasn't been bad since my last visit. I'm hopeful maybe we can make it to the holidays, at least.

I tell her about the test I just crushed when she suddenly eyes me suspiciously and says, "Why are you smiling so much today?"

I've noticed that look the last few times we've chatted, when she's asked about my plans for the evening or if I've made any new friends—not the kinds of questions she normally asks. She's probing for something.

"Guess I'm just feeling good today," I lie.

I know why I'm feeling good. Because I'm only one more class away from meeting up with Luke at the library so we can chill…and, well, *not* chill together.

"Okay, it's more than that," I confess. "There's a guy, since I know that's what you keep dancing around."

Her eyes widen. "A guy? Really?" she says, appearing genuinely shocked.

"Why are you acting surprised? This is what you've been hinting around all week."

"I figured that's what it was, but I wasn't expecting you to tell me this soon. You've never mentioned a guy to me before."

She grins like she already knows how into Luke I must be to tell her that. And I must admit, I'm getting pretty hung up on him.

Even with all the Sinners bullshit we have to navigate, I like spending time with him. Getting to know him better. Finding out the little things about him. Like how he needs his bangs to have that perfect curl in front. Or that he owns, like, five black thermal sweaters, which look the same, but I can see why they're his favorite because they definitely show off his assets best. Or trying to guess how long I'll see him with the book he's reading—the one from last night might last until tomorrow.

And now that I'm thinking about those things, I'm smiling even more.

"So how do you know him?" Mom presses.

For some reason, that sets me on edge.

I met him because I'm part of a group that fucks around

with magic, and we're pretty sure between our botched spell and this guy arriving at the school, an evil monster has escaped from an alternate dimension, and we're trying to stop it from going on a killing spree.

Not the kind of thing to tell Mom, you know?

"We go to the same school. Not a big mystery, is it?" I shrug.

"You planning to bring him home for Thanksgiving break or maybe Christmas?"

"It's kinda early for that. He has an uncle he might spend it with, but…I'd like to introduce you two. I think you'll like him."

"Going by the good mood you've been in the past few weeks, I like him already."

I can't help grinning, a big, goofy grin, the sort only Luke can put on my face.

And really, it's nice having this kind of conversation with Mom, when she's healthy and in good spirits. Reminds me how far we've come from the bullshit Dad put us through.

"YOU GUYS GONNA make out as soon as I leave?" Matteo asks as he packs extra clothes into his bookbag.

Luke scoops some pad thai out of his container with chopsticks. "You think we're *only* gonna make out?" he asks before taking a bite, which makes Matteo laugh.

"Knew I liked this guy." Matteo has quickly warmed up to Luke, and even now, on a Tuesday night, I know he's made plans so we can have our space.

"You can stay, though," I say.

"So you guys have to creep over to the showers and sneak around? Please. No. Besides, I'm really into this new girl, Lena. She's a lot of fun, so for the same reason Luke would rather be over here, I'd rather be with her. And I don't need to be around you now that I know about these mystical powers you have..." I tense up, thrown by the comment, before he goes on, "...to sway the straights into needing it up the ass."

"What—I did not ever say that," I tell Luke, hoping he knows I wasn't going around blabbing about our private conversations. And especially not anything to do with powers. Or him bottoming.

Luke chuckles. "Relax. When you went downstairs to grab the Asian fusion, I may have mentioned I thought I was straight before I met you. But now I know I'm definitely not."

"You don't have to call your bi hookup *Straight Boy* in secret anymore," Matteo says with a wink.

So clearly Luke told him about the nickname too.

"He's not a hookup," I snap.

"Ooh, careful," Matteo says. "I was just gauging where you're at, but you need to cool it down around this guy, or he's gonna know you caught some serious feels."

"Shut up," I say, but Luke's smirking.

Like he doesn't already know.

"Okay, I'm done ragging on you," Matteo says. "I'm gonna head out. If I stick around much longer, you might use your evil powers to rope me into a threesome."

We all laugh, and he tosses his bag over his shoulder, leaving Luke and me to ourselves.

"You told him about Straight Boy?"

He shrugs. "Just as a funny thing. I'm sorry. I didn't know you'd be uncomfortable with that."

"I'm not," I assure him. "Just not something I thought you'd be chatting with Matteo about. When he said that about magical powers, I was worried I'd said something—"

"Oh, trust me, I knew what you were thinking, and I was trying to psychically project to you not to blurt anything out."

I let out a nervous chuckle. "Well, I like that you and Matteo get along. Wish Alexei was this cool about us hanging at your place."

"Guess I'm more likable than you," Luke says with a shrug. "Or maybe it has something to do with when you were an asshat to me during those pickup games."

"Yeah, but Alexei and I have always been cool with each other. We've hung out because of the games, and also had some classes together. It's weird suddenly being on his shit list."

"He's nice when you come over."

"He's *polite*," I clarify. "But he feels off, and like he wants to go somewhere else, and not in the way Matteo is trying to get out of our hair."

"I'm confident that if you guys hang out enough, after a while, he'll get used to you again. And he'll realize you're really good to me."

"I am really good to you," I say, which makes him smile, but just as quickly it fades and he groans.

"This sucks. I don't want to train tonight. I want to just lie here and watch a movie."

Meditating has been far from relaxing for Luke. I feel for him.

"Maybe tonight we could stay in."

Seth and Cody wouldn't be happy with that, but Luke's only human. We've been trying since last week, and if Luke's really this frustrated, maybe it will be a waste of time anyway.

"No, I need to go," Luke says, fishing at his pad thai with his chopsticks.

"Hey," I say, reaching over and resting my hand on his shoulder. "I'll be right there with you."

His lips twist into a smirk, and he nods. "Just not how I figured I'd be spending the first semester at St. Lawrence."

I trail my hand to the back of his neck and offer a gentle rub, leaning close and kissing his cheek.

After we finish up dinner, we prep, then head out to the old church.

While we assume our usual positions, I receive a text from Seth: **Good luck tonight. Keep us posted.** I've been getting these sorts of texts since we started Luke's sessions.

"That Seth?"

I nod, and I can see the frustration in his expression, like he already knows tonight is gonna be another failure.

"Wish me luck," he says.

I get out of my meditation pose and crawl close to him so that my lips are right in front of his. "Good luck," I say before planting a kiss on his lips.

I can feel his tension and uneasiness, but the more we kiss, the more he relaxes, and once I feel he's eased up enough, I pull back, enjoying his smile as I cross my legs.

Luke closes his eyes, and I direct him through his breathing to start, like I usually do. He's not cracking any jokes or shifting around, just obeys my instructions, and once he's into it, I close my eyes and try to quiet my mind.

It's not easy. I have plenty of my own bullshit rattling around in here...memories of my dad being an ass to me.

"You're just like your mother."

"The world's not gonna be nice to you just because you're my son."

"Such a waste that you're the one to carry my family name."

Words that are always there, in the back of my mind,

haunting me.

"Fuck," Luke mutters, and I open my eyes. His eyes are closed, his expression twisted up, his cross floating up near his chin. He's using his powers without touching me, seemingly without even realizing it. He raises his hand and hits his palm against his head. "Fuck, fuck, fuck," he mutters.

"Hey, hey." I lean over and rest my hand against his wrist, which rests on his knee.

"I need a break," he says, and opens his eyes.

I'm expecting to see his blue irises, but his eyes—even the whites—are pitch black. For a moment I think it must be in my head, but Luke's eyes widen, and he searches desperately around the room.

"No, no, no!" he calls out.

"Luke?"

He thrashes about, pulling away from my hand and screaming, "Make it stop! Make it fucking stop!" His hands cover his face as he calls out, and then he pulls them away and the black is gone. I'm relieved, but that only lasts a moment because he continues searching the room, catching his breath.

"What the fuck just happened?" he asks.

"You were using your powers. Your necklace was floating without you touching me. But other than that, I don't know. You tell me."

His gaze keeps shifting about, like he's still trapped in what just happened. "The memory I told you about the first time we tried this… Every time we've come here, I try to focus on my breathing, but that memory keeps coming back. And the harder I try to push it away, the more intense it becomes. This time, though, I was sucked back to the worst of my pain—like when Cody brought it up in the showers. And then when your hand rested on me, something happened. Not a memory. I was right there in that moment, and I wanted to get out. But when I opened my eyes, I was still there, sitting at Dad's funeral."

"I'm so sorry, Luke."

"No, I had this realization—it's that thing you described, where you know but don't know how you know, like in a dream. I think that memory is what's keeping me from having the Moment. I must face it. Sit with the pain and despair of it until I get through to the other side."

Even as he says the words, I see the terror in his expression.

"Does that sound right?" he asks, as if wishing it wouldn't be true.

"I'm not sure. For me, I didn't have to face any bad memories to have the Moment, but you're not experiencing any of this like we did, so it could be that you have to do something different to get there."

"Fuck," he says, his chin quivering. "Not that. Anything but that."

"Oh, Luke…"

He pulls away and pushes to his feet, heading toward the other side of the cellar, and I let him have his space. I wish I could tell him he's wrong, that he might have misinterpreted what he just felt, but I know better. I know what those kinds of realizations feel like, and if he picked it up that strongly, it's likely he's right.

"You said my necklace was floating?"

"Yeah."

He tears up. "I don't want to do this."

"You don't have to do anything right away."

"What choice do I have? I can't let this go on any longer. We both know what will happen if I don't find a way to get on top of this."

We do, and he wouldn't be the Luke I know if he didn't consider that over himself. But in this moment, I selfishly want him to do what's best for himself.

He takes a few more seconds before returning to me and sitting back down. His expression is full of worry; he won't look at me, and when he does, I notice a tear break free, slide down his cheek.

"Do you need me to do anything for you?" I ask.

He shakes his head. "No. When you touched me, that's when I knew I needed to do it on my own. No shortcut. The only path is through. The only way to have this Moment is to walk through the fires of hell." He shakes his head. "Fuck my life."

Silence stretches between us as my heart breaks for him. This is wrong. He shouldn't have to do this. No one should have to relive the worst moments of their life.

"You should go," he whispers.

"What?"

"It's gonna be bad. Really bad."

"I want to be here for you."

"I know you do." He reaches out and takes my hand. "And that's very sweet of you, but I don't want you to see me like this."

That, I have to respect, but I have other concerns. "I want to be nearby. At least, in case something happens."

"Maybe you can wait upstairs. Listen out? But you can't come in unless I call for you. I have a feeling it's gonna be painful. Excruciating, so even when it's hard, you must let me feel it."

I dread the thought of hearing him in pain. Will I be able to stop myself from bursting in when it was hard enough just to let him continue meditating when I saw he was distressed?

"You can't disturb me too soon. This is what has to happen. The only way. And I don't know that I can do this more than once."

There's not a trace of doubt in his tone. He knows what needs to be done, and it's clear he's doing this whether I want him to or not.

I cup his cheek, running my thumb across his smooth flesh.

"A little kiss before you go?" he asks.

I don't give him a little one.

But despite his enthusiastic response, this isn't like before we started this session. He stays tense, on edge.

I accept that my kiss isn't enough to make that better, and when I pull away, he wears a solemn expression. "Go on. I'll be okay," he assures me, which only makes me feel like this is gonna be so much worse than I can imagine.

I grab my things and head upstairs, taking one of the desk chairs with me and setting it up on the other side of the door. I keep the room illuminated with my phone light, mentally prepping myself for whatever we're about to experience.

It's quiet for some time, giving me hope that maybe it won't be as bad as Luke thought. But then I hear grunts, groans, and cursing before a wave of pain hits me, followed by an anguished cry from the cellar. It shakes me to my core, and I clench my fists, starting to my feet.

As Luke screams again, there's another jolt of pain. I grab the doorknob but stop myself. There's an impulse in me to just say fuck what we agreed upon and get down there and end his pain, but then I remember what he said: I need to keep it together. He'll do this on his own.

Over my dead body.

"Fuck," he calls out, followed by another cry.

I clutch the doorknob and press up against the door, gritting my teeth, knowing instinctively that the worst is yet to come.

21

LUKE

I STAND IN *the atrium of the church, silent.*

It's not real. He's not gone.

It's a lie, I keep telling myself, as Mom thanks the attendees.

Wake up, Luke. Wake up, and you'll find out none of this is real. Only a nightmare.

But the more people who talk to me, who say things like, "I'm so sorry for your loss, my poor boy," the angrier I get that my eyes aren't opening, pulling me from this horrible place.

When Brad touched me while I was enduring that horrible memory, a flash of awareness moved through me, and I knew what I had to do.

It's not something I wanted to do. I wouldn't think anyone would want to force themselves back through the worst memories of their lives. But I know like I know who I am that this is the only chance I have of having the Moment. It's the only chance of saving people from the Slasher.

I've already been through the pain of being at the hospital with Mom, but my torment isn't over. Not yet.

It's after the service. We're in the cemetery, watching as the coffin is lowered into the hole in the earth.

It's not him, I assure myself, though I know better.

He wouldn't leave me like this.

I turn to Mom, who puts a handkerchief to her face, unable to stifle her sobs.

Why does she keep crying when it isn't even him?

"No!" I call out as I experience the pain I wouldn't let myself feel the depths of that horrible day. It's like nails driving into my chest, tearing me apart. I won't survive this, I'm sure of it.

I should stop, but now that I'm in these memories, it'd take more effort to leave than to stay with them.

A flash between weeks, then months after the funeral, to a day when I'm sitting at the kitchen table in the afternoon.

He's gonna come home. He has to. But why doesn't he?

In my dreams he's there, and he's real, but then I wake and he's not. Why?

Then comes a moment I remember too well, but it's not like the other memories. It's much later.

I'm in high school, and I finish my 5A championship, breathing heavily as I search for Mom, who hurries to me. Yet a part of me, some part that's forgotten, even after four years, looks for Dad.

But he's not around.

Tears stir in my eyes.

Don't let her see. Don't let her know.

But as her gaze meets mine...

Fuck, she knows.

I stuff all my emotions away. Push on like that didn't just happen.

Now I'm in the hospital, and my uncle approaches, teary-eyed. He looks just like Mom did back when Dad died.

No, no. It's not real. It can't be.

It all comes flooding back. Every cruel moment. Her funeral. Stuffing down my emotions to keep it together long enough to make it through. Then the haunting moments, like with Dad, not the terrible, nightmarish moments, but beautiful moments when I wanted them to be there.

To see me.

To be proud.

To show me they loved me.

I'm opening a letter.

My acceptance to St. Lawrence. A rush of excitement runs through me, and I search around as if they're some-where here with me, for me to share it with.

But they're not here.

They're gone.

The pain burns within me like fire. It overtakes me, and suddenly there's just darkness again, and I thrash about wildly as the sensations don't cease with the memories. They go on, terrorizing me, and I cry out to the unjust universe for taking them from me.

I cry out, knowing only Brad can hear my pain.

Finally, the sensation releases me, and I collapse on my back, breathing deeply. The pain has ceased, and I feel something else move through me.

I know what this is even before it hits me fully. It doesn't feel like relief, but like a quiet embrace of all that's horrible and beautiful. An acceptance of this powerful grief. My body vibrates with energy, tingling all over, and it reminds me of the feeling I got when Brad first touched me.

As I close my eyes once again, I feel like I'm being embraced in a warm hug. I'm floating in what in my mind's eye looks like an orange light, moving through me. It's the energy Brad told me about, from the Rift.

Suddenly I'm aware I'm not just floating in my mind, but levitating, without needing Brad inside me. It's not me doing it this time, though. It's something beyond me.

As I open my eyes again, I find myself steadily drifting to the floor, before settling against it, this energy that possessed me dissipating, leaving me trembling.

The door at the top of the stairs opens, followed by footsteps. I don't have to turn to know it's him.

He hurries over and kneels at my side. "Luke?"

"It happened," I whisper so softly, I wonder if he heard me.

"I know. I felt it."

Despite the ease I feel now, I notice the terror in Brad's expression.

"What's wrong?"

Being so captivated by the experience, I'd momentarily forgotten what happened just before. And as the realization hits me, I look away.

"You don't know how hard it was to keep from coming in here," he says. "Knowing how much pain you were in. I can't imagine how so much pain can fit inside this body of yours. God, Luke…"

I feel so vulnerable, so exposed. Like he didn't just hear my pain, but witnessed those memories in my mind.

"I was right," I say. "Those memories were getting in my way somehow."

"What happened?"

I sit up, still unable to make eye contact. "It was like I was paying a price for not feeling so many powerful emotions at times when I just wanted to break down."

I turn to him and notice his wrists; there are red marks around them.

"What are these?" I ask, taking his hands to assess them.

He looks to the floor. "When it got bad, I had to keep myself from coming down here. There was some rope bound around some old boards upstairs, so I knotted it around my wrists to distract myself. If I hadn't, I would have broken the damn door down and forced you to stop."

The wounds are deep, and in a few places, he's drawn blood. "Oh God, Brad. Was it that bad?"

He hesitates, then says, "There was a moment toward the end where it sounded like you were dying. It was blood-curdling."

Now it's not just embarrassment that he's heard me like that; there's guilt too. "I'm sorry. I should have asked you to go. You shouldn't have had to hear that."

"I wanted to be here, and I'm glad I was. It was like someone was hacking my arm off with a handsaw, so I had to restrain myself. But I would have rather that than leave you."

My heart warms. Doesn't surprise me. It's the kind of guy I've learned he is.

"Luke…Luke, please look at me."

He pulls his hand out of my grasp and runs his finger under my chin. Just like I did with those memories, I force myself to face him.

"You have nothing to feel guilty about. That was so brave. I don't know that I could have done that even with half the shit I've dealt with in my life."

I thought if our gazes met, I'd feel ashamed of what he saw, but I feel his sympathy, this tender side of him. I never would have wanted anyone to see me like that, but if someone had to, I'm glad it's him.

I raise my hand to his face, stroking gently. He closes

his eyes, and as he rests his face against my palm, he takes a deep breath. When he opens his eyes, his expression has relaxed.

I kiss him, hoping to soothe what remains of his worry for me. He doesn't resist me, lets my tongue slip between his lips before his greets me.

Despite how much energy it took to have the Moment, as we kiss, my strength returns. I push against his chest, guiding him onto his back and straddling his waist.

Brad feels just as greedy for my kiss and touch. His hand slides under my shirt, running up my abs, around to my back.

A wave of inspiration overtakes me. I know what I want from Brad.

"Can I—I want to fuck you, Brad."

Since we started messing around, I've been so obsessed with getting him inside me that, though it crossed my mind, I never fixated on it the way I am now. Maybe it's because seeing him so distressed by my pain, I just want to put him at ease the way he's put me at ease all those times he's taken this ass.

"Please let me fuck you," I beg, and fighting to speak between kisses, he says, "You can...do whatever...the fuck you want to me."

He's all fucking mine.

It's not something I take for granted.

We remove each other's clothes, our lips and bodies

parting just as long as they have to until we're naked. He fetches a packet of lube from his pants pocket.

That's my Brad, always prepared.

We position our shirts and jackets so he can lie on them. There's a chill in the air, but it's quickly forgotten as we latch back on, our combined body heat and this special magic between us making it easy to forget about things like temperature. It's like we're not even in the church cellar anymore, but in our own world, one we've constructed from each fuck.

I'm lost in kisses until I manage to pull away from his mouth, kissing down his neck and body, nipping at his flesh, biting gently, licking. I make a quick stop at his cock to give it a teasing lick before running my tongue down around his balls, to his ass. I hook my arms under his thighs, raising them to display his ass.

I take a moment, just looking at how pretty it looks.

And it's all for me.

I place a gentle kiss against Brad's thigh. Then I ready myself with the lube and push my head against his tight hole. Our gazes meet, a gentle smile tugging at his lips as he waits in anticipation.

He nods, and I push the head inside, watching as he closes his eyes and rolls his head back.

I take my time, steadily inching my way inside, watching as his muscles twitch and his cock firms beneath me. Slow and steady, I push in as he opens up for me. As I get that last inch in, he arches his back, and

I lean down, resting my forearms on either side of him as I offer a kiss, appreciating how tight he is. How firmly his ass grips me.

"God, your cock feels so good."

I pull out and then thrust back into him, then do it again, steadily building up my movements, watching Brad's open-mouthed expression as he takes each push. We work together—as I push, he rocks his hips as we find that familiar, natural rhythm between us.

"Fuck me harder," he begs. "Fuck me, Straight Boy."

His lips tug into a smile, and how can I not laugh? This is what I love about messing around with him. The play, the fun that helps us escape all the bullshit.

But then I give him what he wants, putting in the work as I give him broad, intense thrusts. The way he rocks his head either way, opening his eyes enough for me to see them rolling, it's clear I'm hitting the spot just right, which only encourages me as I continue to fuck him. His muscles shake with my movements as he moans before his eyes open, his gaze meeting mine.

Despite what he heard earlier, me at my absolute worst, I don't see pity in his eyes, only appreciation. He sees past my defenses, past the pain in my soul, but it hasn't scared him away, only drawn him in more.

I see this beautiful man, whom I'd once thought the biggest asshole I'd ever met.

But he has his own wounds. His own aches.

These aren't things I look past. They're part of what

make him so beautiful to me. They're part of what has given him this big heart. Part of what makes seeing his smile or hearing his moans of pleasure all the more intoxicating. Because I know what it takes to overcome that darkness in his heart.

And I just want to be here for him, allow him to use my body as an escape from it all.

Our instincts guide us through our experience as we change positions, like Brad won't be satisfied until he's tried my cock at every angle. I remember that feeling with him all too well.

We fuck until we're panting and sweaty, both of us on our knees, me behind him, thrusting still. With my arms hooked around him, his cock in my firm grip, his ass claps as my hips slam against him. His muscles tremble as I kiss and bite at his shoulder.

"I'm not gonna make it much longer," he admits. He sounds ashamed, like he's disappointed he can't give me more.

"Don't worry, I'm about ready too."

"I don't want to blow until you've come in me."

I lick my lips. Just the thought of my cum pumping into him makes the pressure swell.

"Look at me," I tell him, and he turns his head, his gaze meeting mine once again as his hot breath pushes against my face.

And it's all too much for me.

The pressure builds to its peak, and my movements

pick up until I feel that explosive sensation.

"Yeah, give it to me," he says, and I do, my body smashing against him as I fill him up. His cock tightens in my grip, and it's clearly too much for him too because a moment later I feel the warmth spreading over my fingers as I pump him good.

I cling to him, our bodies shaking as we come down from the high.

After I pull out of him, he lies on his back against our clothes, and I curl up against him, tucking my face against his chest as I massage his abdomen with my cum-soaked hand.

"Thank you for that," I say.

"I should be thanking you. That was amazing."

It was.

But as I glance up at him, I see the worry has returned. As wonderful and necessary of an escape as it was, we both know what this means.

"Now that I've had the Moment," I say, "we need to—"

"No," Brad says, stroking my cheek. "Not tonight. Tonight, let's just make this about you and me. We can deal with everything else tomorrow."

I like the sound of that, but I know it won't be that easy. There's too much at stake. Still, I'm determined to make the best of it, so I rest my head against his chest, tugging him close. Clinging to him the way we plan to cling to tonight.

22

BRAD

THE AIR'S THICK with tension as I strip down.

"This is creepy," Luke says.

Already nude, he sits on the edge of Cody's bed.

The day after he experienced the Moment, we arranged a meeting with the Sinners. Unsurprisingly, Seth fought against this as much as he could.

"It's too soon."

"We don't know what will happen."

"I want you guys to know I'm totally against this."

Despite his adamant objections, in the end, he was outvoted. We've come this far, and if there's a chance this could work, it's worth the risk. I only hope I still feel that way once Luke and I finish.

"At least Cody put on fresh sheets," I say, trying to make light of the situation as I finish removing my pants and briefs.

Do I want to fuck Luke in my friend's bed? No. But considering why we're doing this, we can't afford to be interrupted by Alexei or Matteo, so this is for the best.

I stack my clothes beside Luke's and grab my phone, checking to see if Seth or Cody have messaged. Once Cody's prepped at the old church, he'll give us the go-ahead.

And we'll begin.

As I sit beside Luke, he has a far-off look in his eyes. I hook my arm around him, resting my head against his shoulder.

Last night with him was perfect.

Heavenly.

Not just how good he fucked me, but as hard as it was to hear what he was going through, I was honored to be the guy there for him when he needed someone. He'll never understand how much I respect him for what he went through, what he endured to get through that. Just like he can't understand the feelings I've developed for him over this short time we've shared.

"I feel like a sacrificial virgin," Luke says.

"Don't worry. I worked hard to make sure you'd never feel like a virgin again."

He chuckles.

To think that, even with everything on his mind, he's able to laugh, it's some kind of miracle.

I pull my head away from his shoulder, and he turns to me. "That first vision wasn't too bad," he says. "Cody talked me through what to do, so we'll see if I can get a handle on this enough to figure out something that will help us find this thing and stop it from hurting anyone else."

As his gaze meets mine, he looks so serious. He shouldn't have to think about this. His biggest worries should be if he's gonna get an A on his French test. Deciding whether he'll go to the next Alpha Alpha Mu party. Maybe thinking about someone he wants to ask out...

Not having Luke in my life like this isn't something I like to think about, but if there were a way to spare him all this dark shit, even if that meant a lifetime of misery without him, I would choose his happiness over my selfish desire for him to be with me. Guess that's easy to say when we can't change the past.

My phone buzzes on Cody's nightstand.

"That must be them," Luke says. He crawls back on the bed as I confirm it's Cody.

All set here. We'll give you a few minutes to get set up on your end. ;)

I doubt it'll take us that long, but maybe it'll give me some time to set Luke at ease.

As he lies back, his head against the pillow, he's on full display for me, nude, but clearly stressed.

"This isn't like the other things we've done," he says. "It's like getting a physical."

"You know you're not obligated to do this, right? At any time, you say the word, and I'll explain it to the guys."

He turns to the window, his lips twisting into a frown. He takes a moment, and I already know he's not gonna back down even before he shakes his head.

"I feel guilty enough for that guy I saw before. I'm not gonna let that happen to anyone else."

"Can't blame me for trying." I lie alongside him, and regardless of all that's on our minds right now, we both perk right up.

I run my thumb across his cheek, stroking gently. His breath hitches, like he's bracing himself, before he closes his eyes. I give him a kiss, savor his mouth, our tongues working through a familiar dance as I reposition so I'm straddling his leg, our bodies pressed up against each other. Luke's arms hook around me, drawing me close.

I reach over to the nightstand and grab the lube I placed there earlier so we'd be ready. I pull away from our kiss long enough to ready myself, then rise to my knees, crawling between his legs, which he spreads wide. Once I'm positioned, he raises his legs, gripping the backs of his thighs. Offering himself up to me.

I lube up my fingers and pump plenty for that tight hole before pushing the head of my cock against it. He's tenser than usual, surely from the stress.

"Sorry," he whispers, his expression straining, though I'm not applying any pressure.

"Hey, hey. It's fine. It's just you and me," I assure him, massaging his thigh.

He takes a few deep breaths, then nods. "Okay."

I go slow, and gradually he eases up for me. After some time and effort, I finally get inside him. I lean down and give him a kiss he eagerly accepts.

"Here we go," he whispers into my mouth.

He closes his eyes, and when he opens them, they're black, like that day he had the vision and last night.

I still as a wave of sensation moves through me. It's gentle at first, but then there's a powerful blow, like a gust of wind slamming into me from the front.

I'm not looking at Luke anymore.

We're at a party. Kids our age all around with red Solo cups, chatting.

Is this the fairgrounds?

No, I recognize where we're at: the backyard of Alpha Alpha Mu. They're dressed in sports gear—a theme night, I'm guessing.

Suddenly, there's blood splattering across the side of the house before I'm beside a man with a spear through him. The impaled guy from Cody's vision.

A fireball explodes, fire all around me, and there's the charred man Cody saw, crawling across the ground.

These flashes are so quick before I find myself back in bed, staring at Luke, whose wide eyes are back to normal, his jaw hanging open as he gasps. He's pale, trembling beneath me.

"Luke?"

He continues trembling, like he's having a seizure.

Though his eyes are on me, it takes him a minute to recognize me.

"Oh my God," he mutters as tears well in his eyes. His arms wrap around me, and his shaking intensifies.

"It's okay, Luke," I say as I pull out of him. "I'm here. I'm here."

I hold him close. Cling to him so he knows he's safe as long as he's in my arms.

"I saw," I say. "At least some of it."

He leans back and looks at me with wide eyes, studying my expression. "What did you see?" He listens as I tell him, then says, "Yeah. It really rattled me seeing those kids screaming and the two bodies again."

I comfort him some more before texting Cody.

Fortunately, Cody's fine, and like the first time with Luke, he didn't share the vision.

We dress and head out to meet the guys at the old church. Even though his shaking has subsided, Luke keeps holding his hands like he's trying to steady them as he gives Cody and Seth a quick summation of his vision. He glosses over bits, so I fill in gaps and details he may have missed.

"Why is it different from the first vision?" Seth asks.

Cody's lips twist into a frown. "Something must've changed."

"What if it's something else Luke did without realizing it?"

"We can't put this on Luke," Cody says. "It is interesting there's no fairgrounds, but then the same two deaths after? Maybe those happen at a different time than we thought?"

"The kids we saw were dressed up," I say, thinking the detail might help something click into place. "One of the frat's theme nights. A girl was dressed as a cheerleader, one guy as a football player, and another as a hockey player. We need to talk to someone who lives there and find out when they're having a sports-themed party."

Seth closes his eyes. "No need. There's one this Saturday."

The blood in my face drains. "What?"

"They sent out reminders about it today."

"Then we're just in time," Luke says, sounding more hopeful than he has since he had the vision.

"*In time?*" Seth asks. "We're supposed to figure out what to do about this in two fucking days?" He curses. "We don't even know what we're dealing with."

"We do have some information," Cody says. "It's a large creature, for one."

"And now we know when and where," I add.

"Seth's not wrong, though," Luke says, a first from him. "What the hell are we supposed to do about a fucking monster? This thing was like nine feet tall when I saw it torturing that guy. Are we gonna get a gun or something?"

"I've already considered all this," Cody says. "There's a spell in the Sinners' bible. We can create a circle that can trap animals or people."

Luke's eyebrows tug closer together as he makes a face like when we were first telling him about all this stuff. "And you know this works?"

"We've tried it on each other," I assure him. "When we were first playing around with the book. It works. We don't know that it'll work on something from the Rift, but it's not that far-fetched."

"It's worth a shot," Cody says.

Luke glances between the three of us, like he's waiting for someone to point out that this is a horrible idea. "And what are we supposed to do with it once we have it trapped? Is Cody gonna tell it its future? Is Seth gonna push it to kill itself? Is Brad gonna fuck it to death? Am I gonna fuck Brad and lift it off the ground?" He huffs, rolling his eyes and turning away from us.

Everyone's quiet for a moment before Cody says, "As far as killing the thing, you guys know what we can do."

He looks at me like it should be obvious, and I turn to Seth, who seems just as thrown.

Cody motions to the stack of bricks in the corner of the room, and it fucking hits me.

I cringe. "Really?"

"It could work!"

"*Could* being the operative word," Seth adds.

Luke spins back around. "What are you guys talking about?"

"It's something else we learned we can do," I say.

"Together. If we concentrate, we can—"

"It's probably better just to show him," Seth says, and I have to agree.

I fetch a brick from the stack and set it in the center of the pentagram. Cody, Seth, and I position ourselves to form a triangle around the pentagram.

"Luke, you need to get behind me," I say.

He glances around the room like he's trying to work out what we're about to do. Then he steps close to the wall.

Cody, Seth, and I glance at each other, then grip our crosses and focus on the brick. Despite having done it before, it's been a while, so we might be a little rusty.

I steady my breathing, feeling a familiar sensation swirling in my chest, radiating from there out to my arms. It moves into my hands, like they're vibrating with energy. The more I concentrate on the brick, the more I lose awareness of time and my surroundings.

And then the brick starts vibrating.

I can't see it, but I feel it in my gut as it speeds up, and a second later a sound like a shotgun fills the cellar. Dust explodes in the air, bits of brick launching at bullet speed, only to be stopped by an invisible barrier inside the pentagram. The pieces drop to the floor, and the dust begins to settle.

I turn to Luke, whose mouth hangs open.

"Fuck," he mutters.

"Did you really think you knew all our secrets?" Seth

asks snidely.

If Luke wasn't here, I'd fucking throw Seth against the wall and demand he get over himself and treat Luke like the Sinner he is. But I quiet my rage, ignore the asshole remark, and explain to Luke what just happened. "It's something we stumbled upon in the Sinners' bible and tested out. We can't do anything as powerful as you can on your own, but if the three of us focus, we can cause some motherfucking damage."

"Apparently," Luke notes. "But is that gonna do anything to this creature? Something that's alive?"

"Why don't you get in the middle, and we can test it," Seth says with a nasty smirk.

"Seth," I snap. "That's not funny."

His gaze shifts to the floor; he knows that was too far.

"I've researched this," Cody says, pulling our attention back to his proposed solution. "Imagine how much pressure it takes to make a brick explode. If that can't kill that thing, then nothing else is gonna do it either."

"Yeah," Luke says, "but if we can't trap it, then we're fucked because I doubt this thing will stay still long enough for you to focus as hard as you need to pull it off."

"Do you have any better ideas?" Seth asks, and I shoot him another glare. "That one wasn't me being an asshole," he says. "I'm genuinely curious."

My tense jaw relaxes.

Luke's gaze wanders around the room. "I feel like we're being too hasty here."

"We only have two days," Cody reminds him.

Luke nods. "I agree that we have to do *something*. Let's at least arm ourselves with some real people shit. Dobbers used a shotgun."

"He was also from a family of hunters," Seth says. "How about we do ourselves a favor and not wind up shooting each other while trying to kill the Slasher?"

Luke chuckles. "I wasn't suggesting guns. More like baseball bats and pepper spray."

"That's not a bad idea," I say. "If our powers don't work against it, at least we're armed."

"Okay," Cody says. "We'll text about the details as we figure out what's what. Sound good?" He glances around.

Not sure if any of us are making very comforting expressions. Our solutions are speculation, but it's all we've got.

After Cody calls the end of the meeting, he and Seth head out, leaving Luke and me alone in the cellar.

Luke faces the full-length mirror, staring at his reflection, clearly lost in thought. I can't imagine what's going through his head.

At least the guys and I have some experience with this. Not trapping a monster, but with our powers. We managed to develop these over time, acclimate to the realization that there was much more to the world than we'd ever considered. Luke hasn't had that advantage.

I approach him. "I know it's a lot to trust that we can pull this off, but we are strong. You saw what we did with that brick."

His gaze meets mine briefly before he looks away. "It's not that," he mutters.

I step behind him, hooking my arms around his waist. He doesn't resist me, relaxing in my hold.

Since the vision, it's the first time I feel like as long as I can protect him, everything will be all right.

I kiss his cheek, then whisper, "Please, Luke. Talk to me."

His reflection looks into my eyes. "Brad…" He hesitates. "There's something from the vision I didn't share with you. I was worried you might have had the same experience, but I can't imagine you did; you would have brought it up." He presses his lips together, and a subtle shake returns. "I tried to approach the impaled man, but I couldn't. The burned man, for some reason, I could. He was writhing on the ground in agony…such excruciating pain. Then he reached out to me, and I saw his eyes. And I just knew…"

"Knew what?" I ask, though the way he's acting, I fear I might already know the answer.

"It was me."

My heart sinks. My gut twists up. "No…no, that can't be right."

"I know it in my fucking blood."

A jolt of certainty moves through me. "We have to tell the guys. We'll handle this ourselves."

I'm about to head out to catch them, but Luke grabs my arm. "No, Brad. That's why I was worried about telling you all. I need to do this. I'm not leaving you to fight this thing alone. If we can stop it from killing others, then we can stop it from killing me too."

After what I heard him do to himself last night, I'm not surprised by his courage, but at the same time, unlike him, I'm such a selfish fuck. I'd rather know he's safe than worry about anyone else.

"Luke..." I choke up as I say his name. My vision blurs with tears. "You can't do this."

His reflection breaks eye contact, and he turns to face me, my arms still keeping him close, since he's activated this primal protective instinct within me.

"Even if you guys got it without me, I'll always feel like a coward if I don't. So I don't want you to tell the guys. Please. There's already enough to figure out without having to deal with that too. I don't want them to worry about me. Between the two of us, we'll be worried enough."

Looking at his face and thinking about the one I saw in the vision, it's horrifying to consider that this could be a possible future for my Luke.

"I—" I don't even know what to say. Everything's an objection or an attempt to trick him into not following through with this.

Before I can say anything else, his lips crash against mine.

I firm my hold around him, welcoming his tongue into my mouth as we embrace.

Despite the terror he's awakened within me, now that I know I might lose him, I just know I must take advantage of every moment...every fucking second with him.

As long as I fucking can.

Because I know nothing I say will change his mind.

23

LUKE

*T*HERE HE IS, *the burned man Cody told me about, crawling across the ground.*

Does he see me? Is he coming for me?

I fear how quickly he moves toward me, wide-eyed, his jaw shifting about wildly. But as he nears, he rolls onto his back. His blistering skin is black as coal, except for streaks of red between creases. He writhes in agony, eyes closed as he forces a few breaths.

He reaches up, opening his eyes, looking right at me with familiar blue irises.

At first, my instinct is that I know this man. These eyes are so familiar.

And with that comes a much deeper understanding.

This isn't just a man—it's me.

Flesh and blood charred black.

Struggling in excruciating pain.

Is this my fate?

When I first came to after the vision, I was so shaken I could hardly think straight. After recovering from the shock and discussing it with Brad, I was relieved he hadn't made the connection, but as we talked with the guys, I realized it was too weighty a secret to keep from him.

I knew if I told him, he wouldn't want me to help take on the Slasher, but something in me knows as deeply as I knew those were my eyes that I must do this.

Over the next two days, we prepare for Saturday night. A part of me believes it's too soon, but another part knows nothing can prepare us for what we're about to face.

Before this realization, my time with Brad has felt as though we've been in our own little world, outside of time...and when we fuck, even losing track of space as we're only sensation and passion. Now time races by, slipping from our grasp as it hurtles us toward Saturday night.

I consider skipping my classes, but they're the only thing keeping me from losing my goddamn mind.

Before I head out to the old church to execute our plan, I FaceTime with Dan.

A familiar pang of guilt knots up in me. I should have called him right after I discovered I was the man in my vision. But I couldn't bring myself to talk to him, to look at him.

I've been torn between my desire to see the man I love nearly as much as I loved my parents, and the fear that if I spoke with him too soon, I'd fucking lose it and he'd know something's wrong. Even worse, he's been looking forward to this work conference in Maui, and I don't want to fuck up his good time because of all this shit going on in my life right now.

Just keep it together.

When he answers, he's lying in his hotel bed. He must've placed his phone in his mount because he's relaxed, not struggling with making sure he's framed right.

"Hey, Luke. How's it goin'?" He sounds so at ease. More so than normal. Blissfully unaware of the nightmare my life has become.

"Hey, good." The knot in my gut twists even more from the lie. "How's Hawaii?"

He tells me about how beautiful it is, removing his phone from the mount and taking me over to the window to show me his view.

I can feel the tears creeping up.

A flash of a memory comes back to me: Dan in the hospital, approaching me to tell me about Mom. His voice trembled. His eyes watered. I know how hard he was trying to keep it together for me, wanting to make one of the most agonizing moments of my life bearable.

Now it's time for me to do the same.

Deep, steady breaths. Just like Brad taught me during our meditation sessions.

But even trying to keep it together, it tears me up knowing that, regardless of how I manage this conversation, I'm still putting myself in harm's way, setting him up for another loss.

He's sharing some office gossip that's bled into the trip, but as he places his phone back on the stand, he winces, studying my expression. "You sure you're all right?"

"Yeah. Just been a hectic week with school."

"What's up? Talk to me."

Now the tears I felt creeping up are trying to break free. I battle them back, proud of myself for how I keep them from falling as I say, "Nothing too bad. Just some friend drama."

"Okay...well, if you want to talk about it, I have plenty of time. Finished up my last meeting twenty minutes ago."

I do want to talk to you, Dan. But I can't.

I shake my head. "I'll figure it out."

And I really hope that's true.

I try to think up a way out of this when a thought springs to mind. "You know, I've met someone..."

I'm not just telling him to distract from what he's caught on to, but because I genuinely want him to know, especially if anything happens to me tonight.

His eyes widen with excitement. "Really?"

I nod. "His name's Brad."

Considering I've never said anything about being interested in guys—haven't even known that about myself—I wait to gauge Dan's response.

He blinks a few times. "Oh…that's not what I was expecting you to say."

"You and me both."

He opens his mouth, clearly struggling, but then says, "I appreciate your sharing that with me. Is he nice?"

"Long story short, he was a dick to me when I first got here, but then I found out there was a misunderstanding, and after that we hit it off. He's cool. More than that…" *I have feelings for him—strong feelings for someone I haven't known all that long.*

"Well, now I'm gonna have to meet him, you know. See for myself if this guy is worthy of you."

"Oh, he's definitely worthy," I assure him. "And I definitely want you to meet him." The truth pulses through me as I say the words.

But Dan's expression twists up. "This thing that's on your mind, was it about telling me you had feelings for a guy?"

"Um…sure," I say, since that gives me an out. "Anyway, I'll tell you all about it when you get back from your trip. In the meantime, I'd rather hear about what you're gonna be up to over the weekend."

"Okay, but if you do want to talk more about this, whenever you're comfortable, I'm here. I'm always here for you."

Don't I know it. That's what makes this so hard.

"Thank you," I say before insisting he change the subject, so he tells me about his plans as well as some shows he wants to catch up on. I bask in the moment, cherishing this time I have left with him, wishing I could give him a great big hug for the amazing man he's been to me.

I check the time on my phone. Nearly a quarter to eight. About time to head out.

"I'm off to a party soon, but I wanted to call and…" I don't know how to say this without being awkward as fuck, but it's not something I can go without saying. I don't want to be burned to a crisp, about to lose my life, wishing desperately I'd taken better advantage of this moment. "I want to thank you for always being here for me," I blurt out. "For taking me in and being a great guardian. I know that couldn't have been easy, and I know you didn't have to. It means the world to me that you did."

As I make eye contact with Dan, I see the light catching the tears in his eyes. "Well, Luke, it was hell what happened to you as a kid. Something no one so young should ever have to deal with. And as unexpected or difficult as it may have been for me, and as much as I may have struggled to figure out the right things to do or say, being in your life has been the greatest honor of my life. Seeing you growing into a young man, well, it makes me proud to be here to see it. I know your parents would have been just as proud, and they'd want you to know that. And they'd want you to know they'd love you just as you are."

Keep it together, I urge myself, but I'm fighting a losing battle. My face spasms, my chin quivering as the tears break free, sliding down my cheeks in quick succession. I turn away from my phone, but it's too late.

"I should probably get ready for that party."

"Luke?"

"Sorry, I just miss them and have been thinking about them a lot lately."

I hope he buys that that's the only reason, but his forehead's wrinkled up with worry.

"I love you, Dan."

"I love you, Luke. Always."

When I hang up, losing that image of him, I accept that might very well have been the last time I ever chat with him.

The guilt knotting in my gut intensifies, and I let the tears flow freely, taking my time with them so that I can get it all out before meeting the guys.

AFTER I RECOVER from my conversation with Dan, I meet up with Brad and we head out to the old church.

There are stacks of boxes in the cellar, things we've ordered online over the past couple of days, which we get right into.

Cody collected our stats and purchased matching costumes so that if we happen to get caught behind the

Alpha Alpha Mu house, we can say we're there for the party.

As we toss on the navy-blue football jerseys and matching spandex pants, Brad growls, and I turn, catching him sneaking a glance at my ass.

"Fits nicely," he says, arching an eyebrow before licking his lips.

I study myself in the mirror. "It's weird being dressed in something so silly for the night we're supposed to take on a vicious monster."

"Maybe it'll bring some levity to the situation."

"I doubt much will do that."

"Yeah…"

After we finish getting dressed, we throw on our jackets, and Brad digs through a few more boxes, finding the pepper spray and stun guns—the latter Seth's idea. We ran a test on the pepper spray yesterday, and despite being advertised as shooting to ten feet, it was more like seven. Although, I'd rather shoot at this thing from seven feet than be up its ass with a bat or stun gun.

As I tuck my spray and stun gun in my jacket pockets, I say, "You know, I love the idea of having some weapons on me, but I keep having this image of me trying out the pepper spray. Doesn't work, so I go for the stun gun, giving this monster enough time to rip my fucking throat out."

Brad's expression sobers.

"Relax," I say. "We both know that's not what I have

to worry about tonight."

As he winces, I realize that didn't help any. "Sorry. I'm just in my head."

"Okay, no," he says, approaching me. "You're not getting all apologetic on me. Not tonight."

But there's this creeping fear that this could be the last night I have to be apologetic about anything.

He hooks his arm around me and draws me close. He doesn't go right for a kiss, like he has in the past. He gets close, studies my expression.

With everything we've had to plan, we haven't really had time to mess around. And the Lust hasn't been as intense since we shared my vision, so we haven't needed to fuck just to keep on. But as his lips meet mine, a familiar relief sweeps through me. A relief I need so fucking desperately right now.

Brad must feel the same because before I know it, he has my wrists pinned against the wall, tongue sweeping against mine.

"It's gonna be okay," Brad whispers. "I'll protect you. I'm not letting anything happen to you."

He can't know that, but his words ease up all that tension I've been carrying around in my chest, relaxing that twisting knot in my gut.

"Brad, I care about you so much." Like with Dan earlier, I feel like if I don't fucking say this now, I might not have the chance again. "I didn't know I could feel about someone the way I do about you. I—"

"No," Brad says before his lips crush against mine. I'm greedy for him as my body comes alive with pulsing desire, anticipating him sating my needs once again. When he finally pulls his mouth away, he whispers, "Don't. No confessions. Nothing until we're through this."

"But I might not get another chance."

"It's gonna be fine, Luke. We're gonna get through this, and it will be just a fucked-up thing we had to survive."

"Brad, please, I need to say it."

He grits his teeth, then nods.

"I'm falling for you. Like...ridiculously falling. There's so much I'm scared about tonight, but one of the worst thoughts is that I might miss out on getting to know you so much better. Or getting to do homework together. Or have more study time in the library...or even not studying on the fourth floor together."

He snickers.

I run my knuckles along his cheek. "I want to order more Asian fusion, and calzones, and I want to catch up on fucking *Real Housewives of Salt Lake City* with you so that you can chat with your mom about it. I want to fight with you about stupid, dumb crap that doesn't matter. The kind of stupid stuff that boyfriends do together."

"Boyfriends," he says, tearing up. The word hits my ear just right. "I like the sound of that." His gaze drops to my lips, and he takes my mouth once again.

Before we'd used the word about each other, it just seemed like any other word. But it's not anymore. There's something different about this kiss, knowing I'm not just kissing this guy I'm falling for. That he's my boyfriend. And I'm his boyfriend.

I grip the back of his head, firming our kiss. Wanting to live in this moment for as long as I can.

In case it's one of my last.

24

BRAD

NOT LONG AFTER Luke and I confirm our relationship status, Seth and Cody arrive, and we go over our plan.

Seth doesn't give Luke any attitude. Seems like he's more concerned about making sure we're on top of everything than giving Luke hell, which is good for him because I don't know what I'll do if he gives my boyfriend trouble tonight.

Boyfriend.

There was something so satisfying about hearing that word escape his mouth. Now we just have to survive the night so that we can enjoy all the things that come with the label.

We take stock of our weapons before heading out, cutting through the woods to get to the Alpha Alpha Mu house. Some guys are hanging out in the back, but it's not nearly as busy as in Luke's vision.

The calm before the storm.

Using the night-vision apps on our phones, we navigate through the woods, creating three large salt circles, and then Seth, Cody, and I run through our ritual to cast a spell of entrapment. Once we finish, there's some commotion behind the house, and as we check, we see some guys cracking up as they head through the yard, carrying something large. I can't make out what it is until they prop it upright—

Bucktooth Beaver.

"Holy hell," Seth mutters.

"You think they snatched it from the fairgrounds?" Cody asks.

Luke stares at the statue, surely as unsettled as I am at how things are lining up. I rest my hand on his shoulder, but he doesn't take his eyes off the beaver.

"It is what it is," Cody says. "It doesn't change anything. Now, Seth and I will take the other side of the yard, and you guys take this side. If anyone comes out here, get them to back the fuck off or at least make sure they step around our traps."

Seth smirks as he caresses the head of his baseball bat. "Kind of amusing thinking about drunk frats getting stuck in these things."

Cody ignores his remark, sticking to business. "Anything I'm not thinking of? Thoughts? Feelings? Reservations?"

"All of the above," Luke says, his eyes still locked on the foreboding reminder of what's to come.

Cody glares at him. "Okay, I get it. This isn't ideal,

but it's the best we can do on short notice."

He's right, but fuck if that isn't a bleak truth.

"Come on, Seth." Cody starts toward the other side of the yard.

"Wait, wait," Seth says. "Shouldn't we do like, a *go team* or everyone puts their hand in or something?"

"You know we're not actually playing football to-night, right?" I remind him.

"Shut the fuck up. It'd be good for morale."

It's not gonna hurt anything, so I put my hand in front of me, and Luke finally shakes free of the grip the statue has on him before joining us.

"On three," Seth says, and he counts us down before we all give varying levels of feigned enthusiasm for the moment. Despite how dumb it seemed, I must admit it gives me a much-needed boost of confidence as we brace ourselves for a night of uncertainty and impending doom.

"We'll text if we need backup," I say.

"Or…" Seth begins, "scream like you're being ripped from the inside out by a creature from another dimension."

He searches our faces to see if his joke landed, which it didn't. Then he and Cody head to cover the other side of the house, disappearing into the darkness.

"Here we go," I mutter, turning to Luke, who scans his phone around the darkness, already alert. I consider asking him how he's feeling, but I don't really have to.

We wait in silence, watching from the distance as Alpha Alpha Mus usher guests into the backyard for drinks and games. Gradually, more and more people step into the backyard, which makes Luke and me even more on edge, knowing how many of them could become the Slasher's victims.

It's a little over a half hour before we accept that this could be a long night. I sit on a fallen tree, facing the woods, searching around via the night-vision app.

It's not like us to be around each other without speaking, but the chatter and bass of the music has kept it from being awkward. Besides, why chat when we can spend our time imagining all the different ways a monster might tear through this crowd, decapitating and tearing out entrails?

Luke eventually sits down beside me, and I notice that despite his jacket, he's rubbing his arms, so I hook my arm around him and pull him close.

"Fuck," he whispers.

"What's wrong?"

"I just remembered I have a paper due on Monday."

"You think you can get an extension?"

"Yeah, but my professor has a policy about deducting the grade for every day it's late. It's nothing. This is the last thing I should be worried about right now."

"You still have tomorrow."

He shoots me a look I read as, *You know damn well I might not have tomorrow.*

He pulls his gaze away and searches around before adding, "I talked to Dan today."

The comment seems out of nowhere, like mentioning his paper.

"Just wanted to make sure I told him I loved him and appreciated everything he did for me growing up. And as I was telling him all this, I kept thinking about when Mom and Dad died. This is gonna sound fucked up, but I felt like they abandoned me. Even knowing the circumstances, it was like part of me believed they'd done this on purpose. Like they'd just left me one day without notice. And I felt so guilty every time I had that thought. I hated myself for so long because I know that's wrong. And it wasn't fair to put that on them. I know neither wanted to leave me, but that's how it felt."

I hold him tighter. "Luke, you can't help how you feel through shit like that."

"I've told myself that so many times, but earlier, when I was talking to him, all I could think was how many times I was mad at them for leaving me, and now here I am, putting myself in danger. And he cares so much about me, and I don't want to leave him with that awful feeling..."

Tears flow freely from his eyes, and there's relief in seeing them. I prefer this to when he feels like he has to be strong or tough.

I kiss his cheek, his warm tears pushing up against my flesh.

As I pull away, he turns to me, really looking at me for the first time since we came out here. "If anything happens to me tonight, promise me you'll meet him. He's a great guy. I think you'd really like him."

And now he's got the waterworks going for me.

"Luke—"

"Please just say you will. I want you guys to meet."

Again, I'm tempted to tell him nothing will fucking happen and that he shouldn't think like that. But that won't do any good. Not now.

I press my lips together, stifling words I know won't help. "Of course I will. And when things turn out all right, maybe you can invite him to come with you to Thanksgiving, to meet my mom."

Despite how forlorn he looks, a gentle smile tugs at his lips. "I'd like that."

There's a light in his eyes—it's the first time since the vision we shared that I see hope in them. I take his hand, interlocking our fingers, gripping gently. He grips back.

"Thanks for listening to me...*boyfriend*," he says, stressing the word in a way that gets my pulse racing with excitement.

"That's what a boyfriend's for," I assure him.

He chuckles, and I lean in to take another kiss.

He closes his eyes as he's about to receive me, when an unusual sound catches my attention—

I jump into action, readying my bat, before I realize it was just his phone vibrating.

"Fuck," he mutters.

My heart's racing, muscles tense, nerves on edge.

I settle back on the fallen tree as Luke checks the message. "Alexei's asking if I'm coming to the party. I'll say I'm not so he won't look for me." He replies to Alexei, puts his phone on silent, and returns it to the night-vision mode.

As the night wears on, more of the guests head out to the back.

Drinking. Loud laughter. Loud music.

Kids celebrating life, blissfully unaware of the danger awaiting them.

My anxiety's already high enough, when I notice two guys heading out the gate, which clangs behind them.

"Looks like we have company," I mutter. I'm hoping they'll stay along the trail, where we intentionally didn't set any traps, but they move toward Cody and Seth.

Fuckin' A.

Luke and I tuck our bats down near the tree, and then I flash on my phone light and start toward them. As I near, I recognize Preston Wade and Finnegan Holmes, both members of Alpha Alpha Mu.

Preston flashes his signature charming-ass smile. "Hey, stud," he says with a wink. "You're missing a hell of a party."

"I kind of got distracted out here," I say, indicating Luke.

Preston glances between us, and I can tell the moment he understands what I'm suggesting.

"Oh, is this your plaything for the night?"

A low growl escapes my lips. "He's my boyfriend."

"Boyfriend? Oh, really?" Preston says. "Now I'm intrigued. Word's gotten around that you kept hanging with a guy. Breaking a lot of hearts, you know?"

"Yeah, I guess…"

"Uh…is your boyfriend okay?" Finnegan asks.

I turn to Luke.

He isn't exactly being discreet as he continues searching around, holding his phone high, like he's waiting for that monster to jump out and grab us at any moment.

"Sorry," Luke says. "I was just thinking I might have forgotten something back at the dorms. I was debating with Brad if we should head back."

"We'd offer to walk with you, but we're heading the other way." Preston and Finnegan start to go around me, but I block their path.

"Really? Where are you guys off to?"

Preston's forehead creases. "Not really any of your business, is it, stud?" He pats my shoulder, then tries to get around me again.

"Where's this attitude coming from?" I ask.

I notice Luke texting, I assume to get backup. I just need to buy some goddamn time.

"Back off," Preston says. "It's none of your business."

"I'm only curious."

"We're gonna go to the pond and smoke some weed.

Why? Did you want to come with?"

"Uh, no. We really want to hit the party, but you guys should stay. We can all do shots."

Preston winces. "How about you meet us in there when we get back?"

He tries to get around me yet again, but I block him.

Preston sneers. "Brad, what is this weird-ass game you're playing? Step the fuck out of our way and enjoy the party."

"Why are you being such an ass tonight?"

"Me? I only want you to get off our fucking backs." He gives me a shove.

God, this is gonna get real messy, real fast.

He and Finnegan start to head on, right toward one of our traps, so I throw myself at Preston, giving him a shove that sends him tumbling to the ground.

"The fuck, man?" Finnegan calls out, and as I turn to the yard, I notice some gazes shifting toward the woods.

Finnegan helps Preston to his feet.

There's rage in Preston's tense expression as he comes at me, fists at his sides, but fuck, a fistfight might be the only way out of this.

Preston gives me a shove. "What the fuck is your problem?"

I shove him right back.

"You fucking ass." Preston comes back for me when I hear from behind me, "Stop!"

Preston halts just before me, and I turn to see Seth

and Cody jogging toward us.

"Hey, hey, guys, what's up?" Cody asks.

Preston glances himself over, then looks around, clearly unsettled.

"Everything's fine, guys," Seth tells them, and Preston's and Finnegan's expressions fall, the tension diminishing as they just stare at me.

"You were heading back to the party," Seth pushes.

"Yeah, we were…" Preston says, searching around.

He and Finnegan exchange a look, as though neither can figure out why they're even in the woods to begin with.

"I guess we wanted to see if you guys were gonna join in on the fun," Preston says.

I unzip my jacket and display my jersey. "Eager to join in on the fun."

He smiles, though he still looks unsettled.

As they start back toward the gate, Finnegan spins around. "You guys coming?"

"We'll be a minute," Seth says, pushing on them, hopefully for the last time. They both nod, and as they turn back, a cracking sound catches our attention.

Preston and Finnegan stop in place.

It could be anything, I tell myself, turning with the rest of the gang toward the sound, which comes from where Seth and Cody were guarding.

Luke and I retrieve our bats, figuring Seth can manage this just like he has everything else.

"What's going on?" Preston asks.

"Quiet," Seth snaps.

It's hard to tell whether he's pushed on Preston and Finnegan again or if they're scared enough to just follow the instruction, but they remain silent with us as we listen and use our phones to look for whatever's making the sound.

Part of me wishes it's a deer. Another part wants to fucking end this, find the monster that threatens my goddamn boyfriend and kick its fucking ass.

I move closer to Luke, readying myself, when another *crack* fills the night air. Then another, on the opposite side of the yard.

"We're…gonna…get back to the party," Preston says.

Luke taps my arm. His wide eyes are fixed on his phone, which points toward the house. I follow his gaze to a tree between Preston and Finnegan and the party.

Backlit by the light coming from the party, on a branch maybe ten feet up, a silhouette, tall enough to be a person, perches. There's a quick movement, then something flies through the air—part of a branch, maybe. It lands farther in the woods, that same noise coming from behind us.

That's how it's been sounding like it's in different places.

Fuck.

I don't take my eyes off the shadowy figure, but in

my periphery, I see Finnegan and Preston starting in that direction. The black mass drops from the branch, landing in front of the guys.

Everything happens fast—

Seth, Cody, Luke, and I don't hesitate, racing for Preston and Finnegan to pull them out of harm's way. But before I can get to them, Finnegan is struck, and warm moisture hits my face. For a moment, I think spit, but no, this is blood.

I was expecting an animal, but it's wearing something to cover its body, like a cloak, which makes it look like Death coming to collect. By the time I reach the Slasher, it's got Preston by his jersey collar with long, narrow fingers clutched into a fist.

"Release him," Seth pushes, but it doesn't faze the Slasher, who keeps Preston held high.

I slam my bat against its neck, and Seth and Luke grab Preston and yank him back, tearing him from the creature's grasp.

As I strike at it again, it snatches the baseball bat, demonstrating its superior power as it pulls me off the ground and tosses me over its shoulder like a dirty rag. My body slams against a tree, then plummets to the ground.

While I'm recovering, I hear the guys freaking out.

And something else…growling?

"What the fuck? What the fuck?" Preston calls again and again.

"Preston?" Finnegan groans.

By the time I reorient enough to crawl to my knees, I see the creature's divided the group—Luke and Cody on one side, Seth and Preston on the other. And then it lurches at Luke and Cody, who shoot off into the woods, the monster on their heels.

25

LUKE

THIS SURE AS fuck isn't how I expected to spend my first semester at St. Lawrence.

Cody and I are off in a sprint, Cody's phone light shining our way as we dodge trees and jump over branches, rocks, and logs.

Seeing the Slasher catapult Brad into the air like he was weightless has helped me grasp how strong this thing is.

As it pursues us, I hear something like gurgling and dog growling. As far as I can tell, the Slasher is gaining on us—fast—and I fear looking back will only slow me down.

Even with my track past, I doubt I can outrun this thing, and Cody's starting to fall behind, his intense panting suggesting he's not gonna be able to keep on like this much longer.

I have no doubt what the Slasher will do if it catches us, and while I can't stop it, maybe I can slow it down.

I listen carefully as that growling/gurgling sound

nears, keeping my pace just behind Cody's so that if it grabs for one of us, it'll be me. Then I bring my bat in front of me, gripping the handle with both hands.

"Just keep running," I tell Cody.

"What the…fuck…are you about to do?" he asks between breaths.

"Maybe kill myself, so don't let it be for nothing."

He's about to say something—object or tell me what a dumbass I am—but I'm already spinning away from him, swinging. My timing's just right because the bat slams against something, and as my eyes adjust to the moonlight, I see the cloaked monster. It snatches my bat, just like it did with Brad, but now that I've seen what it can do, I know to release. And as it discards the bat, I slip my hand in my pocket and retrieve the pepper spray, since I'd prefer not to have to get that close to the Slasher for an attack.

It takes a swipe at me, and I aim and fire, dispensing the stream straight into the hood of the cloak. The Slasher withdraws its hand, the gurgling sound intensifying as it claws at its face.

It worked! At least somewhat, so I take advantage of the opportunity, sprinting toward the light from Cody's phone. He's a decent way ahead of me, giving me confidence that even if that thing isn't down for long, it'll likely get me before him.

I sneak a glance over my shoulder, then scan my phone behind us. I can't see it in the night-vision app.

Maybe that pepper spray has bought us some time.

But what if it backtracks and goes for Brad and Seth?

Hopefully, now that they know what we're dealing with, they'll be smart enough to get the hell away from it.

Navigating through the foliage, I speed up a hill. I assume Cody must be on the other side, but I can't see his light anymore. When I reach the top, I hear, "Luke, no!" before I lose my footing, sliding down some kind of trench.

As my momentum carries me over the edge, I manage to spin around and grip on to a sapling, which is rooted enough to stop my fall. Hanging from it, I reorient myself and grab at the sides of the trench. I start to climb the side when I hear, "Luke," behind me.

Glancing over my shoulder, I search the trench and see Cody poke his head out from a shadow, into the moonlight.

"I didn't see it either," he says, clearly referring to this big-ass trench.

"Come here. I'll help you out."

He hisses. "I can't. I sprained my ankle. Also, my phone's busted from the fall. I'll just hide here, but you keep running."

"Not fucking happening."

I use the ridges and roots in the trench to climb down—it must be at least eleven feet deep. I hurry to Cody and kneel beside him. He cringes as he removes his bookbag. "Can you get out the salt? If it gives us a few minutes, I can make a circle of protection."

I'm tempted to say fuck magic and hide, but from what I've seen so far, it seems to fare well in the dark, so I doubt it'll have any issue discovering our whereabouts.

I fetch the salt and pour it in a circle around us.

Cody uses the ground and my shoulder to get on his knees, and as he gets into position, I search overhead, waiting for the Slasher to discover us and jump down to finish us off. Fortunately, it seems my pepper-spray attack bought us more time than I expected.

Cody grabs hold of the cross on his necklace and whispers to himself...not loud enough for me to make out what he's saying. Even with the extra time we've earned, I fear he's not gonna have time to do this and we're both gonna die.

He's still muttering to himself when a *crack* comes from outside the trench. My heart races as I place my hand on Cody's wrist.

He quiets.

Fuck, did I stop him too soon?

Are we sitting ducks?

I retrieve my pepper spray from my pocket, readying myself in case I need to strike again.

A dark silhouette steps into the moonlight, and the hood of the cloak searches around before zeroing in on us. I wait for it to pounce, come down like it did from that tree, but it moves backward quickly, disappearing into the darkness.

Did Cody's spell work? Or is it fucking with us? Toying with its next meal?

We wait a few moments before Cody says, "I'm pretty sure it worked."

I catch my breath, not just from holding it while that thing was searching for us, but from that intense sprint.

Maybe it really worked after all.

But a rustling comes from overhead.

I keep my finger under the safety of the pepper spray and pull the stun gun from my other pocket.

The rustling gets closer.

There's a hope in me that it's Brad and Seth, but suddenly, a figure appears, looming over Cody and me.

It's not them.

But it's not the monster either.

"Luke? Cody?" Alexei asks, moonlight illuminating his face.

The fuck?

"Alexei, come down here. Quietly."

"Quietly? And why were you guys running through the woods?"

"Please. Just get down here."

"Quickly," Cody follows.

Alexei's expression is scrunched up like he's confused as fuck, but he nods and searches around.

The *crack* of a branch heightens my senses once again, followed by a sound I can't make out until I see something push through Alexei's torso, like a long, straight rod. Too straight to be a branch. Alexei cries out in agony as he's yanked back.

"Alexei!" I shout just as something tumbles over the side of the trench, landing away from us, in a depressed part of the ground, like a spot that used to hold water.

It's Alexei, impaled on—

Bucktooth Beaver.

"Oh God," Cody whispers.

The blood that scattered across Brad's face and mine. Now this.

The vision is coming to pass.

Alexei grabs at the rod in him and curses.

"I have to help him," I tell Cody.

"You'll break the spell if you cross the salt," he warns.

"You can heal, right?"

"Cuts and scrapes. Not *that*."

Fuck.

"We can't leave him like this," I say. "He's still alive. We can make another circle around him."

"We might not have time."

"Isn't it worth it if we might save him?"

"Of course."

"The pepper spray bought us some time before," I explain. "If it comes again, I'll spray it. I'll electrocute it. I'll keep it back. You think you can get that thing done in thirty seconds?"

Cody grimaces. "I can try. Help me over."

"Luke?" Alexei groans.

"We're coming," I whisper.

Cody tosses his bookbag strap over his shoulder, and I keep my finger under the safety of the spray as I help him to his feet, out of the circle, checking overhead. Cody hops alongside me as we settle in the depressed part of the ground near my fallen roommate and friend.

As Cody gets back on his knees, I tuck the stun gun in my pocket since I need my hands. With one hand, I hold the spray. With the other, I run the salt along the sides of the trench.

Cody's gripping his necklace and muttering to himself before I'm even finished, and as I complete the circle, there's a sound from above. My head snaps toward it, and a black mass comes at me. I raise my pepper spray and shoot, the stream flowing into the hood of our attacker.

Another perfect shot.

I jam my finger down on the spray, and the Slasher's claws withdraw to its face again, pulling back the hood, the moonlight shining off a jaw of lengthy teeth. But it doesn't back away, like it's getting better at enduring the pain, so in a panic, I fire up the stun gun, pressing it up against the back of its wrist.

The Slasher unleashes another cry, and I dodge a swipe before it retreats over the side of the trench, its screeching so high-pitched I need to cover my ears.

Another victory!

Maybe we'll make it out of this alive after all.

Cody continues his spell as I hurry to Alexei, whose eyes are wide open, mouth agape as he struggles to breathe.

"Fuck, Luke. Fuck," he says, but my gaze is focused on the spot where he's impaled. Not just because it's horrifying, but because this is the exact image from my vision, as if someone recorded what I was seeing in this moment.

Alexei grunts. "It hurts."

My gaze meets his, his usual playful expression locked in strain as he grits his teeth. "Cody might be able to do something for the pain," I say. "Just give us a moment, okay? Hang in there."

Oh, please, Cody, fucking get this sorted out.

I turn to see how he's progressing. He has his necklace in one hand, and he's moving the other about vigorously. Again and again. This isn't part of what he did before, and he's not muttering the spell. What the hell is he doing?

I hurry over to him. His eyes are open, black as the night, and he's not just moving his hand about. It looks like he's writing something in the air.

Something's happening.

I unzip his bookbag and retrieve a notebook and pen, placing the pen in his grip and holding the notebook out for him. I glance between his writing, the opening of the trench, and Alexei, my adrenaline keeping me on top of my surroundings.

Cody writes gibberish at first, but then I start to make out letters:

I AN KARM
I AM KYMS
I AM KYS...

He goes on like this, which is not getting us any-where, so I release the notebook, but just as I do, Cody lets go of his necklace and grabs hold of the notebook, writing:

I AM KYSAR
LUKE LUKE LUKE

This is followed by squiggly lines, and then my name again, with even more squiggly lines.

"Cody, did you finish the spell?" I ask, but he doesn't reply. Just keeps on writing the same thing over and over again, then turns the page and keeps going.

"Cody—"

A growl comes from overhead, sounding different than before—deeper, more menacing. This thing is fucking pissed.

I was so busy trying to keep the Slasher off us that I hadn't considered how much I was irritating it. Like spraying a hornet's nest with vinegar instead of Raid.

A few yards along the trench, something shifts, and I turn to see that black mass again, hunched over, making its way toward us, slowly, like something out of a horror movie.

We're fucking dead.

And then I hear:

"Cody?"

"Luke?"

Brad's and Seth's voices.

The Slasher stops in its tracks, then turns in their direction.

"Luke?" Brad calls again as the creature climbs up the side of the trench.

"Brad! Seth!" I call. "Don't come here!"

I turn to Cody, who's still writing *Luke*, but the squiggly lines aren't as erratic. It's a drawing of…

Fire.

The image of me, burned to a crisp, springs to mind.

But I can't think about that right now. I have to make sure the guys get the fuck out of here.

Before I can give that another thought, Cody drops the pen and snatches my wrist.

"Cody, what the—"

I'm lightheaded all of a sudden, and then a familiar sensation sweeps through me before everything goes dark.

I'm standing in the woods, over two bodies. I recognize Seth's and Brad's jackets. Seth lies facing away from me, the side of his face covered in blood. Brad lies with the Slasher squatting next to him, concealing everything above Brad's neck. As I walk around it, I see the Slasher's mouth wide as it crunches down on Brad's face.

As my chest constricts, I'm transported over the trench, looking down to see Cody lying alongside Alexei, his face covered in blood, his jacket torn open as a mess of what looks like black ground beef spills out of a gaping hole in his torso.

"Luke!" I hear Brad's voice again, and my eyes pop open.

I'm back in the trench with Cody and Alexei.

I turn to the page Cody wrote on, with my name and the image of the fire.

An awareness moves through me.

It reminds me of the Moment.

There's no doubt. No confusion.

I raise my hand, concentrating, and there's a sensation…heat swelling in my chest. It moves down my arm to my hand, and as I roll my hand toward me, a flame pushes from my palm. It's so fucking hot that I cringe at the sting before cupping my hand to put it out.

That horrifying image from my vision returns to me, then the words Cody received from the Guides: *He must go. It's time for him to go. Go now.* And suddenly, I understand what it means.

"I have to go now," I mutter.

If I don't, the Sinners and the people at Alpha Alpha Mu's party will die tonight.

26

BRAD

"LUKE!" I CALL out. "Cody!"

"It had to have come from this direction," Seth says as we stop in a clearing. He pulls out his phone and scans around.

"Anything?"

"No," he says in a hostile tone.

Both of us are still reeling from the wild goose chase.

After the Slasher tossed me against the tree, it took me a moment to get back on my feet.

"It was a bear," Seth pushed on Preston. *"Call 911. Get Finnegan help."* I doubt he pushed that last part—didn't need to—before Preston took off.

I found my bat, then headed in the direction the Slasher chased the guys. Since we lost sight of Luke and Cody, we searched for clues. There was Luke's baseball bat, then some blood on a tree trunk that I assumed—or hoped—was what remained on the Slasher's claws after assaulting Finnegan. We found Cody's thermos, which must've fallen off his bookbag. I hoped we were that damn lucky, but then I started getting suspicious, especially as we kept on with no sight of the guys.

We shouldn't have been so quick to trust what we found. It was all too perfect, something that really hit me once we heard the screech coming from the opposite direction we'd taken, on our way to little more than an echo.

The Slasher may be a monster, but it isn't an un-thinking, feral creature. It's clever. Tricky. It already showed us that with what it did from the tree, tossing sticks to throw us off its whereabouts.

Would've been nice if the original Sinners had given us a heads-up about that, but now Seth and I just have to hope we can make it to Luke and Cody before it does.

I heard Luke call out, but it's a struggle to tell which way it's coming from.

We keep quiet, listening for any other sounds that might indicate where we should head next, hoping Cody or Luke might call out again.

Something. Anything.

Seth scans our surroundings again, and as he faces me, aiming up at the trees, he freezes in place. "Brad—" He doesn't have to say more. I've already got my bat up, spinning in the direction he's pointing his phone.

The flashlight reveals a dark figure flying toward me, and I jump out of its path just in time for it to drop where I stood.

As Seth backs up, his phone light catches the cloaked

creature, which no longer wears its hood, exposing wide black eyes in a narrow face and sharp fangs. It crouches, then steadily rises, towering over us before displaying its lengthy fingers with sharp claws at the ends.

I tighten my grip on the bat, and the Slasher hisses before coming at me.

"Stop!" Seth pushes, but it keeps coming.

I strike, and it moves out of my path. As I give it another go, it snatches the end of the bat and tosses me once again, throwing me as effortlessly as it did the first time. I release the bat as I hit a tree and tumble to the ground.

As I push back to my feet, the Slasher starts for me, when I hear Seth shout, "Hey, asshole!" He rushes the monster from behind, his phone in the clip at his waist so the light's still illuminating the clearing. When he's a couple of yards from the monster, he raises his arm, and a stream of pepper spray nearly hits the Slasher's face, but it turns so it catches the back of its head. It cries out, but it's not the sound we heard before, when it sounded injured. This sounds annoyed. It swipes at Seth, catching his wrist, and Seth curses as the spray goes flying out of his hand. He jumps out of the creature's reach, inspecting the blood on his wrist briefly before readying his bat as the monster redirects its attention to him.

"Stop!" he cries out of desperation, but like his other attempts, the monster keeps moving toward him, assuring us Seth's power has no effect on it.

Seth strikes, slamming his bat against the thing's neck, but it doesn't faze it. Just stands strong before unleashing a deep roar. Seth tosses the bat aside, retrieving the stun gun from his pocket. Realizing the bats are useless against this thing, I discard mine as well, arming myself with the stun gun and heading to join my fellow Sinner. I don't know that I'll get to it before it can get its hands on Seth, when something comes flying from the woods—a rock?—and hits the creature's head. If only because of the surprise of being hit, it doesn't attack Seth, turning instead to see where that came from, and I notice a figure moving quickly through the clearing.

The light catches a face, and I realize it's Luke.

Luke!

The Slasher spins around and goes for him.

My boyfriend is unarmed, his arms spread to either side as he runs at the thing full force.

What the hell is he thinking?

"Luke, no!"

The Slasher roars again before lunging into the air. Luke mirrors the move, on a collision course toward this thing that could easily tear him the fuck apart.

I call out in vain, and the next moment there's a blinding flash of light, so bright I have to momentarily avert my gaze. It's followed by a *pop*, then a wave of heat and a piercing screech. A fireball surrounds Luke and the monster, and at its center, Luke's clinging to the creature, the fire searing through its cloak, revealing its lengthy arms and legs.

Fire…

No.

I start toward them. "Luke, stop!"

Luke turns to me, then looks away. "Seth, stop him!"

Like hell he will!

"Brad, stop!" Seth spits out, and I freeze in place against my will.

Fuck!

I struggle against the directive, trying to continue to Luke.

"Luke, what are you doing?" I call out. "You can't do this!"

Luke's face strains as he cries out. As the creature unleashes its own agonized cry, its flesh burns like paper. Luke's own flesh starts to turn gray, then black.

I struggle to rush toward him. "Seth!" I shout. "Let me go!"

"You can't help him now," Seth says.

Fuck him.

I drop the stun gun, lock my fists, and punch through the air, willing my limbs to obey my command when Seth shouts, "I said stop, Brad!" My muscles stiffen like I've been turned to fucking stone.

Dammit! "Fuck you, Seth!" I scream, battling his push as Luke and the Slasher are consumed by flames, their screams becoming one.

I continue fighting my body. Even with how burned

Luke is, I have to believe there's still a chance. If I can just get him away from the Slasher.

My struggle takes me to my knees as I claw at the earth, trying to pull myself even an inch, but my body won't allow it.

"Seth!" I turn to him, and his gaze meets mine as tears well in his eyes.

"I'm so sorry, Brad," Seth says before turning back to the fire.

"I'll never forgive you for this!"

But he doesn't reply, and when I look back to the fire, I see Luke's victim has finally stopped moving, and Luke looks as though he's been painted black.

Just like in the vision.

His haunting, strained cry fades with the flame, until both cease.

"Seth, let me go! Let me go *now*!"

"You can go to him," he says. "I'll call the police."

The release from this psychological bondage clicks. I crawl to my feet, but then get quickly back on my knees as I reach Luke's charred body, now lying on top of a pile of ashes the monster has become.

Luke's body's a fit of shivers. I want to grab him, to hold him, but I don't want to cause him any more pain than he's already in.

"Why did you do that?" I ask, tears streaming down my face.

This can't be!

Not my beautiful Luke.

His chin shakes, and he opens his mouth like he's trying to say something, but all that comes out is a choking sound.

"No, God no!" I cry out.

Is this really how we end?

I refuse to believe it! I refuse to lose him.

27

LUKE

AM I DEAD?

Is this darkness the afterlife?

I vaguely recall bright white lights and faces—maybe the light was heaven and the faces were angels. If that's the case, why haven't I seen Mom or Dad?

And why do I keep hearing Brad's voice?

I still hear it now, calling to me, and my eyes flit open.

The light's so intense, it takes me a few moments of blinking and wincing to adjust before I can scan the room. I'm lying on a bed with rails along the side, a TV mounted on the wall across from me. Brad sits in a chair next to the bed, reading out loud from a book.

It comes to me—I'm in a hospital room, and while I can't recall being here before, I have a feeling I've seen it, maybe coming in and out of consciousness.

I run back through the moment I followed the light in the woods to Brad and Seth, who were confronting the Slasher. I knew what it would do to them. And though I'd only just discovered this power, I had to believe my instinct was right—I had to use it to destroy the monster.

As I charged, this primal instinct, a connection to the Rift, moved through me.

Then there was the fire.

Blinding, excruciating fire.

Like nails driving into each nerve as the monster sliced into my flesh with its claws.

I felt.

Everything.

And now Brad's still alive. Maybe this means it worked.

Maybe this means the others are alive too.

But what about me?

Shouldn't I be dead?

Oh fuck.

I start to look down at my hands but stop myself as I envision what's been haunting me—crawling around, covered in black blisters. Surely, I'm bandaged up—is that what the coarse sensation at my fingertips is? But shouldn't I be in pain? Given what I remember of the vision, this will be brutal.

I wait for it to hit me, the intense pain from the severity of what I sustained, but…nothing.

How is that possible? No meds can be that strong. Or maybe the Sinners performed a spell to ease my pain? Or what if it's like with Brad's mom and his presence helps me somehow?

Whatever it is, it's likely temporary and at some point I'll have to feel it again—those nails driving into me, searing to my soul.

Brad looks up from the book, and he must notice I've woken up because he sets it on the edge of the bed and rises up.

"Luke? Can you hear me?" His expression is tense with worry.

My thoughts return to those last moments, when I asked Seth to stop him. How Brad cried out, his agony mixing with the horrible screams of the Slasher.

I try to say his name, but it catches in my throat.

"It's okay. You don't have to say anything. Just nod."

I can manage that, and a gentle smile tugs up on his beautiful face, his eyes watering.

"What happened?" I force out.

"You did it. You killed it."

Relief courses through me.

In our brief interaction with the Slasher, we discovered it was more powerful than we'd expected. And clever. If it hadn't been destroyed, it would have killed everyone in sight.

And who would have stopped it?

As grateful as I am to have succeeded and still be here, I tear up at the thought that I'll never be the same me. That I'll always carry these scars with me. Will I even be able to walk?

I push those thoughts away. Plenty of time for self-indulgence later.

I fight to speak, finally managing, "How long have I been out?"

"Maybe ten…twelve hours."

That can't be right. Not for the injuries I sustained. And this doesn't look like an ICU room. Shouldn't I be intubated? What's going on?

"Luke, you're fine," he says, intuiting my concern.

He reaches under the blanket and takes my hand. I feel his touch, so it's not bandaged, which throws me. And then he displays it for me. "Look."

My jaw drops. My hand looks a little paler than normal but unharmed.

"What—*How?*"

"It was bad. Really bad. Just like in the vision. We called the paramedics, and as they were transporting you, they were trying to work out what the black stuff on your skin was. They discovered it was some kind of film covering your body. When they removed it, you were fine underneath. At least physically. They brought you in because of how they found you and because you'd passed out. They're running tests on the black film. And they've done an MRI and other tests to make sure you're all right, but everything looks fine so far."

He releases my hand and pulls out his phone, turning the camera to display my face.

I'm not just fine—my skin looks better than it did

before the attack. I'm even missing a lone faded freckle I used to have on my forehead. I gasp with relief, tears welling in my eyes.

Thank fuck.

"It's okay," Brad says. "You're alive. And you're here. With me." He runs his knuckles across my cheek.

Here? With him? Can it be real?

No, it has to be some kind of dream.

His touch soothes me as he asks, "Are you in any pain? I can get the doctors to come in to give you something."

I shake my head, and as relieved as I am that I'm all right, I have to know how the others fared. "Alexei?"

"He's fine. Finn's fine too. He checked out this morning. Needed some stitches and he was concussed, but that was it."

I'm happy to hear that Finnegan's okay, but with Alexei, how's that possible? "No, it stabbed something right through Alexei."

Brad opens his mouth like he's about to explain, but then presses his lips together. "I don't get it either. Cody was there when it happened, and he and Seth are in the waiting room now. But just know, everything's okay."

I wasn't expecting to hear those words after the night we had.

He leans over the bed rail, puts his arm around me for a hug, then kisses my cheek. "I was so scared," he whispers. "I didn't want you to have to go through all that pain and suffering."

He continues kissing my face, and I bask in the sensation of his lips against my flesh and his warm hold around me. It's something deeper than the Lust, something that fuels me.

I run my hand through his hair as he kisses down to my neck, tightening his hold.

Despite everything he's said, given the moments I remember before this room, it's hard to accept.

As he buries his face in my neck, warm tears push up against my skin. I want to freeze this moment, cherish it for as long as I can, since as far as I knew the other night, I was never gonna see him again.

Once we finally manage to pry away from each other, he texts Seth and Cody to come to my room. When they enter, I sit up.

"Brad said Alexei's fine, but I'm trying to understand what happened after I left that trench."

"He has a little scar where the Slasher stabbed him," Cody says, assessing my skin in a way that makes me uneasy. "And you don't even have that much, but from how you looked last night, you should have something."

"Cody, tell me what happened. Just give me the quick, thirty-second version, at least."

"Thirty-second version: When I was working on the spell to make that circle of protection, something connected with me from the Rift. And it started controlling my movements. That's why I was writing in the notebook."

"I remember that. You wrote *I am Kysar*."

"We've seen that name before," Brad says. "Kysar is one of the Guides."

"So when Cody grabbed me and I had that vision…"

"That was him," Cody says.

"When you touched me…or he touched me…the vision was showing me what I had to do to save everyone."

"I didn't see it," Cody says, "but I assumed based on what the guys said happened after."

"And then what happened?" I ask.

"After I finished transcribing for him, he…possessed me. Went to Alexei, put my hands on him, and did something—the rod in him split in two and pushed out either side. Then his skin healed in seconds. At least that's how it felt."

"When I found them," Seth says, "Alexei was unconscious but breathing normally."

"Did he say why he was out there last night?"

Seth shakes his head. "When he woke, he wasn't sure. Seemed really confused and out of it."

"It's weird that he happened to find us even before you guys did," I say, having a hard time making sense of that.

"The Slasher sent Seth and me on a wild goose chase," Brad says. "It laid clues to make it seem like you ran in the opposite direction, and we fell for it."

"That must've been why we had time to make that first circle of protection," Cody says.

"But why didn't it just kill them?"

The room falls silent. Cody looks to Brad as if seeking permission to share.

Brad nods.

"Because it was after you, like we suspected. We think it could sense your power and that it could feed off it. I don't think that's what the Guides were telling us before, though. I assumed because the Slasher could prolong killing to get more power, that was why it chose fire for one of the victims—before we knew it was you. But now I believe they were trying to tell us that you were the one who could destroy it with your powers."

"That makes sense," I say. "After I discovered my ability to start the fire, I suddenly knew things, like I know my own name. I knew something was different about this Slasher."

"Yeah, that's for sure," Brad adds. "The Slasher described in the bible wasn't as cunning as what we faced."

"It was from something older, wiser in the Rift," I say, filled with some intuitive wisdom planted in me after Cody touched me in the trench. "And a blow to the head or even tearing it apart wouldn't have been enough to destroy it. It had to be incinerated to prevent it from coming back. And I knew the message they gave you was intended for me. That I had to go right then, before it could strike again. Save Brad and Seth."

"If all that's true," Cody says, "then Kysar must've known everything would play out like it did." He spins his backpack around front and fishes through it, retrieving the notebook he wrote in last night, flipping the pages before displaying more writing. It doesn't look like his handwriting, but more like the scrawling I'd seen when he was in a trance.

Cody reads out, "*I'm the Guide of the original Sinners. I was here to protect Mark and Josh. I am here to protect you.*" Cody flips the page. "*You didn't unleash the Slasher. Something is happening. Something is shifting in the Rift.*"

"What's happening in the Rift?"

"He didn't elaborate," Cody replies. "But this is more than I've ever done before, and I think it's more similar to how Dobbers used to communicate with the Guides. Here, look: there are a few lines that say *This isn't your fault*. When all that stuff started happening, just based on the timing, we assumed it must have been from what we'd done, and then maybe involving your arrival, but he must know more."

It's not that comforting, especially when we don't know much about Kysar or why he's helping us. But what he says lines up with the things I felt in the trench, and at least he gave us some answers through Cody, even if they're not wholly satisfying.

"Anything else I need to know?" I spit out.

"I think that's enough for now," Brad insists sternly. Cody and Seth glance at one another.

LUST

"Why did you say it like that?" When he doesn't answer, I turn to Seth and Cody, who won't make eye contact. "Why did he say it like that?"

Seth glances at the door, as if longing to make a break for it.

"It's just a lot all at once," Brad says. "But if you really think you're up for it…"

"I don't mind tearing off the Band-Aid." After what I've been through, what could be so terrible?

Cody licks his lips, then says, "Kysar's message included a warning: *Something's coming. Something worse than the Slasher. You need to be ready. Train. Train. Find me.*"

"But you contacted him. Last night."

Cody's face twists up. "Sort of. I channeled some information, and then he basically took over my body to help Alexei. But that was a struggle for both of us. And that's why I think the messages are so vague—like when I just saw your silhouette initially. I had a hard time understanding everything I was receiving. We need to be more attuned to the Rift so I can translate better."

Despite my reservations about this Guide, after what happened, I accept he's the reason I killed that thing. And not only did he give me the answers I needed, he must've known I had the ability to heal from the burn. He's the reason we're all alive right now, and that's not nothing.

"Now can we talk about what we're gonna do about

325

the cop situation?" Seth asks.

My eyes widen. "Cop situation?"

Seth winces. "You didn't think they were just going to be totally chill about the naked guy covered in goo in a pile of ashes in the middle of the night, did you?"

"We'll figure that out," Brad snaps. "You'll sit in while they talk to Luke and help them along, right? Didn't have any problem doing it last night with a friend you vowed never to use it on, so should be easy with them."

Seth and I exchange a glance. His expression's rife with guilt.

"Brad, I told him to do that. If you had intervened, you would have died senselessly and I would've been fine."

Brad blinks a few times. "Sorry, Seth. I just... That situation messed with my head. I know you were only trying to keep me from..." He doesn't finish, doesn't acknowledge that he was willing to die to save me.

"I am sorry," Seth says, and it's one of the few times I've seen him when he's let his guard down, shown something other than being a total dick around me.

"I know you are," Brad says.

Seth nods. "I can figure out the cop thing."

"And there's one more thing," Brad tells me.

"More?"

"Your uncle's on the way here."

"What? Why?"

"The cops wanted to contact your parents, and I mentioned you had a guardian and that I'll let him know. So I found him online and sent him an email. He called me, and we've gone back and forth. He's on a flight from Maui now."

"Fuck…" Of all the people I would rather not have to worry about this, he's top of the list. "I need to call him."

"He's on a plane, Luke. He won't be in for another three hours."

"I'll send him a text, then. He can get it through the Wi-Fi."

But fuck, I hate that he dropped his Maui trip just to come make sure I was okay.

"Fuck, is my phone even—"

"Incinerated," Cody says.

"Of course it is. Brad, can I—" But he's already passing me his phone.

"They're gonna want to keep you here for observation," Brad says, "do you want me to run by the dorm and grab some things? Clothes, your laptop maybe?"

As much as I want him to stay here with me, I could use a little time to myself to digest everything.

"Honestly, before you go, I could use some water."

"I'll get that," Cody says.

"And I'll check with the nurse," Brad says, "and then maybe pick up some food on my way back."

We coordinate plans before he and Cody head out,

leaving Seth and me alone together, Seth avoiding eye contact as I text Dan.

My uncle is worried, I can tell by the half words and no punctuation in his reply, but I assure him I'm all right.

Dan: be there soon love you.

Me: I love you too.

With that out of the way, I relax against my pillow, noticing Seth lingering awkwardly near the bed.

As much as he's pissed me off since we've met, something changed last night. And I know I asked a lot of him.

"Thank you, Seth."

"Huh?"

"For stopping Brad. You didn't have to do that, but you knew it was right."

His gaze meets mine briefly before he nods. "No problem. Guy would have thrown himself on that fire to save you."

I knew it too. I saw the determination in his gaze as he started toward the fire. We both would have died to save the other.

Seth's quiet for a few moments before he adds, "I've been a dick to you since you got here. But what you did…that was really noble. If I'd been in that situation, I doubt I'd have been able to sacrifice myself like that."

It's a sincere remark, a rare occasion for him. At least with me.

"I guess you don't know until it happens, right?"

"I think you're the only one between us who'd know the answer to that. It was just a fucked-up situation. I've never betrayed him before. I would do anything for these guys, so it was a mindfuck for both of us. Seeing him hurting, knowing I was the one doing it… I don't think Brad hates me, but it must be hard for him to reconcile what happened with the fact that I'm his friend. Just like it's hard for me not to feel guilty, despite telling myself I was doing the right thing."

Like most of this shit, and like life in general, it's complicated.

"I don't know that any of us will ever be the same after last night," I say.

And that seems like a massive understatement.

28

BRAD

THE FOLLOWING EVENING, after Luke is released from the hospital, we return to the dorms. I'm wondering if we'll encounter Alexei, but he's not here.

Luke steps into the room, glancing around, not like he's looking at anything in particular, but at something in his mind's eye. It reminds me of how he stared out the window on the drive back. He has plenty to think about, so I'm not surprised he's out of it.

The past couple of days have been surreal.

Seeing Luke ravaged by fire.

Battling in vain against Seth's push so I could reach him.

And then...the end.

At least, that's what I thought, but Luke didn't die. His eyes closed, his body shivering, he was still breathing.

Felt like an eternity before the paramedics arrived. Luke was rushed to the hospital, and fortunately, Seth's powers got us intel from the doctors and access to see him.

But trying to piece together everything that happened is a whole other beast. From Cody's scribbling about Luke and fire and the other messages, it's apparent there was more to all this, and it's weighing on all of us.

Luke turns to me, and I move close, hooking an arm around his waist and resting my hand against his cheek. His gaze finally meets mine.

I offer a kiss, and as he receives it, his tongue plays across mine. Each time we've kissed since he woke up has been a consoling reassurance, reminding me he's safe.

And that's what really matters.

I firm our kiss, my hands greedily probing his body as I guide him back until his ass is against Alexei's desk.

He moans, then pulls away. "Let me at least take a shower. I feel so gross having been in the hospital."

"I don't mind kissing you dirty," I say, which makes him chuckle.

But then his expression turns serious again. "Dan was really worried."

After all those revelations yesterday, not only did he have to contend with visits from Alexei and the cops, each stressful for different reasons, but then Dan arrived at the airport. I borrowed Luke's car to pick him up so he could pay his nephew a visit, and as much as Luke wanted to see him, it had to be a lot. I hate how much he's had to deal with in such a short span of time.

"He was relieved to see you were all right," I assure him.

"Yeah, it was just tough. He was trying to keep it together, but I could tell he was struggling. And then Alexei seemed so out of it. Like he wanted to push more about what happened but knew that wasn't the time, and I don't know what the hell I'm gonna tell him when he actually asks."

I know what he means—Alexei was agitated, uneasy in a way that's unlike him. But it sounded like he was mostly trying to figure out how the hell he wound up in the woods with the strange scar, which is far better than if he knew the truth.

"Hey, hey, we don't have to figure all that out to-night," I say.

"You're right. I'm just glad Seth was there for the cops. Hopefully that was enough to get them to let it go."

"From what Seth told me, he sowed enough doubt about the stuff covering you that they won't get anywhere near the truth. Probably think it was a prank gone bad, since they're already pissed they found Bucktooth Beaver behind Alpha Alpha Mu's house. But they won't push because Alpha Alpha Mu's guys have powerful dads who can really fuck over this town if the cops start rumors about what happens at that frat."

"Nice to see dirty politics come in handy for a change," he says with a wry smirk.

"We'll see. But again, all this can wait. Go take that shower. It'll make you feel better, and then we can watch a movie. Maybe order some Lucky Buddha."

"Ooh, you know me so well." His smirk expands into a grin, but I detect tension in his expression. What he's been through isn't something he can just shake off.

He grabs his towel and toiletries and heads out to the communal shower, leaving me in the room. I lie in his bed, start an episode of the *Real Housewives of Salt Lake City*, and watch for a bit before calling Mom. I tell her Luke's back from the hospital and that it looks like everything's going to be all right. Luke's back just as I end the call, a towel around his waist and his clothes tucked at his side.

He throws the clothes in the hamper, then joins me in the bed, curling against me. His body radiates the warmth from his shower, and a drop of water falls from his bangs onto my chest. As he sighs, I can feel his exhaustion.

"It's just…too much," he mutters. "That night. The stuff Kysar wrote for us. That we have to train for something worse. And all I can think is, something worse than that? I don't know what to focus on first."

"How about…what you want to order from Lucky Buddha?"

He chuckles. "Maybe pad thai. And while we're at it, can we order some cookies from that place nearby…and ice cream? I'm fucking starving."

"Anything you want."

He angles his head up to me. "In that case, I'm ready

for some more kisses."

I submit to him, taking what's mine and giving him what's rightfully his. God, I missed these when he was under. Desperately.

"Thought these lips…might never be…mine again," I fight to say through our kisses.

"I thought…they might not…be either."

He pulls away, studying my expression. As I look at that beautiful face, I'm overwhelmed with emotion. "All I keep thinking about is how close you were to being gone. The things I'd never be able to tell you. About how obsessed I am with you. How even in this short time I've known you, I can't get enough. I've seen your passion. I've seen your desire to help others. And I've seen your willingness to sacrifice yourself so selflessly."

"Says the guy who was willing to die to save me."

"You know why I wanted to save you. Because I'm totally, hopelessly in love with you. I love you, Luke, my Straight Boy."

His gaze meets mine, and he smirks. "I love you too," he says softly before our lips collide.

There's relief in his words and his touch, each kiss assuring me he's back in my arms. And most important-ly, he's mine.

I assumed he might want some time to recover, but I feel desire pulse through him.

His want for me.

His hunger.

Unlike the rhythm we'd developed, there's something more frenzied about this time—more like those original fucks.

Now that I know how easily I could have lost him, I'm desperate to share this experience with him again, to remind myself of how good it feels, flesh to flesh, soul to soul.

I tear off his towel and toss it to the floor. We part lips just long enough to get me out of my clothes and grab some lube.

Soon, I've got the head of my cock against his hole as he lies beneath me, looking as eager and ready as ever.

"Are you sure?" I ask, still thinking about how fragile he seemed the past few days.

"At this point, I'll be pissed if you don't fuck me," he says with a mischievous smile.

I grin, and as I push into him, he opens right up for me, like his hole's been waiting for me. He rolls his head back, and I lean down, kissing along his throat, tasting his flesh again, reminding myself how good he tastes and smells.

As I begin thrusting, I tell him, "You scared me."

"I'm sorry."

"Don't be sorry. Just take me. Take everything I have to give you."

"I will," he whispers.

I take hold of my necklace, intensifying the sensation between us, seeing him writhing beneath me. My cock firms inside him, and he rocks his hips, our rhythms matching as we speed up.

I cherish this precious time.

Given what we've been through, I keep waiting to wake up from this dream. But I don't wake up.

It's just Luke and me, our bodies pressing up against each other, his ass massaging my cock, the steam we work up building up pressure within, making me speed up my pace as we become a frenzy of thrusts and passion.

His inspirations, his every whim, carry us through the experience, until he's on his knees, grabbing the headboard as I take him from behind. With each thrust, the clap of his ass echoes around the room.

My chest's against his shoulder blades, and he twists his head to kiss me, until he's so caught up in passion that he's just open-mouthed, eyes rolling back as he revels in the satisfaction my cock offers him.

Watching him in his fit of pleasure, I'm determined to make it even better, so I grip my necklace and send another jolt coursing through him.

I want to take him to the very edge. To build him up until it feels so good, he nearly can't stand it. Then and only then, I want to give him release.

As he moans, I nibble at his bottom lip, raising my free hand to his nipple and toying with it between my finger and thumb.

"I'm getting close," he warns.

I keep hammering away, drilling his ass, as his desire

feels like commands.

I slide my hand down to his cock, taking it in a firm grip. As it pulses, I offer a kiss, and his ass grips my cock, tightening as I feel him erupt into a fit of spasms and thrusts as I milk him.

It's too much for me.

The pressure mounts, and I seize another kiss before calling out into his mouth, pulling away and grunting as my orgasm tears through me. I thrust like I'm trying to get every drop of cum in that ass.

He glances over his shoulder, watching me as I finish my work, feeding him my cum.

And when I'm done, I pull close to him, and he reaches back, resting his hand against my face as we gasp and pant together, recovering from the much-needed release.

Finally, as I come back to my senses, I lean back. We lock gazes, and as I look into his eyes, I'm hypnotized.

He was right when he said there's so much to consider. So many unknowns, and we don't know where the hell all this is leading, but I know as long as I'm with him, that's all that fucking matters.

EPILOGUE

LUKE

"THIS IS REALLY good turkey," Brad's mom, Cheryl, says after she finishes swallowing a bite. "You said you used an air fryer?"

"It's the only way I'm willing to make it now," Dan replies. "Keeps all the moisture in. Makes the meat nice and tender."

"It definitely is that," Cheryl says as she cuts into another piece.

Initially, Brad was planning to head home for Thanksgiving, but when his mom pushed about meeting his new boyfriend, we came up with a plan for her to fly into town to have Thanksgiving with Dan and us.

She's everything I would have expected based on what Brad's shared with me. Fun, playful. To our relief, her symptoms have been kept at bay since their previous visit, so we're hopeful this time together over the holiday will serve as a booster, tiding her over until he can see her again sometime next semester.

From meeting her, I'd never have known how bad

it'd gotten, had Brad not told me. Just like I wouldn't have known about all the pain she endured at the hands of his asshole father.

And as assuring as her health and vibrant personality are, the way Cheryl's taken to me since she arrived, it's clear she wants to know everything about the guy her son's told her about.

After everything we've been through together, I'm proud to be the one—something I'm reminded of every time he sneaks me a glance from beside me at the dinner table.

Or gently strokes my thigh.

Or licks his lips, as though thinking about how he wants to pull me away from his mom and Dan and give me a firm kiss.

It's been a while since either of us has felt that agonizing pull of the Lust, but not kissing him through dinner is starting to remind me of what that felt like.

And I don't like it.

Still, I'm appreciative of these little moments because they help distract me from the fact that something's missing from this occasion. The people I love who I can never get back.

"Turkey's great," Alexei says, "but the mashed potatoes are where it's at."

Since it was going to cost him a small fortune to travel back and forth for Thanksgiving and Christmas, Alexei stayed at the dorms through Thanksgiving. Dan only lives a few hours from the university, so I suggested Alexei join us.

Despite the awkwardness that followed our interaction with the Slasher, things have gone back to normal. Well, as normal as they can be under the circumstances.

I've been training with the guys, and it's apparent that the power I managed to access the night we fought the Slasher, I can't access it anytime I want. At least not yet.

But I've caught up on schoolwork, made sure I keep my grades up. And there haven't been any other emergencies of dealing with monsters, which really, what more could I ask for?

Even better, Brad and I have had more time for dates and fun. Enjoying life the way two college kids who've fallen for each other should.

After we finish the meal, we all pitch in to help Dan clean.

Alexei and I take on dish duty while Brad, Cheryl, and Dan chat in the living room.

"I'm glad I came," Alexei says. "This was really nice. I appreciate your inviting me."

"I'm glad you said yes. Dan loves entertaining, and compliments, so you were a perfect addition."

As I hand him a plate to place in the dishwasher, I notice him eyeing me, and it catches me off guard. "What is it?"

He shakes his head. "Just thinking about that wild

night."

I tense up, struggle to read his expression. After the incident, we only talked about it a little, and only for him to say he didn't really remember what happened. I lied and said the same. But I keep wondering if any of it will come back to him. If one night he'll suddenly sit up and start screaming at the horror of what transpired.

"You remembering anything else about that night?"

He stares at me for a few moments. "No. You?"

A familiar guilt rises in me over the lies I've had to tell Dan and Alexei. I tell myself it's to protect them, but that doesn't make me feel any better.

"Just going to the party," I reply. At least it's partly true.

He nods, studying my expression as if trying to work out if I'm lying. Or that's how it feels, but I can't imagine why I'd think that when Alexei doesn't have any reason to think I'm lying.

"Maybe it'll come back to us at some point," I say, returning to our task.

"Maybe." He's quiet as we pack a few more dishes into the dishwasher before he says, "Luke…is everything okay?"

Our gazes lock.

No, it's not, Alexei. Something's coming. And I have a feeling it's going to be terrible.

But I can't tell him that. "Why do you ask?"

"You seem…different…since that night."

"I could say the same about you."

He lets out a nervous laugh. "Yeah. I bet."

"Are *you* okay, Alexei?"

He hesitates, his gaze wandering before he says, "I'll be better once we get these dishes done." He offers a charming smile, then changes the subject, which I embrace. Once we finish up, we join the others in the living room, and Dan encourages us to play a board game. It's what Dan and I would do with Mom and Dad for holidays, and it picks at a familiar sting, like the one I felt on Halloween when I went to that party at Alpha Alpha Mu.

I can tell Brad's caught on by the way he keeps eyeing me, how he moves closer like he wishes he could protect me from my past. But just like that night with the Slasher, he can't protect me. Not from this.

I don't want to spoil the night, so I do my best to get through it before Cheryl has to head to her hotel for the night.

"I really wish you'd stayed here," Dan says as we say our goodbyes to her in the foyer.

"I didn't want to be any trouble," Cheryl says. "And it worked out, since now Alexei can get your guest room. I really just wanted to meet the guy who won my Brad's heart."

"Mom," Brad mutters. It's one of the few times I've seen him blush.

As Alexei snickers, Dan says, "Well, Luke's a good

kid."

"I can tell," Cheryl says. "And I don't doubt my Brad to know a good man when he meets one."

As she and Brad exchange a look, I sense the pain behind that statement...since he knew such a bad man when he was growing up.

She offers us all hugs before leaving, though we'll see her again tomorrow.

Afterward, we all head to bed, where Brad and I finally have some alone time to make up for all the kissing we missed throughout the day.

"Mmm..." he says after pulling away from a kiss. He's got me backed against the wall of my old room. "Did you see how good I was by not making out with you in front of Mom and Dan?"

"Did you want an award?"

"Think I deserve one," he says with a cocked brow.

"If you want an award, you're gonna have to earn it tonight," I say, excitement pulsing through me at the thought of having a good fuck after our day of being decent.

But Brad's expression turns serious. "You good?"

I know he's asking because he knows this was a hard day for me. And while there were difficult moments, having him here with me made it better. "No worse than usual," I say, but with the mood spoiled, I feel it's a good time to bring up what's been on my mind. "Alexei mentioned that night."

"What about it?" Brad asks, and I can hear the concern in his voice.

"Seems like it's in there somewhere. He wanted to make sure I was all right. I don't know. It was a strange conversation. Sometimes I wonder if it'd be easier on him to know the truth. But the truth is so fucked, revealing it seems even more cruel."

Brad raises his hand to my face, caresses his knuckles along my cheek. "I'm sorry you're in this position. But if you do think it's better to tell him, you say the word, and I'll advocate for it with Seth and Codes."

I nod. "Let me think on it. In the meantime, I'd rather do things to help me forget about it...at least for tonight."

"Mmmm." He leans close and kisses the side of my throat. I roll my head back against the wall, and as I moan, there's a knock at the door.

I growl softly and feel Brad smile against my flesh. "Guess you're gonna have to be a good Straight Boy a little longer."

"Pretty confident you violently murdered Straight Boy, but sure."

When I answer the door, I find Dan standing outside.

"Mind if I grab you for a minute?" Unlike earlier in the day and throughout dinner and our game, he's glancing around uncomfortably, as though he's just received some bad news.

I head out into the hall and close the door. "Everything okay?"

"Just wanted a minute with you, if you don't mind."

"Of course."

He leads me down the hall, into the primary bedroom, closing the door behind us.

"Are you sure everything's okay?"

"First, I wanted to tell you that I really like Brad."

"Glad to hear that. He's been very good to me. In ways that are difficult to explain." *In ways I wish I could explain to you, Dan.* "But I'm assuming you didn't bring me in here just to tell me that?" I press, unable to shake the discomfort in his expression.

"No, there's something I'm supposed to give you." He bites his lip and holds up his finger. He opens his dresser and retrieves a narrow, rectangular wooden box. Opening it, he reveals a necklace. It bears a cross, like the ones we wear.

Does he know?

"What is this?"

He seems to hesitate before saying, "It was your father's, then your mother's. She once told me I would need to give this to you and that I'd know when the time was right. I didn't understand what she meant, and honestly, it slipped my mind."

He passes it to me, and I run my finger along the cross, thinking about how this is one of the only things aside from the Sinners' bible that links me to Dad's secret past. And Mom's too, it appears.

"Thank you, Dan."

"Can I ask what that means to you?"

"Uh…"

His lips twist into a frown. "Remember when your parents went on that trip when you were younger, for a few weeks?" I struggle before he adds, "Their anniversary trip."

"Oh yeah." Mom and Dad always said they didn't have much of a honeymoon, so they wanted to redo it, and Dan babysat.

"I remember. That's a weird thing to bring up."

"It was a weird thing to happen. They didn't seem like they were ready to go on a big fun trip. They were on edge. Agitated. Like how you were acting before you wound up in the hospital."

The way he looks at me, he must've realized something else was up.

"When they returned," he goes on, "your dad was wearing that necklace. I thought it was a souvenir. I never saw him wear it again after that. Then when I came to the hospital to see you, I saw your friends' necklaces and the one you had on—the one you're wearing now. Even then I didn't think much of it. But last night, I woke up in the middle of the night, and the day your mom gave it to me was like it happened yesterday, her telling me I needed to wait to give it to you. Even now, I'm wondering why I forgot for all this time or why it came up just now, but all I know is that this belongs to you."

The way he tells the story, it's clear he's somewhat disturbed by his memory lapse, and I can't help thinking there might've been some magic involved. But Mom wasn't a part of the Sinners stuff. Was she…?

He studies my expression. "Is there anything you want to tell me, Luke?"

Like with Alexei, part of me wants to share the truth with him, but my parents must've had their reasons for not sharing this with him. And I fear that if I tell him the truth, it might pull him into this with me.

I'd rather spare him. Not give him a reason to worry about me attending St. Lawrence. Or about what's to come.

"Nothing right now," I make myself say, since I don't like lying to him.

"Well, I'm here if you need anything. Anytime. I hope you know that."

As always, I can feel his love, his acceptance, his care for me. The love and care of the man who took me in as his own and selflessly gave so much of himself to me.

"Thank you, Dan," I say, hugging him tight.

I put the necklace on with mine and return to my old bedroom, where I tell Brad about the odd exchange. Still with the necklace on, I sit up in bed, assessing the cross.

"How would your mom have known to put a spell on Dan?" He slides close to me, places his hand on my abs. "She couldn't have known that all this would happen."

"But what if she did? It sounds strange, but maybe the answer is as strange as everything else. I just wish I knew what my parents knew about all this. Like, did Dad tell Mom? And what was that trip about? And this on top of all the other questions related to Kysar. Too many questions, too few answers."

"Now you know what it's been like for us since we found out about this stuff."

"I don't like it."

"Well, come here and let your boyfriend make it better."

Just hearing him refer to himself as my boyfriend has this strange power over me.

He leans close and offers a kiss. It's a gentle reminder of how far we've come from the Lust-fueled kisses we shared early on, back when it felt beyond our control. Inescapable. Now that we spend so much time together, it feels more natural. We're more at ease, like this is the way it's supposed to be for us.

He rolls onto me, and I reposition comfortably under him as he pushes his weight against me. He nibbles at my ear, then kisses down my throat, stirring that familiar desire, as something moves through me.

I'm no longer looking at the ceiling, images flashing through my mind in quick succession. Like memories, though not mine.

"There's something I need to do," Dad tells Mom, and I somehow know I'm in his body. *"I must go back to St. Lawrence. It's life or death."*

"I'm not letting you do whatever it is by yourself."

"You have to stay here. For Luke."

And then I see Josh Dobbers and Dad and Mom in the church cellar.

A series of images collide, moving so fast, I can't keep up. One moment I'm sitting in a room with recliners and IVs, the next I'm walking around an office, and finally, I'm in a car and hear an ominous voice before I snap back to the present with Brad lying over me.

"Luke? Luke?" he asks, panic in his expression.

"What happened?"

"Your eyes went black like you were having a vision."

Despite only seeing flashes, I have a deep awareness of what took place in the past, as though it downloaded into my brain. As though I've known it all my life.

"The cross," I say. "It stored the memory of what happened to my parents. When I was a kid, Kysar called them to the Rift—my dad and Josh. Something evil had escaped. A monster they knew could tear apart our world. After Dad told Mom the truth about the Sinners, she insisted she go with them. She didn't want them to fight this on their own. She didn't know what she was getting into, but while working with them, she discovered her telepathic ability. Once they found the monster, they couldn't find a way to get it back into the Rift, and knew it would be fatal to fight it, but the Guides told them it was the only way to keep others from dying. Mom used her power to split its consciousness between them, locking it in each of their bodies. They thought they could use their combined powers to keep it at bay, but after Josh got cancer, Mom and Dad knew it was only a matter of time before it broke free and took control of their bodies. When it started to take over Dad, he used his powers to give himself the aneurysm. Stored the memory for Mom to see in the necklace. Then when she felt the same thing happening to her four years later, she drove herself into a wall to keep the creature from driving into oncoming traffic. It was different than the Slasher they killed while in college. This thing could only survive as long as they were alive, so once they were gone, it was too."

"They sacrificed themselves," Brad says, wrapping his arms around me. "Just like their son did."

I nod, tearing up. "They debated what to do. They didn't want to die because they had me, but they knew if this monster got out, there might not be a world here for me. They died so that I could live." Tears stream down my cheeks.

"I'm so sorry, Luke."

But there's a relief in knowing the truth. More than that—a sense of responsibility. My duty.

"This is what I'm supposed to do," I say, and Brad pulls away.

LUST

"What?"

"I always thought the reason I wanted to go to St. Lawrence was because Dad went there, but now I feel like it's been calling me. Like it's my destiny to guard the Rift with the Sinners, like my parents did."

Brad raises his hand to my face, caresses gently. "Is that what *you* want, though?"

I consider it briefly, maybe too briefly given the weight of the consequences. "I don't know that I have a choice."

"You do have a choice. But knowing who you are, and that you want to do the right thing, I know you feel you only have one choice. It's one of the reasons I'm so in love with you."

I gaze at Brad's beautiful face, and fucked up as it is to discover all that's on our shoulders, there's comfort in knowing he's mine. "This is very dangerous," I warn him.

"You think I'm scared of a little danger?"

"I know you aren't, and neither am I." Not now that I grasp just how important this work is.

He takes my mouth again, and I cherish every moment of it, realizing how fragile it is, how quickly it could be taken from me by the looming threats. When we pull away, he presses his forehead against mine. "We'll figure this out, Luke. Together."

"Together."

We seal the promise with another kiss, his words

351

reminding me how lucky I am that I'm not on my own in any of this.

But also vividly aware that, for the Sinners, this is only the beginning.

THE END

CONTINUE THE ADVENTURE WITH:
FEVER (SAINTS & SINNERS #2)
mybook.to/SaintsSinnersFever

SIGN UP FOR DEVON'S NEWSLETTER:
eepurl.com/gi1Zzn

ABOUT THE AUTHOR

Devon McCormack

Devon McCormack grew up in the Georgia suburbs with his two younger brothers and an older sister. At a very young age, he spun tales the old-fashioned way, lying to anyone and everyone he encountered. He claimed he was an orphan. He claimed to be a king from another planet. He claimed to have supernatural powers. He has since harnessed this penchant for tall tales by crafting worlds and characters that allow him to live out whatever fantasy he chooses. Devon is an out and proud queer man living in Atlanta, Georgia.

Find Devon:
www.devonmccormack.com

Made in United States
Cleveland, OH
27 February 2025

14738000R00197